Praise for the Jaya Jones Treasure Hunt Mysteries

"Charming characters, a hint of romantic conflict, and just the right amount of danger will garner more fans for this cozy series."

– Publishers Weekly

"With a world-class puzzle to solve and riveting plot twists to unravel, *Quicksand* had me on the edge of my seat for the entire book...Don't miss one of the best new mystery series around!"

– Kate Carlisle,
New York Times Bestselling Author of the Bibliophile Mysteries

"A delicious tall tale about a treasure map, magicians, musicians, mysterious ancestors, and a few bad men."

– Mystery Scene Magazine

"A joy-filled ride of suspenseful action, elaborate scams, and witty dialogue. The villains are as wily as the heroes, and every twist is intelligent and unexpected, ensuring that this is a novel that will delight lovers of history, romance, and elaborate capers."

– Kings River Life Magazine

"Forget about Indiana Jones. Jaya Jones is swinging into action, using both her mind and wits to solve a mystery...Readers will be ensnared by this entertaining tale."

– RT Book Reviews (four stars)

"*Quicksand* has all the ingredients I love—intrigue, witty banter, and a twisty mystery that hopscotches across France!"

– Sara Rosett,
Author of the Ellie Avery Mystery Series

"Pandian's second entry sets a playful tone yet provides enough twists to keep mystery buffs engaged, too. The author streamlines an intricate plot....[and] brings a dynamic freshness to her cozy."

– Library Journal

"If Indiana Jones had a sister, it would definitely be historian Jaya Jones."

— *Suspense Magazine*

"Has everything a mystery lover could ask for: ghostly presences, Italian aristocrats, jewel thieves, failed actors, sitar players, and magic tricks, not to mention dabs of authentic history and academic skullduggery."

— *Publishers Weekly*

"Move over Vicky Bliss and Joan Wilder, historian Jaya Jones is here to stay! Mysterious maps, legendary pirates, and hidden treasure—Jaya's latest quest is a whirlwind of adventure."

— Chantelle Aimée Osman,
The Sirens of Suspense

"*Pirate Vishnu* is fast-paced and fascinating as Jaya's investigation leads her this time to India and back to her own family's secrets."

—Susan C. Shea,
Author of the Dani O'Rourke mysteries

"Pandian's new series may well captivate a generation of readers, combining the suspenseful, mysterious and romantic. Four stars."

— *RT Book Reviews*

"Witty, clever, and twisty... Do you like Agatha Christie? Elizabeth Peters? Then you're going to love Gigi Pandian."

— Aaron Elkins,
Edgar Award-Winning Author of the Gideon Oliver Mysteries

"Fans of Elizabeth Peters will adore following along with Jaya Jones and a cast of quirky characters as they pursue a fabled treasure."

—Juliet Blackwell,
New York Times Bestselling Author of the Art Lover's Mysteries

THE NINJA'S
ILLUSION

**The Jaya Jones Treasure Hunt Mystery Series
by Gigi Pandian**

<u>Novels</u>

ARTIFACT (#1)
PIRATE VISHNU (#2)
QUICKSAND (#3)
MICHELANGELO'S GHOST (#4)
THE NINJA'S ILLUSION (#5)

<u>Novellas</u>

FOOL'S GOLD (prequel to ARTIFACT)
(in OTHER PEOPLE'S BAGGAGE)

THE NINJA'S ILLUSION

A JAYA JONES TREASURE HUNT MYSTERY

GIGI PANDIAN

HENERY PRESS

THE NINJA'S ILLUSION
A Jaya Jones Treasure Hunt Mystery
Part of the Henery Press Mystery Collection

First Edition | October 2017

Henery Press
www.henerypress.com

Trade Paperback ISBN-13: 978-1-63511-251-1
Digital epub ISBN-13: 978-1-63511-252-8
Kindle ISBN-13: 978-1-63511-253-5
Hardcover ISBN-13: 978-1-63511-254-2

Printed in the United States of America

To my critique partners—I couldn't do this without you

ACKNOWLEDGMENTS

Writing a book is far from a solitary pursuit. Huge thanks to critique readers Nancy Adams, Stephen Buehler, Adam Gratz, Emberly Nesbitt, Susan Parman, Larissa Reinhart, Brian Selfon, and Susan Spann, and my incredible Henery Press editorial team of Kendel Lynn, Rachel Jackson, and Erin George. And special thanks to two people who believed in this series from the start: my agent Jill Marsal and Malice Domestic Grants Chair Harriette Sackler.

Writing about a historian involves a lot of historical research, including the fun of discovering obscure facts, visiting mysterious locations, and talking with fascinating people. My research for *The Ninja's Illusion* benefited from the help of many people, most notably Jacob Pandian, Larissa Reinhart, Susan Spann, Chizuko Goto, and Yuichiro Yamashita. Any mistakes in these pages are my own.

I'm forever grateful for the friends who kept me sane as I wrote this novel. I'm blessed with a wonderful community of more people than I can list individually with the space I have here. I need to at least mention local writers Emberly Nesbitt, Mysti Berry, and Michelle Cruz Gonzales, who keep me going at our café writing dates. Fellow members of the board of Sisters in Crime, who inspire me with all they do for this genre we love. And Diane Vallere, who never blinks an eye when I ask her the silliest questions.

And the reason Jaya got to travel to Japan is James, who first suggested we visit Japan. At the time I had no idea I'd fall in love with both the country and Japanese mystery novels.

CHAPTER 1

I'm better at finding lost treasures than a phone buried in the bottom of my bag. Handwritten notecards for my lecture. A granola bar squished nearly as thin as a hand-pressed sheet of parchment. A magnifying glass. But no phone.

My students had kept me after class asking questions. Normally having engaged students was a wonderful thing. But not today. The text message I'd received before class told me this was urgent. He'd be calling any minute now.

I rushed through the building, hoping I didn't crash into any of the students who filled the hallway. With only two days to go before a week off for Thanksgiving break, a flurry of academic activity was keeping us busy. I wanted to answer the call privately inside my office, but this was taking too long. He was a stickler for promptness. Accurate timing meant the difference between life and death in his act.

I stopped next to a corkboard adorned with colorful flyers and rooted through my bag. A light from my phone illuminated the depths of the cavernous red messenger bag. I smiled as I saw the face of my best friend on the screen. In the photo, his thick black hair was partially obscured by his bowler hat, and a mischievous smile hovered on his lips.

"How goes it, Houdini?" I said as I answered the video call. I thought that would get a smile out of him. I never called him by his stage name, The Hindi Houdini.

"Don't get on the flight, Jaya," Sanjay said. "Don't come to Japan."

I stared back at the video image on the small screen, my smile wavering. "What are you talking about? I've got my ticket for the day after tomorrow."

"There's something—" He stopped speaking and glanced nervously over his shoulder. When he spoke again, his voice was quieter. "There's something odd going on here. You're not going to believe me, but I'm serious. Someone is—"

His voice broke off in the middle of the sentence. The screen went dark.

"Sanjay?" I said to a blank screen.

I tried calling him back as I walked to my office. He didn't answer.

Seeing the scowl on my face, the undergraduate students in the hallway parted to let me pass. Surely it was just a dropped signal. Sanjay was on the other side of the world from San Francisco, after all. But what had he been trying to tell me?

"Lecture bombed?" a voice next to me asked.

I jumped and dropped the phone. Why was I so shaken by Sanjay's call? He made his living as a performer. He was bound to be dramatic. I told myself that's all it was. But that look on his face...It was difficult to believe the rational part of my brain.

"No," I said, picking up the phone. "Class went great."

"If this is what you look like after a good lecture," Tamarind said, "I'd hate to see you when a class goes badly. Your face is pale. Good thing I brought caffeine." The librarian smiled as she held up two paper cups of coffee, their lids covered in raindrops.

Tamarind Ortega had been hired at the university library two years before, after completing her Library Science Master's degree. She was a brilliant librarian who knew how to track down even the most obscure information, but the library staff also appreciated her size and temperament. Big-boned with clothing that indicated she was not to be messed with, the post-feminist post-punk was five feet ten inches of tough love. Our university was in the heart of San Francisco, and colorful characters who weren't students would sometimes wander into the library. Tamarind was great at relating to people the other librarians didn't want to deal with, and she wasn't afraid of using her strength and size as an implicit threat if disruptive people didn't leave the library. We met shortly after I got my job as an assistant professor. As two women starting out in academia who didn't fit conventional expectations, we'd quickly become friends.

I unlocked the door to my office. My six-foot Ganesha statue and his broken tusk greeted us. I'd fallen in love with the statue in a craftsman's workshop in Kochi, India. Lane Peters, the man whose presence never failed to make me feel more alive, had noticed my reaction to it and bought it for me. Tamarind handed me one of the coffees and set the other in front of Ganesha. I'd told her repeatedly it wasn't necessary, but she said it couldn't hurt.

"It's not the lecture," I said as I looked for a safe spot on my cluttered desk to set the coffee. "I'm distracted. Sanjay called me for a video chat, but we got disconnected."

"Bummer. I'm sure he'll call you back when he gets a signal."

The phone was still clasped in my hand. I willed Sanjay to call me back. *What had he seen over his shoulder?*

"Let me try him one more time." I deposited my bag underneath the messy desk and tried him again. I once again failed to reach him. I flopped dejectedly into the desk chair. It squeaked more miserably than usual, as if commiserating.

"Spill," Tamarind said. "What's going on?"

What *was* going on? I took a sip of coffee to give myself a moment to gather my thoughts. I smiled at Tamarind. "You remembered I like four sugars."

"Oops. I put in six. Hey, stop avoiding the question. Spill."

I looked out my small sliver of a window at the gray sky and misty rain. "You know Sanjay is performing as the opening act in an Indian Rope Trick show in Kyoto next week. The fabled illusion that's supposedly impossible."

Sanjay was a professional stage magician—an incredibly successful one. Performing as The Hindi Houdini, he'd been doing his show at a theater in the Napa Valley until a California wildfire last summer had burned the theater to the ground. He didn't have a backup plan, so after the theater where he'd established his career was destroyed, he didn't know what to do with himself. An invitation from Akira, Japan's most famous stage magician, came at the perfect time. Sanjay was aimless and vulnerable. The controversial magician who claimed to perform real miracles had swept in to take advantage of the situation to fill a hole in his new show. With a much more scrupulous magician friend in Japan, Sanjay could have been doing a show where the theatrics remained on the stage. Unfortunately, his friend Hiro's career wasn't doing nearly as well as Akira's, so Hiro hadn't been the one to extend an offer.

Tamarind nodded. "That's old news, Jaya. Why do you look so freaked out about it?"

"Sanjay texted me earlier, saying he needed to tell me something urgent. When he called, he said something 'odd' was going on." Goosebumps swept over my arms as I remembered Sanjay's face. "He told me not to come to Japan."

"Shut. Up. Why would he say that?"

I bit my lip. "He looked over his shoulder...and the connection went dead." I gripped the paper coffee cup so hard that coffee splashed onto a stack of papers.

"Seriously?" Tamarind gaped at me as she tossed me a box of tissues from my bookshelf. "Of course you're serious. You don't have that kind of sense of humor. But Sanjay does. He's messing with you. I'm all for pulling a good practical joke on one's friends, but if he could see how tense he's making you, he'd call you back."

"This isn't a joke. It's not only what he said to me today. Sanjay was desperate to sign onto this gig, but it made him uneasy. Something has been weighing on him since the first time Akira contacted him. But he wouldn't talk about it."

That, I realized, was why Sanjay's dropped call had been so unsettling. He was already nervous about something. Something he wasn't telling me.

"Because of Akira's reputation as someone who possesses real supernatural powers?" Tamarind asked.

"That's part of it. Akira cons people into believing he performs real miracles. But Sanjay already knew that about him when he signed on. Something changed."

"Let's ask my assistant." Tamarind enunciated as she spoke into her phone. "What has Japanese magician Akira done this week?" She frowned at her phone and shook her head. "No public scandals to speak of. Oh, but here's something worth our time."

Tamarind grinned as the sound of a Japanese pop song filled my office. She held up a music video with four teenage boys dancing on a stage and thousands of fans in a stadium audience.

"There's so much happening on this screen right now," I said, "I think I might have a seizure." Small rectangles with additional videos played in both the top left and lower right corners of the screen, in addition to text that scrolled across the bottom.

"That's the norm with Japanese television. It engages all the senses. But I don't know how you can look at anything else besides that beautiful face of his. Akira is the one with silky-smooth long hair."

"He looks like he's sixteen."

"This video is from more than a decade ago. So my reaction is totally age appropriate. I'm not really into J-pop, though, so I don't know the story of why the boy band broke up. But that's when Akira became a magician."

"Sanjay told me how it took Akira a while to make it as a magician. Challenging starts to their magic careers is one thing they have in common."

"Sanjay never had an accident like Akira's, though."

"What accident?"

Tamarind began dancing to the catchy song. I took the phone and silenced it.

She sighed. "Sanjay didn't tell you?"

I shook my head.

"All I know," Tamarind said, "is that a few years ago, Akira nearly died. It was an accident in his show—and it looked like he was dead. The press initially thought it was a publicity stunt, but when it took him a whole year to recover, and he returned with a crippled hand, everyone realized it wasn't. He lost the use of his left hand, but he gained something else. He came back with the power to perform miracles."

"He doesn't really perform miracles."

Tamarind shrugged. "He's much more famous now. And he has legions of fans who believe he does."

"I know. And that's how he claims he's going to pull off performing the 'impossible' Indian Rope Trick. I don't understand how Sanjay convinced himself it was okay to work with Akira."

"Sure you do."

"I do?"

"Ambition, Jaya. That hunky best pal of yours has got more of it than anyone I know."

"I know Sanjay is ambitious," I said. "I wouldn't be so worried if that's all it was."

What was so dire that had him looking over his shoulder and telling me not to join him in Japan? Sanjay had escaped from a coffin sinking to the bottom of the Ganges. He'd kept his wits when there was a mishap during a stunt where he was buried alive. I'd never seen him nervous about a performance.

Until now.

Chapter 2

"You need a distraction until Sanjay calls you back," Tamarind said. "That's why I'm here, after all."

"It is?"

"No, not really. I'm delivering a message from Miles that he was too scared to give you himself. He's not going to get caught up before you leave for Japan."

I'd recently hired my underemployed poet neighbor, Miles, as my part-time assistant. I hadn't been able to keep up with the email messages and letters people had been sending me since I'd helped find treasures from India that had been lost for centuries. After missing an important message over the summer, I knew I needed help. Tamarind was dating Miles after they met through me, and she'd suggested the idea.

"I'm behind too." I pointed to the stack of papers I'd just spilled coffee on. Several of the people who got in touch with me had serious ideas that merited a personal response from me, not simply a polite form letter from Miles.

"You're replying to all these yourself?"

"An academic in south India thinks he may have stumbled across a temple cache like the Padmanabhaswamy temple in Trivandrum." It was easy enough to refer to Bombay as its reclaimed name Mumbai, Madras as Chennai, and Calcutta as Kolkata, but the south Indian city of Thiruvananthapuram was a mouthful in casual conversation. "And a retired businessman found a buried hoard of coins in his backyard in Texas when he began gardening."

"Since when did you become that kind of treasure hunter, Jaya?"

"The coins had Sanskrit writing on them."

"Oh."

"Obviously neither one is my kind of thing. But I need to figure out who to put them in touch with. And then there are people like Dr. Nakamura, a professor I met at a history conference a few years ago. He has some questions about my work on East India Company trade routes in Europe and Asia. It's my specialty, so I can't punt him to someone else."

"You're too responsible for your own good."

"Says the person who trekked across campus in the rain. You didn't have to give me Miles's message in person."

"The real reason I wanted to come," she said, "is because I found this." She reached into her plaid backpack and held up a hardback book with library markings in the corner.

She opened the book to a full-page reproduction of a magic poster from the early 1900s. "Ta-da. May I present the most magical illusion the world has ever known: The Indian Rope Trick."

The illustrated poster was filled with vivid reds and bright yellows. Framing the poster was the arch of a Mughal palace, and the Taj Mahal was visible in the distance. In the center, a young Indian boy climbed a rope that stretched to the sky from a woven basket. At the bottom of the poster, a conjuror waved his hands in the air, directing the magical feat.

"Pretty cool, huh?" she said. "This is one of the oldest posters advertising the trick. I couldn't resist looking it up when you told me where you were going. I also found an eye-witness account."

"There aren't any real eye-witness accounts. Since the Indian Rope Trick is impossible and hasn't been performed in its true form."

"You doubt me, Jaya?" Tamarind asked with a grin. She closed her eyes, and when she opened them and spoke, her voice was that of a different person. One with a faux British accent.

"The most famous illusion in the world, and I saw it with my own eyes, I did. There I was in a dusty open field outside New Delhi, the stifling sun beating down on us." She glanced down at the book in her hands before resuming the story. "A wisp of a boy gathered us Westerners together. He explained we were about to witness the most amazing things we'd ever beheld. My friend and I crept closer. It was then we saw the old man with a white beard that reached his heart. But Jaya, what a black heart it was."

Her kohl-lined eyes grew wide with mock horror. It was a superb performance, and I found myself successfully distracted from my worries.

Her voice fell to a stage whisper. "This was the great magician to whom the boy was enslaved. Once a dozen of us were gathered around the two of them, the black-hearted magician showed us a wicker basket, about two feet high, empty except for a coil of thick rope. The magician lifted the rope from the basket and tossed it into the air. To my surprise, the rope stayed there, hovering in the air." Tamarind glanced again at the book. My gaze followed hers, and I noticed for the first time how modern the book was. I found myself disappointed it wasn't a centuries-old book containing a real eye-witness account.

"We weren't near any buildings, Jaya," she continued. "It was an open field. You can imagine how much my heart raced. It nearly popped out of my chest at what happened next." She picked up one of the figurines that cluttered half my desk, small tokens of appreciation from people I'd helped or who hoped I'd help them. Tamarind selected the palm-sized Leprechaun. "The small boy climbed up the rope suspended in midair. My friend is an artist, so he began to sketch the amazing scene before us. I took a photograph. I was glad I did, because a moment later, two of the most unimaginable things occurred." She paused, meeting my gaze, as if daring me to ask her to continue.

"I'll bite. What happened?"

"The boy *disappeared*. Into. Thin. Air. As soon as he reached the top of the rope, high above us, he simply vanished." She unsurreptitiously flung the Leprechaun into the plaid backpack at her feet. "The magician became angered at this, so he climbed up the rope after the boy—with a machete in his hand." She stepped forward, brandishing a Swiss army knife. "The magician climbed higher and higher, then disappeared at the top of the rope as well, along with his machete. But from the ground below, we could hear them arguing. I didn't understand the language they were speaking, but it was clear they were fighting."

She shivered, as if she were reliving the moment she'd never experienced. "Before we could ask any of our fellow onlookers what they were saying, an arm fell from the sky. Then a foot. I took another photograph, because I knew nobody would believe what I'd witnessed. The black-hearted magician was killing the boy with magic that tore him apart without any blood. I was too shocked to act as the magician climbed down the rope. Other members of the crowd drew closer, rage in their eyes, looking as though they were about to attack the murderous old magician. He must have seen the look in their eyes. As soon as he jumped to the earth, he lifted his hands in a placating gesture and raised the lid from the wicker basket. The boy was inside. The 'limbs' we'd seen falling from the sky were nowhere to be seen. The boy bounded from the basket, unharmed."

"I've seen many astounding feats by the magicians of India," Tamarind concluded, "but none as amazing as the Indian Rope Trick."

"Weren't magicians in India called jugglers at the time?" I asked. "If you're being historically accurate."

She narrowed her eyes at me. "You broke the illusion, Jaya."

"I especially loved the bit about the magician's black heart. I didn't remember that detail from what Sanjay told me or any of the articles I read."

"You like that bit? Creative license on my part." She tapped on her phone and frowned. "You're right. Performers who did magic tricks in India in the 1800s and earlier centuries were called jugglers. And mystical magicians were known as *fakirs*. I'm losing my librarian superpowers."

"You're not losing your edge. I liked the formal language as well. It was really like you were telling the story from 1890."

"I've been binging on the History Channel at night. Their actors read a lot of original documents. But you're distracting me. That's not the end of the story."

She cleared her throat and resumed the fake accent. "The most interesting thing happened when my friend and I returned from the British Raj to the States. I developed my film, and imagine my surprise when I beheld *there was nothing there*. The old magician and the young boy were simply seated next to the wicker basket. My mouth hung agape for several minutes, I can tell you. We'd been *hypnotized*. There was no rope trick, only mass hypnosis." She paused and curtseyed, lifting the sides of the fuchsia skirt she wore over black leggings and silver combat boots. "Okay. Now I'm done. No, I lied. I have questions. I know Akira doesn't possess real magical powers. Or at least I'm pretty sure. So is he a mesmerist who's actually going to pull off hypnotizing hundreds of people?"

"I doubt it," I said, "since there will also be tens of thousands of people watching on television. Maybe millions. Even if it were possible, the camera can't be hypnotized."

"Then how is he going to pull it off?"

"I wish I knew." And I wished I knew where Sanjay was.

CHAPTER 3

The rain had let up and the sun was setting when I arrived home, a semi-legal attic apartment above a Victorian house in San Francisco's Haight-Ashbury neighborhood. I found my brother on the front porch with his laptop open on his lap and a pitcher of green liquid at his side.

"Green juice?" he asked me.

"What's in it?"

"You know, green things. Kale, cucumber, green apple."

"I'll pass. Did the power go out?"

"Because I'm sitting on a rocking chair on the porch? It's a porch, JJ. A porch! With both a porch swing and a rocking chair." He proceeded to rock back and forth a few times. "Remember when Dad found that squeaky rocking chair at a thrift store when we were little? How could I not take advantage of having such a charming place to work?"

My landlady, Nadia, was on a cruise with her paramour, Jack, so my brother was housesitting while he searched for an apartment in San Francisco. He'd recently accepted a job at a local law firm, claiming he needed a change from Los Angeles. In truth, I think he needed to get away from memories of his girlfriend who told him she needed a temporary break from the relationship to reconnect with her son, who'd been having a tough time at boarding school.

I knew the truth about why Ava was staying away, but there was no way I could tell my brother that it was her past, intertwined with mine, that hovered dangerously close to catching up with her.

Still, I could tell that somewhere deep down, he knew there was something more going on than Ava had told him. He was a perceptive guy. It was one of the things that made him a great lawyer. He could read people. He was the one who'd seen Ava's truly good qualities, when I'd been the one who hadn't been able to see past the superficial ones.

I pushed thoughts of difficult relationship choices from my mind and sat down on the swinging bench. I kicked off my heels and eyed the juice suspiciously.

"It's good," he said, closing his laptop.

"I don't know, Fish. Maybe now that the sun has gone down and I can't see that I'm drinking something green."

My brother's given name was Mahilan, an Indian name that meant happiness—just like my middle name, Anand—but when we were little kids I called him Mahi Mahi, like the fish, which morphed into my calling him Fish. I was the only person he let get away with it. As many a woman had pointed out to me, he was far too attractive to be called Fish. His bright green eyes set against dark skin were certainly a striking feature, but I'd always been told he was all-around classically attractive. Since he was my brother, it was impossible for me to judge.

He poured me a glass. It wasn't half bad, but I would have preferred a whisky after the afternoon I'd had. We sat in the near-darkness for a few minutes, drinking our strange green cocktails and talking about nothing and everything, just like we used to when I'd crashed on his couch in my twenties while completing my dissertation.

Neither of us got up to turn on the porch light. The house was located on a side street close to the main drag of Haight Street, so it was fun people-watching from the shadows. The sidewalk became more crowded as people returned from work, walked their dogs, and went out to dinner.

"It's funny," Mahilan said, "but now that I can barely see you, I can tell from your body language that something is up. Your hand is gripping your phone so tightly, I'm surprised it hasn't shattered."

I'd been burned by keeping secrets from my brother before. I wasn't going to make that mistake again. I flipped on the porch light. A faint scar was visible on Mahilan's nose from our exploits in Italy a few months before.

"Sanjay called from Japan, but the video chat got cut off"—I gripped my phone even tighter—"right after he looked over his shoulder—like someone was after him."

"JJ, I concede that your good imagination saved our lives last summer, but that doesn't mean there's a nefarious plot at every turn."

"I wish you wouldn't use words like 'nefarious' to convince me there's nothing to worry about."

"Fine. How about—"

"It doesn't matter, because you're wrong. He told me something odd was going on."

"Odd like what?"

"No idea. But he told me not to go."

"To Japan? He invited you and now uninvited you? I can't believe he'd be so rude."

"You're missing the point, Fish. What's making him so worried that he's keeping watch over his shoulder and he doesn't want me there?"

It had been over an hour since Sanjay's call had dropped. I stole another worried glance at my phone. This time, I was rewarded. An image of Sanjay's bowler hat popped up on the screen of my phone as the device began to ring. Sanjay was calling from his mobile number rather than a video call.

"Sanjay." I stood up so hastily the swinging bench crashed into the back of my legs. "Are you okay?"

"It wasn't a good idea for me to have invited you."

"What's happened?" The wooden beams of the porch were rough and cold on my bare feet, but I didn't care.

"Nothing," he snapped. "It was just a bad idea."

"Nothing? But you said something odd was going on—"

"If I knew what it was, it wouldn't be *odd*, would it? It would be fascinating or annoying or—"

"I get it." I rolled my eyes. Maybe Tamarind and Fish were right after all and I needn't have worried about Sanjay. "Start with what happened an hour ago. Why did you hang up on me?"

"My pocket Wi-Fi died. I forgot to charge it overnight. And I couldn't get a cell signal where I was."

"But you were looking over your shoulder—"

"False alarm."

"False alarm for what?"

"I'll be fine," Sanjay said. "But you shouldn't come. Okay? Good."

"If you hang up on me again I'll strangle you."

My brother's eyes grew wide. I stepped off the porch and onto the sidewalk. The concrete felt damp on the balls of my feet. I ran a hand through my hair and avoided Mahilan's gaze.

"That would be some magic trick from five thousand miles away," Sanjay said.

"I assume you're not staying in Japan forever."

"Maybe I will. They love magic here. Though I don't like how restaurants don't like to customize orders. It's far too easy to accidentally end up with way too much spicy wasabi."

"Stop distracting me. Why don't you want me there? Is Sébastien uninvited as well?" The ninety-year-old Frenchman was one of Sanjay's mentors, and after meeting him the previous summer, I'd come to care for him a great deal.

Sanjay mumbled something incomprehensible.

"I didn't catch that."

"Would you"—Sanjay cleared his throat—"sign a nondisclosure agreement?"

"Why would I—"

"It's not that unusual for a magician to ask for one. It ensures you won't reveal Akira's secrets."

"Why is he going to tell me his secrets?"

"He's not. But you might accidentally see them."

"No." My brother spoke from my side.

"Fish?" Sanjay said. "Is that you?"

"Yes. Mahilan Jones, *Esquire*, here." He took the phone from my hand and put it on speaker. "My sister isn't signing a Japanese legal document. That's what you asked her about, isn't it?"

"I didn't think she would," Sanjay said. "Even if I thought it would be a good idea for her to come—which I don't—Jaya won't even have fun because she can't see us practice."

"Why didn't you tell me this earlier? Didn't you tell Akira more than a week ago that I'd be there?"

Sanjay's contract included an extra hotel room in Kyoto for an assistant, which he didn't currently have. Since all of his larger illusions had been destroyed, he was traveling solo and performing a smaller-scale act. Therefore, he decided to use the free extra room for moral support. Me.

"I did. But..."

"But *what?*"

"It has to do with the odd business I was telling you about."

"You didn't admit anything," Fish said.

"This call is costing me a fortune," Sanjay said.

"You have a fortune," I pointed out.

"That doesn't mean I want to waste it on a phone call."

"I'll reimburse you," Fish said. "This is important. I want to make sure my sister is safe if she goes to Japan."

Sanjay groaned. "It's not dangerous. But it's complicated. That's why Jaya shouldn't come."

"It's not just about you anymore," I said. "I've already committed to helping a Japanese professor with some research."

"You did?" Sanjay asked.

"There was no harm in agreeing to help since I thought I'd already be in Japan," I said. I didn't add that I hadn't agreed to help Professor Nakamura in person. Or that I hadn't actually gotten back to him yet. Or looked into his questions at all.

"But she's not signing any contract," Fish added.

I glared at my brother. The light from the porch illuminated his head like a halo. "Do you care more about my safety or my liability?"

"It's the same thing. Money is safety."

"Can you two have this philosophical conversation another time?" Sanjay said. "I accept defeat. I'll see you Sunday, Jaya."

"Wait," I said. "Aren't you going to tell me what's going on?"

"Since it won't make any difference to your decision, it'll be easier to show you in person."

CHAPTER 4

I had three hours until I needed to leave for the airport.

It was a beautiful Saturday afternoon, with a bright blue sky overhead and not a wisp of fog in sight in San Francisco. It had been two days since my strange conversations with Sanjay. I'd finished with faculty responsibilities and grading student papers, looked up the trading ship Professor Nakamura had contacted me about, and eaten chocolate and ham crepes for lunch with my brother. That particular combination wasn't listed on the menu, but the staff at my neighborhood crêperie knew me well.

My travel backpack sat next to the door, next to my heels and underneath a poster of coins used by East India Companies and a framed photo of my brother and me in the Berkeley hills as kids, with the Golden Gate Bridge behind us in the distance. The attic studio apartment felt more like home than anywhere I'd ever lived. Though it was small, I'd made it my own. The sloping ceilings of the Victorian house were more than high enough for my five-foot frame, a walk-in closet provided enough space for my tabla drums and books in addition to clothing, and the kitchenette was the perfect size for my style of cooking—meaning just enough countertop space to set my laptop as I looked up a restaurant that could provide me with the type of food I was craving. I loved to travel, but whenever I was gone for long, I missed the life I'd made for myself in San Francisco.

Three hours. If ever there was a good time to see a sort-of-ex-boyfriend and be sure I didn't let myself do anything I'd regret, this was the time.

Lane Peters was in San Francisco to consult with the Asian Art

Museum. I'd put off his open-ended offer to have coffee while he was in town. I still had strong feelings for him, so I didn't trust myself that coffee would simply be coffee.

I caught the N Judah light rail line to the museum. It was a Saturday, but he'd told me he was working weekends in the rush to prepare for the next exhibit. My plan was to call him once I was there, to avoid the awkwardness of figuring out what type of plans to make. But I didn't need my phone after all. As I walked into the museum, I caught a glimpse of him beyond the ticket counters.

Lane's dark blond hair had grown long again in the months since we'd seen each other, and along with horn-rimmed glasses, hid the sides of his face. But I'd know that face anywhere. I even recognized him when he was in disguise—which he wasn't today. He was dressed more formally than usual, in a slate gray suit and crisp white shirt with a stylishly cut collar. But what did I know of his "usual" life? There was no such thing, which was one of the reasons I needed time to figure out my own normal life, whatever that meant.

I flashed my museum pass and hurried into the brightly lit main hall to catch Lane. By the time I got there, he was nowhere in sight.

I walked up to the statue at the end of the grand hall. Hanuman, the shape-shifting monkey warrior from the Ramayana, the epic Indian poem, was bathed in light from the skylight above. Dozens of people stood in front of a mural that showed highlights of the twenty-five-hundred-year-old story of loyalty and deceit, princes and demons, and exile and enduring love. Lane Peters wasn't among the people reading the illustrated timeline. Where had he gone?

At the end of the summer I'd told Lane I needed a break from our relationship. Our long-distance affair had never been easy to categorize. It had been an exhilarating, baffling, passionate, nerve-racking, and blissful year.

I knew Lane cared about me more than was good for him, and that the feeling was mutual. That much wasn't in dispute. He had tried to hold me at arm's length when he believed he'd be forever looking over his shoulder for a looming danger that could befall either of us. But once we'd learned he was wrong about the threat at the end of our time together in Italy, I realized there was more than that keeping us apart. As soon as we knew we *could* be together, openly in the same city, I knew I wasn't ready.

It wasn't Lane. I wasn't ready to be with anyone. This had been the strangest year of my entire life—including the years I spent waitressing all over the U.S. before starting college and the months I hitchhiked across mainland Asia. I'd spent the previous year finding treasures across the globe, being pursued by dangerous thieves, and getting blackmailed into robbing a museum.

The man who'd blackmailed me saw something in me nobody else had seen: with the adrenaline pumping through my veins during that heist, I was the most invigorated I'd ever been in my life. It wasn't the heist that had scared me. It was what I was turning into. I'd lost myself. Who was I? Figuring out where I stood in my own life was the main reason I'd broken things off. But...I also had to admit it wasn't the only one. I wasn't ready to think about that now.

I took a deep breath and forced myself back to the present. Here in the museum I was surrounded by over eighteen thousand pieces of art created over six thousand years. I stood next to exquisite sculptures carved to honor the enduring love story of Prince Rama's quest to save his beloved wife by defeating a demon king. The effect was so strong I even imagined a familiar scent that included a hint of sandalwood. It was both comforting and exciting.

This was a bad idea.

I turned around to leave, and promptly stepped on someone's foot.

"Jones," he said, the emotion in his voice betraying his claim to respect my decision to be on my own right now.

Lane didn't move to give me a kiss, or even a hug, but the expression in his eyes betrayed his feelings. It reminded me of how he'd looked when we were stuck in the dungeons of Mont Saint Michel, the tide filling the old dungeons with water that was soon to drown us, and both trying to sacrifice ourselves for the other.

Without thinking, I squeezed his hand.

That small gesture was all it took. Lane's hug lifted me off the ground. He was a foot taller than me, so it was easy for him to do. He set me down as soon as he realized what he'd done.

"Old habits," he said, an apology in his eyes.

"Don't worry." I straightened my black cashmere sweater. "What's with the suit?"

"I'm supposed to impress some museum donors."

"You don't need a suit to do that."

"Since I'm not an English baron," he said in his impeccable English accent, "nor am I an Italian aristocrat," he said in a gregarious and thoroughly convincing Italian accent that included the movement of his whole body, "the suit will have to do for plain old Lane Peters." That last bit he said with his true Minnesota accent.

I glanced around. "Should you be doing that here?"

He shrugged. "What can I say? I'm bored."

"Me too." I'd graded a stack of papers, and he was about to meet donors. I loved my students, and he loved art history. Still, these weren't the lives either of us had imagined.

Lane's lips formed a smile. "You don't look bored."

"Well...I have a new research project. An eighteenth century Dutch East India Company ship that looks like it didn't follow normal trade routes." I meant to stop there, but more of the story rushed out of me. This was something I wanted to share with Lane. "A scholar who studies the colonial trading port of Dejima, Japan, noticed conflicting records and wondered if my research could resolve the discrepancy. It didn't, but now I'm intrigued. And since I'm going to Japan...Why are you looking at me like that?"

"Your face lights up when you get caught up in history."

"So does yours," I said. It was one of the most attractive things about him, possibly the one that sealed my fate in falling for him.

There are two conflicting reasons that explain why I've always loved history. First, history shows us so much about ourselves and our shared humanity across time and across cultures. Those connections that bridge time and space. Second, there's an inherent drama in history that's fundamentally unlike what we're living through. In the present moment, we're unable to step outside of ourselves and see the bigger picture—yet with its lessons from the past, history can shed light on the present. Lane Peters understood that better than anyone I knew. His own past haunted him, and he was now doing all he could to make up for it.

"Did you need my help with this research?" he asked. "I'd be happy to—"

"No, I'm leaving for Japan in a few hours."

"You're here for the Rama exhibit then?"

I shook my head. When my lips parted I found myself wanting to be doing something other than speaking. "I thought maybe..."

He didn't reply. My old professors must have been right about my wild imagination, because the mischievous sparkle in Lane's eyes spoke to me as clearly as if he'd said the words out loud. In his eyes, I saw the suggestion that we run off to a grand adventure that we both knew was a terrible idea but simultaneously desperately wanted.

Before I could finish my thought, Lane took my elbow to steer me aside. We were blocking the placard that explained Hanuman's everlasting devotion.

"Maybe...?" Lane prompted.

"I thought maybe before I need to leave for the airport—"

"Mr. Peters," a woman in a gold Kashmir shawl said. She stood next to a distinguished woman wearing a stunning ruby necklace. "I'm sorry to interrupt—"

"I'll be with you in a moment," Lane said.

"It's all right," I said softly. "Go."

Lane hesitated for a moment. It was enough time for the woman in the golden shawl to deftly steer him away.

I stood alone under the museum's skylight and whispered the rest of my unspoken sentence to myself. "I just wanted to see you."

CHAPTER 5

I sat on the steps outside the museum. Above me, pigeons fluttered around the stone pillars of the historic Beaux Arts building that combined different architectural styles. With the time I had left before catching my flight, I could have stayed for the Rama exhibit. But seeing Lane had given me an idea. I stood up, disturbing a petulant pigeon, and hurried across the street.

Two years ago, I wouldn't have thought of it. I hadn't always been as creative in how I thought of historical research. Not until I'd met Lane in his cramped and smoky basement office. But now I understood the clues that art could provide when piecing together history.

The San Francisco Public Library was only a block away from the museum. With the help of a librarian nearly as amazing as Tamarind, thirty minutes later I was sitting at a cubby surrounded by art history books. A book on Dutch painting lay open in front of me.

This couldn't be right, could it? My skin prickled with excitement. Thanks to Sanjay's dramatics, I'd taken a small request more seriously—and it had paid off.

Professor Nakamura had contacted me because of my research on trade routes when British, French, Dutch, and Portuguese East India Companies ruled large portions of India beginning in the 1600s. Wealthy merchants from European countries funded trading ships that traveled across the world to bring home spices and significant wealth. More often than not, they never made it home from their treacherous journeys.

The focus of my academic research was the British East India Company, but it was impossible to look at countries in isolation, since they so frequently joined forces or fought one another. The professor's research involved European trade in Japan and centered on Dejima, the Japanese island where the Dutch were allowed to enter Japan during its isolation period.

For over two hundred and fifty years, during the height of European influence, when foreign powers brought colonization and religion on their trading ships, Japan had closed itself off from the world. The punishment for a foreigner entering Japan, or a Japanese person leaving without special permission, which was rarely granted, was death. With one exception: During the *Sakoku* period that stretched from 1600 to the late 1800s, the Dutch were exempted from this law. At Nagasaki, the artificial island of Dejima was built to allow for trade with Dutch and Chinese merchants while maintaining a separation with the mainland, to make sure the foreigners wouldn't enter the country.

Dr. Nakamura was working on a lecture to teach his class how to do historical sleuthing when faced with incomplete information. As he prepared a case study, he'd come across conflicting information about ships that had docked at Dejima in the late 1700s. Sea trade routes were dependent on both weather patterns and political power, and ships didn't generally sail from Europe to India and continue onward to Japan. Yet he found conflicting references to a ship that appeared to have left the east coast of India for Japan. That's where I came in.

Historical research was challenging for many reasons, one being that the scribes who recorded information didn't have a shared understanding of spelling, and in many cases used different names altogether to refer to the same thing. Trading ships were one example of such discrepancies. Modern scholars try to make names consistent, but the people writing ledgers in the 1700s? Not so much. When present-day historians come across ship names that are suspiciously similar and have overlapping records, we try to resolve the discrepancies by using logs and other historical documents.

But sometimes we're wrong.

Here in front of me was evidence of an eighteenth-century Dutch trading ship—one that modern scholars had concluded never existed.

True, it was only a painting. It could have been fiction. But history is a puzzle with its pieces scattered by time and often purposefully hidden by people with an agenda. As a historian, it was my job to hunt for those missing pieces. It was entirely possible that I was wrong about my phantom ship. But I didn't think I was.

I glanced at the clock on my phone and groaned. I'd gotten so caught up in this research it was later than I thought. I was supposed to be at the airport.

I snapped photos of the most relevant pages, closed the books, and ran by the librarian's desk to thank her on my way out the door.

CHAPTER 6

I was the last person to board the flight, but I made it. I landed in Japan the following afternoon. Between the twelve-hour flight and the sixteen-hour time difference, it was already Sunday afternoon by the time I arrived.

I flew into Kansai International Airport, the closest airport to Kyoto. Like the old trading center of Dejima, KIX airport was an artificial island, though the one I stood on had been created over three hundred years after the island that had been built for Portuguese and then Dutch traders. Like Dejima, Kansai was filled with people from different parts of the world. I hurried through the modern terminal, passing multiple smoking rooms as I followed signs that pointed to the train station. I tried not to be distracted by the concourse shops selling items ranging from chocolates flavored with sake and green tea, to computer gadgets in the shape of sushi. I avoided the souvenirs but stopped briefly to buy a red bean paste sweet for a snack.

Sanjay was busy preparing for the magic show and couldn't meet me at the airport, but there was a direct train that took just over an hour to reach the historical city. Even with the noise of announcements on the train, the smooth motion was quite unlike the trains I was used to at home. After the long journey, the train lulled me to sleep—but a restless one.

Even on the other side of the world, where I was eager to see my best friend and witness the Indian Rope Trick, Lane Peters and eighteenth-century Dutch trading ships were on my mind. In my restless sleep, I dreamt that I was standing in the crow's nest lookout-point of an old-fashioned ship that looked more like a painting than a real one. From my perch I looked down on the wet wooden beams of the East Indiaman, while a cold rain threatened to send me tumbling into an icy ocean below. Two men stood on jagged planks of the wooden deck: Lane Peters and Sanjay Rai. Between them, a thick rope floated in mid-air, rising higher every moment, swaying precariously with the force of the storm. They were performing the impossible Indian Rope Trick.

I woke up with a start as an announcement in Japanese boomed through the overhead speakers. Sitting in the plush seat of the train, my jacket I'd been using as a blanket had fallen to the floor. No wonder I was dreaming of cold rain and icy waters.

Stepping off the train and hoisting my backpack onto my hips, I expected to find a calm, historical city. I knew Kyoto was once the capital of Japan, and laws had been passed to retain much of its historic roots. I immediately saw that those ordinances didn't apply to the Kyoto Station hub. As a cosmopolitan assortment of people darted around me, I felt almost like I was in New York City, except with Japanese signage and a more pleasant scent. The mouthwatering aroma of coffee and donuts filled my nostrils. On the train platform stood a coffee stand next to two vending machines with graphics of American celebrities.

While enjoying my donut, I accidentally went down too many levels and found myself walking past station maps that showed multiple underground shopping promenades that stretched for blocks, with everything from restaurants showcasing their signature meals with plastic replicas, to bookstores jammed from floor to ceiling with colorful books. I wished I had time to explore, but I was eager to get in touch with Professor Nakamura now that I'd arrived, plus I knew Sanjay was waiting for me. I found the taxi queue and caught a cab to the hotel.

Within minutes of leaving the train station, the modern part of town gave way not to countryside, but to narrow winding roads, buildings made of thick wooden beams, traditional lanterns, and, as I looked out the window more closely, hidden shrines and temples. *This* was historic Kyoto. Even before I had a history project of my own in Japan, I'd hoped to have time to explore local history. Now I was giddy with excitement for my quest to find a lost trading ship. I wondered what historical secrets Japan would offer up to me.

The taxi pulled into a modern hotel, hidden from the road by a row of bamboo trees. Sanjay had told me he'd meet me at my hotel, but when I checked in the front desk clerk handed me a note. The message was from Sanjay, telling me he'd gotten caught up longer than he'd hoped, but that if I wasn't too tired, I should meet him at a Buddhist temple.

My eyelids twitched with exhaustion, but there was no way I was going to sleep. The clerk checking me in told me about the lucky timing of my visit, which coincided with a long-awaited *netsuke* exhibit opening at the museum across the street from the hotel.

"All but one of a famous artist's collection has been reassembled here," she said as she handed me a map of Kyoto and circled the hotel. Spotting Professor Nakamura's university on the map, adrenaline replaced fatigue.

Once I reached my room I called his number, but it went straight to voicemail. I'd emailed him from the San Francisco airport with my findings, so he was expecting my call. I left a short message, then took a quick shower in the most modern bathroom I'd ever been inside—which included a toilet that sensed when I stepped close and raised its cover in response—before taking a taxi to the location Sanjay had given me.

On the drive, I felt as if I was traveling through time as well as space. Modern buildings of glass and concrete sat beside temples with oversized tour buses idling outside. On the sidewalks, rows of vending machines sold tea, beer, and even designer ties, while throngs of people hurried by wearing suits, school uniforms, stylish jeans and sneakers, and kimonos with wooden platform shoes.

We passed the famous Bamboo Grove. But that wasn't where we were headed. The taxi driver continued past the green stalks that stretched high into the sky and swayed in the November winds. Leaving the tourists behind, we continued on a deserted road not much wider than a footpath. Just where was Sanjay taking me?

The driver pulled over next to a lush forest where the trees parted to reveal a wooden entry gate with a steep hillside beyond. The driver smiled and pointed. I was glad he'd double-checked the destination, because I wouldn't have been sure this was the place. I hoped Sanjay would be there; otherwise I had no idea how I'd make it back to civilization.

There was no sign of Sanjay outside the temple's entry gates. Aside from a smiling young man at the ticket counter, I didn't see another living soul. I bought a ticket and went inside. As I stepped forward, I immediately felt the gaze of thousands of eyes. It was an odd sensation, because I could have sworn I was alone in the tranquil forest.

Moss-covered statues led up to a red-roofed structure that looked like a miniature castle. I was alone except for thousands of hand-carved statues that covered the hillside. I felt as if the figures were watching me. Each rough stone figure, no more than two feet high, captured a whimsical personality. I wasn't the type of person to claim they were open to all possibilities in this world. There's a clear distinction between fantasy and reality. It's a clear line, easy to see. But that didn't appear to be the case here in Kyoto.

I climbed the uneven rocky steps that led to more of the weather-worn sculptures. I stopped at the squat statue of a man wearing a wide grin visible beneath his stone mustache.

"It's perfect, isn't it?" Sanjay said, coming up beside me and stopping next to a statue of a bald man reading a book. "The perfect place for the impossible."

The stone faces welcomed me to the tranquil hillside, a world away from the crowded Bamboo Forest a mile or so down the winding road from where we stood. He knew I'd love it here, surrounded by history so real I could breathe it in with the scents of ubiquitous bamboo and running water from the small waterfall that passed through this hillside.

I turned and gave him a hug. His strong arms hugged me back, and his thick black hair brushed against the side of my face.

"You feel it too?" I asked, pulling back and smiling at his choice of clothing.

He was still dressed in a black tuxedo with black converse sneakers. It was the outfit he performed in. He held the other important piece of the ensemble in one hand: a classic black bowler hat. It was so thoughtful of him to have taken a break from preparing for his show to take me to this place he knew I'd love.

Sanjay tilted his head and gave me a questioning look.

"I'm in awe of the intense gazes of these statues," I said, stepping closer to the bibliophile statue.

Sanjay grinned. "I told you they were perfect for his act."

"What?"

"Akira's act. The utterly impossible act." He looked past the trees' spires toward the sky.

"That's why you brought me here to this spot? Because of a magic act?"

"Why else?"

"Never mind."

I turned away so Sanjay wouldn't see the flush I felt spreading on my face. I'd once thought of Sanjay simply as my cherished best friend. But after he'd been drugged while trying to help me draw out a killer, he'd kissed me. Which had changed everything.

I knew the kiss meant nothing to him. He hadn't even remembered it once the drug wore off. But that kiss had opened a question I didn't think was a possibility. I knew I loved Sanjay, my dearest friend, but that love had always been similar to how I felt about my brother. That kiss was like being spun around in a carnival ride and stepping off into another dimension that looked almost identical to the one I knew, but with something intangibly different. It scared me.

Between those two confused thoughts—needing to find myself and trying to figure out what Sanjay meant to me—I knew I was making the right decision to be on my own for a while. Lane had respected my wishes, and he'd done a better job than I'd hoped. Part of me had wanted him to defy me rather than do what I asked. The fact that he *did* listen made me respect and care for him even more. I couldn't win.

Sanjay would be mortified if he knew I'd ever thought of him as more than a brother, even though the moments were fleeting and confused. And if he ever remembered that when he was drugged he'd once kissed me, he'd die of embarrassment.

"What's up?" Sanjay asked.

I shook my head. "Akira can't possibly perform his show in this sacred, historical temple."

"I know. It's really too bad. If he could, it would be thematically perfect. This temple has been destroyed multiple times over the years, yet it gets resurrected each time. The real location of our show is just down the road from here."

"Speaking of the show," I said, "what exactly is going on?"

Sanjay's face relaxed. "In spite of everything, I'm glad you're here. It all started—" He broke off abruptly and swore. He pointed toward a grouping of statues and whispered, "He's here."

"Sanjay, I know you like theatrics, but—" My words died on my lips as I followed the direction of his index finger.

It hadn't been my imagination. One of the statues was moving.

CHAPTER 7

I shook myself. This was real life. Statues didn't come alive. The very idea was ridiculous. But men were alive. And that's what this was. A man hidden behind the statues. He'd been watching us.

And now, the man knew we'd seen him. He gave up hiding in his crouched position and stood up, giving me a clear view. Not that I could identify who he was. The figure was clad in black from head to toe, save for a space that revealed his eyes.

A ninja.

Was I really seeing a ninja? A medieval Japanese spy? That was certainly what he looked like from a few dozen feet away. The sprightly figure in black took off, running down the hillside between the statues and the trees. Even though he was small, I couldn't imagine how he'd gotten so close to us, even partly hidden behind the thin trees.

Sanjay snatched his hat in his hands and bounded down the stairs. "I can't let him get away!"

"What are you doing?" I called, but I doubted Sanjay heard me. He was already halfway down the hill, following the ninja. Was he kidding?

Sanjay paused when he reached the base of the stairs. He grasped the brim of his bowler hat in his right hand and flung it through the air—aimed at the ninja's head. The ninja darted away, and the hat made contact with the head of a stone figure instead. I was surprised to hear the loud clang that echoed through the air. The sound of metal hitting stone. I should have expected it. Sanjay's hat was no normal bowler hat. The custom-made prop was an integral part of his act.

Sanjay swore, but instead of going after his hat, he ran after the ninja. That small decision made me understand the importance of what was happening. If Sanjay thought it was more important to catch this man than save his beloved hat, this was more dire than I thought.

The ninja reached the base of the temple and was about to disappear from view. Sanjay turned away from me and broke into a sprint.

I slipped off my high heels and followed the pair in my bare feet, gripping one shoe in each hand. The rough stones bit into my feet, but I barely felt it. I was used to going barefoot, so my feet responded well.

I'd always worn heels not to be fashionable, but because I was short. It was only my thick black hair that got me to a full five feet tall. In normal life, three-inch heels seemed like the best choice. But what did normal even mean these days? I pushed all thoughts of a sensible life out of my mind as I ran down the uneven stone stairs and through the wooden entrance gate. A few seconds later, I reached the road outside the temple.

I couldn't tell which way they'd gone on the winding road that barely kept overhanging trees at bay—until I heard Sanjay cry out.

I tensed at the sound. I took off toward Sanjay's voice, thinking of how the ninjas from Japanese history were stealthy assassins. I crashed into Sanjay as I rounded the first bend in the road. I stumbled but stayed upright. At first I thought I'd knocked him over, until I realized he was already crouched on the side of the road rubbing his shin.

"He hurt you?" I asked.

Sanjay shook his head and wheezed.

Sanjay was fit, but not a sprinter. Out of necessity for his career success and his safety, he had developed flexibility (to fit into cramped cabinets) and upper arm strength (to break out of difficult spots), as well as fantastic breath control (to survive under water for close to two minutes). His career as The Hindi Houdini did not, however, necessitate being a fast runner.

"Where did he go?" I asked.

Sanjay pointed, and this time I did fall. I hadn't noticed the ninja was standing a few dozen yards beyond us. His eyes were the only part of his face not swathed in black cloth.

His stoic presence unnerved me. He was neither running away nor approaching. He was simply watching us, unmoving. I shivered.

"I need to get a look at his face," Sanjay whispered.

"I'll do it," I whispered as Sanjay helped me up. "I'm faster—"

"No." Sanjay's voice was quiet but firm, and he kept his hand on my arm.

"I'll take a photo so you'll know it's him." I shook free and stepped forward.

As soon as I made a move, the ninja bolted. I broke into a run.

"That's not what I meant," Sanjay shouted after me. I heard him call out the words "be careful" as I sprinted after the black-clad man.

This time our ninja didn't stick to the road, but cut through a field of tall grass.

The ground was prickly beneath my feet, but I pressed on.

Without shoes, I wasn't making much noise. If I was lucky, he'd soon think he'd lost me and slow down. Except my phone rang.

The ninja glanced back at me, but kept going. The open field gave way to thicker vegetation. Wispy tree branches whipped across my face, but I hardly felt them. The man was still several dozen yards ahead of me, but I'd kept pace with him. At the edge of a thicker section of trees, he paused and faced me. I kept running toward him—then stopped as abruptly as if I'd slammed into a tree. The ninja held a shiny metal star in his hand. The sharp kind that ninjas throw at you, the shiny blur of silver the last thing you ever see.

I couldn't see his lips, but I imagined him laughing under the black cloth as he nodded deliberately. He tucked the star into an invisible fold of his costume, bowed, then disappeared into the trees.

While I made my way back to Sanjay, I wondered if I'd fallen into a reality show. Sanjay had appeared on Indian MTV before, after all. I wondered if this could be another television stunt. Because really, how could I be chasing a ninja?

I stopped to get my bearings and rub the sore ball of my foot. I remembered I'd missed a call while chasing the ninja, so I also listened to the voicemail that had revealed my pursuit. It was Professor Nakamura, returning my call.

Sanjay reached my side, panting. "Please don't do that again."

"You didn't warn me he had death stars he'd throw at me."

"They're called *shuriken*, not death stars."

I stared at Sanjay. "You're not the least bit surprised."

"How are you not even winded?" He leaned into his knees and glanced around. "Where's a cold drink dispenser when you need one?"

I looked around the overgrown field to the trees with colorful autumn leaves. Not a building was in sight. We were in the middle of nowhere. "This is why you didn't want me to come. Because a ninja is after you?"

"He's never tried to hurt me before. I didn't know this would happen."

I gasped. "The way you said that...you know who it was."

"I don't know for sure. That's why I wanted to get close enough to grab his head covering and see his face."

"Who do you think it was?"

Sanjay hesitated before responding. "I don't really think it's him."

"Who?"

"Hiro," Sanjay said. He smoothed the edges of his damaged hat and avoided meeting my gaze. "Hiro Matsumoto."

He pronounced the name like the English word "hero." It was a name I remembered.

"Your dear *friend* might be the person who almost killed me?"

"Can you find me a cold drink? It's time for me to tell you everything."

CHAPTER 8

Sanjay polished off a second plastic bottle of cold green tea we'd purchased from a vending machine and threw it into a trashcan. "The ninja," he said, "has been spying on Akira and his assistant, Yako. And once I arrived last week, he began following me too."

"Why?" I looked carefully around the more central part of Arashiyama that we'd made our way to on foot. I spotted the raised platform of a train station in the distance, but no ninjas were in sight.

"It appears someone is attempting to steal Akira's secrets. Or worse."

"Worse? You mean trying to kill him with those ninja weapons?"

"No. Trying to expose Akira as a fraud."

"He *is* a fraud," I said. "His whole act is premised on him possessing supernatural powers."

"He's a great magician and showman. In that sense, he's not a fraud."

I stared at my friend in disbelief. "You idolize Houdini and hate the charlatans who claim to perform real miracles. Frauds like Akira."

"It's more complicated than that."

"Then please explain it to me. I don't get it. You're here in Japan for your Japanese debut as a magician, made possible by Akira, Japan's most famous magician. Akira invited you both because you're somewhat famous—"

Sanjay cleared his throat. I internally rolled my eyes.

"Right, because you're *world* famous," I corrected, but couldn't help adding, "in the magic world. And because Akira's big summer show is based around the Indian Rope Trick, therefore an Indian theme. So he thought getting the famous Hindi Houdini would be a great addition to warm up the crowd and get them in the mood for his grand illusion, which will be witnessed by a lucky few hundred people and also televised to millions. I get all that. What I don't understand is why you said yes."

"My theater—"

"Is a poor excuse. There are plenty of magicians you could work for who don't claim to possess fake powers. And who don't have strange men dressed as ninjas following them around."

Sanjay's lips twitched. "If you'd seen some of his enthusiastic fans, you'd know the spying ninja is one of the least strange among them. Anyway, the man dressed as a ninja, who I really hope isn't Hiro, probably thinks I know the secret of how the trick is done. But I don't. Akira never tells anyone how his illusions are performed."

"That's what's especially weird about this whole situation. Akira is still keeping you in the dark. I thought you signed a nondisclosure agreement so he wouldn't have to keep it a secret from you."

"It's not such a strange thing. The contract was just a precaution in case I accidentally saw anything I shouldn't. Magicians are very guarded with their illusions. Especially in this case. You have to understand, this illusion is different than all others. The Indian Rope Trick is considered the world's greatest illusion."

"Tamarind and I read up on it. It sounds pretty cool. Why haven't you done it? Too cliché?"

"No. Because it's impossible."

"That's what you said before we were so rudely interrupted by your ninja friend. But Akira is going to do it, so I know you're just being dramatic."

"I meant what I said. It goes against all the laws of physics and is truly not possible to do as it's been described—not unless real magic exists, as Akira claims."

"You don't believe that."

"No. And neither does Akira. It's only his public persona. Which is very annoying." Sanjay breathed deeply. It seemed to calm him, because he grinned at me. "Do you want to hear the story behind the Indian Rope Trick? It's big on history, so you'll love it. Hang on." Sanjay pulled his cell phone from what looked like thin air but must have been a pocket. Sleight of hand was second nature to him. He probably hadn't realized he'd done it.

A range of emotions flickered across his face. I knew my best friend well enough to read most of his facial expressions, but not this time. After recognizing fear and anger, I couldn't gauge the emotion he landed on.

"We have to leave," he said. The phone was nowhere in sight. "There's a change of plans."

"What's happened?"

"Not only does Hiro want to expose Akira as a fraud. He's stooped to something far worse. Sabotage."

I realized, then, the emotion that had flickered across Sanjay's face. He was terrified.

CHAPTER 9

I was so unprepared to see terror on Sanjay's face that I knew I had to be missing something.

With the level of illusions Sanjay and Akira performed, a maliciously loosened bolt could kill them. Yet Sanjay lived up to his namesake and had pulled off brazen escapes that rivaled those of Houdini, even after things went wrong. What made this different from all the death-defying situations he'd previously been in?

"Are we heading to Akira's workshop?" I asked. "Is that where the sabotage happened?"

"No. We're going back to the hotel." He began walking briskly in the direction of the train station. "To pack our bags. We're going home."

"Wait...what?" I stared at my friend in disbelief.

"I knew you never should have come. I shouldn't have either. If I'd known it would come to this—"

I grabbed Sanjay's hand and forced him to stop walking. "What's going on with you?"

"Sabotage." He blinked at me. "Weren't you listening?"

"You've coped when things went wrong in your act before. Didn't you tell me one of your assistants screwed up when you were buried alive?"

"That was different."

"In a how-could-it-possibly-get-worse-than-being-buried-alive way."

"Don't you get it, Jaya? Someone is *intentionally* trying to screw up this performance. I can control for risk, which I can calculate. Not deliberate sabotage that could come at me in unexpected ways."

"But it's still—"

"I've only ever been good at one thing, Jaya. I can't lose it. I know you all think I have a big ego, but it's justified."

I would have laughed at Sanjay's ego if it hadn't been for the fear in his eyes. "We all know you're a great magician, but—"

"I didn't drop out of law school because I'd rather perform magic."

"Of course you did. You've told me that story a dozen times."

"I didn't drop out to become a magician," he said. "I dropped out because I was failing." He let the words hang in the air. His eyes were fearful as he watched my face for a reaction.

"Sanjay..."

"I've never told that to another person," he whispered.

"There's no shame in taking a while to figure out what you're good at in life. Now that you've found it, it doesn't matter what the rest of us think. I don't care about you because of your fancy apartment, clothes, and car. Surely you know that."

"You still don't get it, Jaya. Now that I've been working with Akira for a week, I've seen his hand up close. Underneath the glove. It's not an act. His hand was completely crushed when something went wrong. If anything like that were to happen to me, it's not just my career that would be over. It would be my life. I'm not like Akira. I'm not willing to be famous by pretending I perform real miracles. All I've got is my skills. I can't survive sabotage."

I squeezed his hand. "Why didn't you ever tell me?"

His face darkened and he pulled away from me. "That I'm a flunky who can only do one thing right?"

"That's not true."

"Please stop humoring me, Jaya."

"And there are plenty of things you'd be great at if you weren't a magician." I didn't add that playing sitar wasn't one of them. But I sympathized. I couldn't imagine doing something I didn't feel as passionately about as I did history.

"Well I'd rather not find out." He started walking again. This time with his arms wrapped in front of his chest so I couldn't take his hand.

"I'll see you back home next week," I said, not moving.

He whirled around. "Very funny."

"I'm serious. I've got research to do here. My life doesn't revolve around you, Sanjay Rai. I wanted to support you in your Japanese debut, but if you're overreacting and leaving, that doesn't mean I have to."

"Fine," he said through clenched teeth. "You win. We'll go to Akira's workshop and find out how bad the sabotage is. I'll reserve judgment until then." He glanced at his phone. "We have exactly nine minutes and twelve seconds to get to the platform before our train departs."

"Glad your sense of humor is back."

"Sorry to disappoint you." Sanjay resumed walking. "You've only been in Japan for a few hours, so you haven't learned how prompt Japanese trains are. I wasn't kidding."

We walked briskly to the train station, with Sanjay brushing off my questions as his eyes darted around. Did he think the ninja was spying on us beyond the bamboo trees or from behind a building? In this part of Kyoto, I saw only traditional wood buildings, so a sixteenth-century ninja warrior would have fit right in.

"Why aren't we catching a cab?" I asked.

Sanjay frowned but kept walking. "The location of Akira's workshop is a secret."

"I don't expect you to tell the taxi driver we're going to his secret lair."

Sanjay's eyes narrowed. "It doesn't have an exact address. The best way I know to get there is to repeat how I've gotten there before."

We made it to the station with two minutes to spare, and I stepped onto the train at the exact minute Sanjay had declared. I was hoping to hear more about the sabotage, but the people on the train remained silent, mostly reading paperback books with beautiful covers, so we refrained from speaking for the fifteen-minute ride. I was too fidgety to sit in one of the few free seats, so I stood between a Buddhist priest dressed in black and gold robes reading a novel and a man in his early twenties wearing an LA Raiders hat and flicking long hair out of his eyes as he looked at his phone. The sight of long hair falling over an attractive man's face brought on an involuntary memory. I couldn't stop myself from thinking of Lane. I looked across the smoothly running train and let my gaze fall on my best friend, his lips turned up into a small smile as he watched the scenery on the outskirts of Kyoto go by. What was I doing here? What was I doing with my life?

Twenty minutes later, we disembarked at the bustling Kyoto Station.

"You're doing the right thing," I said. "You can at least find out what's going on before you make a decision."

"I should warn you about Akira," Sanjay said as we navigated our way around bundles of businessmen in crisp suits and travelers with shiny rolling suitcases. "I thought I'd have time to tell you more before you met him. Since you're meeting him sooner than I expected, and not under ideal circumstances, I want to make sure you're prepared."

When Sanjay had told me about this invitation, in typical form, the account had been all about Sanjay himself. In what was basically a one-sided conversation, we bounced around ideas about which of his illusions could be best performed outside on a grand scale, with equipment that hadn't been destroyed or that he could recreate quickly. He'd only mentioned Akira in passing. I'd learned more about him from Tamarind and the internet.

"I'm most interested in why you're putting up with him," I said.

Sanjay glanced sharply at me, but didn't slow his pace as we darted around a group of school kids in uniform lined up for a field trip. "This is a great opportunity, Jaya. I can't very well go back to my theater—"

"I know." Part of me didn't blame Sanjay. This *was* a great opportunity. He had passed up the Las Vegas scene back at home in favor of carving out his own niche in the Napa Valley of California. Wineries in the region had realized some years ago that their clientele liked to be entertained once they'd had their fill of sampling the famous wines of the region. Many concert venues had sprung up for the National Public Radio set. Sanjay's magic shows were part of that mix. He was able to charge high ticket prices for extravagant shows. Not as big and extravagant as Vegas, but he'd made a good living at it.

He didn't have a mortgage or family attachments. He rented a luxurious studio apartment in San Francisco, where he had some good friends, including his best friend, yours truly, but nothing was holding him back from traveling or living anywhere in the world.

"He's not asking me to pretend to be like him," Sanjay said. "My act will be the same as always. Akira isn't asking me to change that. I still deserve the name Houdini."

He sounded more like he was trying to convince himself than me. I held my tongue as I hurried to keep up. Sanjay was five ten, compared to my five foot zero. I walked fast, but he was purposefully trying to get ahead of me.

Through Sanjay, I'd learned that Houdini had been a spiritualist debunker in addition to a renowned escape artist. Houdini had been outraged at the fraud that deceived so many desperate people and cheated them out of their money in hopes of reuniting with dead loved ones. Akira played on those same fears and hopes in people; he was the antithesis of the type of magician Sanjay aspired to be. That same difference of opinion had ruined the friendship of Harry Houdini and Arthur Conan Doyle. I hoped Sanjay wasn't setting himself up for similar disappointment.

In my haste to keep up with Sanjay as he zigzagged through the train station, I ran into him when he came to an abrupt halt.

Sanjay swore. I wasn't sure if it was directed at me or the item that had caused him to stop. Plastered to a column in the station was a ten-foot-high poster. The style of illustration evoked a feeling of days gone by, including faux-faded edges. Art Nouveaux lettering across the top of the poster stated "Indian Rope Trick," with Japanese characters underneath. It was a poster for Akira's magic show.

Akira commanded the center of the poster, his illustrated face a mesmerizing mix of power, beauty, and sadness. He wore a white tuxedo, but his reflection in a mirror behind him showed him dressed in a kimono and holding a glass ball dotted with gold specks. Surrounding Akira were three figures of lesser importance. To his left was a beautiful woman with her own altered reflection, a fox dressed in the same clothes. Above Akira's head, a rugged sailor held a Dutch flag. I thought of my Dutch ship. Because of the isolationist period of Japanese history, much of Japan's history with foreign powers was tangled up with the Dutch.

I forgot about the ship as my eyes fell to the other side of the poster. A south Asian man with an outstretched arm pointed at a rope that rose to the sky. I couldn't tell if the illustration had been based directly on Sanjay, or if it was representing the origin of the Indian Rope Trick in general. It looked somewhat like him, but it was missing his signature bowler hat. I thought of the hat as his security blanket. He never went anywhere without it. I don't think I'd ever seen a photo of him without that hat.

"Did you know about this?" I asked.

He shook his head as he took in the poster. "I knew this show was a big deal because of my paycheck, and the fact it's being televised...But this? No."

He lifted his bowler hat from his head and ran his fingers around the brim. He rapped on the top of the hat with his knuckles and a length of rope fell out.

"Show-off." I stuck out my tongue at him.

I expected him to laugh, or at least grin at me. Instead, he looked intently at the poster. I could have sworn he looked suddenly claustrophobic in the bustling train station.

"It looks like," he said, "this is going to be impossible to get out of."

CHAPTER 10

Akira Kimura, whose stage name was simply Akira, was an outdoor performer. There was no theater at which to meet him. Instead, we were on our way to his workshop, a small warehouse where he built the equipment he needed and practiced with it in front of a camera. On the short walk to his workshop, Sanjay impressed upon me the importance of playing along with Akira's act.

"How on earth did you find this place?" I asked as we followed signs written in Japanese characters through a narrow alley off an open-air market street that smelled like fish. Sanjay had zero attention span when it came to anything besides magic, so there was no way he'd learned how to read kanji.

"His assistant, Yako, took me here the first time I visited." He stopped in front of a gray door with a brass fox-head knocker.

"There are no markings," I said. "Are you sure it's the right place?"

Sanjay looked around. "Quite."

He knocked, and a moment later, the door clicked open. Sanjay pushed it in, and we stepped into a dark, dusty room. As soon as Sanjay shut the door behind us, a light turned on. It illuminated a six-foot-long hallway flanked by storage shelves filled with cardboard boxes. A door on the opposite end opened. I could see why this was a good spot for a hidden workshop. It was centrally located and hidden in plain sight. Akira's fans must have wanted to find him. Even if they got through the first door, they'd only find what looked like a storage closet for one of the adjoining businesses.

Beyond the second door stood a man with beautiful lips, silky black hair that fell beyond his shoulders, and the most chiseled jaw I'd seen outside of Hollywood or Bollywood films. It was the same man who appeared in the music video and posters I'd seen. He was even more handsome in person. The boy band producers knew what they were doing.

"Houdini-san," a petite woman with lush red hair said from behind Akira. She bowed to Sanjay, causing her beautiful long hair to ripple. Her bow was more than a nod, but less than the low bow I'd been greeted with at my hotel.

"It took you long enough to get here," Akira said in English with only a hint of a Japanese accent. He wore purposefully ripped skinny jeans and a white t-shirt so bright it must have been plucked from a bottle of bleach. "And you weren't supposed to bring anyone who hadn't signed my nondisclosure agreement." His eyes flicked to mine.

"Jaya's hardly another person," Sanjay said. "You can think of her as an extension of me and can trust her completely. Not that you're going to tell her anything about the act."

Akira sighed as he studied my face, then the rest of my body. "True."

I wasn't the type of person to be easily intimidated. I regarded him and his workshop as openly as he watched me. Images of foxes surrounded us. Ornate fox heads had been carved into pieces of wooden furniture and freestanding fox carvings adorned shelves.

"Being surrounded by spirit fox energy helps me perform my miracles," Akira said, following my gaze.

I laughed. Nobody joined me.

"Akira-san and Yako-san," Sanjay said, "may I introduce Jaya Jones."

"Nice to meet you," I said, unsure of how to address them since I knew using surnames was much more common in Japan, even though Sanjay had used only their given names. Was I supposed to shake hands or bow? I opted for a slight nod of my head.

"I'm pleased to meet you, Jones-san," Yako said.

"Please call me Jaya. And you can talk about what's happened. I won't say anything. You really don't have to put on an act around me."

Akira cocked his head to one side and looked between me and Sanjay. "Houdini-san didn't tell you about me?"

Sanjay shrugged noncommittally. I didn't blame him. How was one supposed to answer that question?

"Good," Akira said. "Very good. You're a blank slate."

"I wouldn't say—" I began.

"What do you know about Japanese mythology?" he asked me.

"I suppose I know the most about Buddhism. Buddhist deities were imported from India and China long ago, so Buddhist temples frequently exist alongside Shinto shrines."

"Then you aren't familiar with *kitsune*—fox spirits. *Kitsune* can be good or evil, ranging from mischievous to malevolent." His gaze moved from me to Yako.

"You're the fox," I said to Yako. "From the posters. Your reflection is a fox."

Yako replied with an enigmatic smile.

"Indeed," Akira said. "She is a *kitsune*, a fox spirit who can take on human form. Yako is one name for a *kitsune*. It suits her, don't you think?" A glass ball with flecks of gold materialized in his good hand. "I possess her spirit ball, so she must follow my will."

He flicked the spirit ball toward the high ceiling of the warehouse, where it disappeared. "Many years ago," Akira continued, "I suffered an accident." He nodded towards his gloved hand. "When I was in the hospital, I prayed for death. Without the ability to be a performer, I had no reason to go on. Sensing my weakness, a spirit visited me. She tried to possess me, as *kitsune* do by seducing men. But I was smarter. I was able to capture the source of her power, her spirit ball. With that prized possession, a person can control his *kitsune*. When I die, it will return to her."

"Akira," Yako said. Her voice was quiet but firm.

"*Hai*," Akira said, a cell phone appearing in his hand. "You're right. We don't have time for this. We need to discuss the break-in. I'll call our uninvited guest a taxi—"

"Cut it out," Sanjay said.

"I'll hold you personally responsible if she reveals anything," Akira said, glaring at him.

"I can make my way back to the hotel," I said. I knew Sanjay must have been dying to find out about the sabotage, and Akira wasn't talking with me there. If he didn't want me there, I had my own work to do. And delicious Japanese cuisine to eat. I was starving.

"Don't go," Yako said. "We need all the assistance we can get."

Akira's lips turned up in a smirk. "If my Yako tells me, so it shall be." He pressed his hands together and bowed deeply, but I had the distinct impression it was a mocking gesture. His physical features became less handsome with each word he spoke.

"Stay," Yako said. "I will make tea." Her English was more formal than Akira's, and her accent stronger. Her long hair, dyed a bright shade of auburn, swished like an ocean wave in a typhoon as she turned away and walked to the back of the cavernous room. I could see why he'd hired her. She'd be a superb distraction for the audience. I made a mental note to ask her what hair products she used. Now that my hair was growing out longer than the bob I'd had for years, I didn't know what to do with it.

"Forgive me for my rudeness," Akira said to me, but again I was struck by his insincerity.

I opened my mouth but Sanjay shot me a warning look.

"Can we please focus," Sanjay said. "What in the name of Heaven and Earth did the intruder sabotage?"

"You're not going to like it, Sanjay," Akira said. "You're not going to like it at all."

CHAPTER 11

Akira pointed toward a wooden barrel that sat by itself on the workshop floor, with nothing around it for ten feet in any direction. "The water escape."

Sanjay swallowed hard and strode to the barrel. He bent down and, without touching it, examined the wooden lid and the black calligraphy painted on the side. It looked like a wine barrel that had been compressed and adorned.

"What's the matter with it?" I asked, looking for signs it had been damaged and seeing none. "It looks like a normal barrel."

Sanjay shook his head. "First of all, this was never a normal sake barrel. Second, it would have killed Akira. Or me."

"I never would have noticed the change until it was too late," Akira said, "if he hadn't moved it when he broke the escape mechanism."

As I drew closer to get a better look, the large door in the back of the workshop began to move—or rather, seemed to move. It wasn't the true door I'd spotted on my way in, but its reflection in a mirror. The workshop was the size of a small warehouse. Besides the door we'd entered, the only way in or out that I could see was a metal garage door large enough for a truck. Lane had gotten me in the habit of checking for exits.

"Hiro has gone way too far," Akira said. "At least I had the diary on me, so he couldn't get his hands on it."

"We might have seen him today too," Sanjay said before I could ask what diary Akira was talking about.

Akira's bravado faltered. He looked rattled for the first time since

I'd arrived.

"A man was dressed as a ninja," I said, "spying on us while we were at the site that Sanjay thought would be perfect for your illusion."

"When?" Akira asked.

"Right before we came here," Sanjay said.

"He must have captured a *kitsune* of his own," Akira said, "to be in two places at once."

"We got lost," I said. "No supernatural explanation necessary. He could have been forty-five minutes ahead of us."

"You didn't call to warn me?" Akira snapped at Sanjay.

"Why would I need to warn you? You already knew he tried and failed before."

Akira shook his head and uttered what I was fairly certain wasn't a complimentary word in Japanese, before switching to English. "That man doesn't give up. I should have realized my security wasn't enough. I have cameras at the doors."

I wondered how many doors there were. The cavernous workshop created a distorted sense of space. There was something off-kilter about the whole setup.

"No guard?" Sanjay asked.

"A live guard would only bring more people here. With my locks, nobody should have been able to get inside."

"Except another magician," Sanjay said.

Akira nodded. "My followers have never gotten inside. They haven't come close. Even the most devoted."

"Followers?" I asked. "Do you mean your fans?"

"You find my English lacking?" he said.

"I'm sure it's better than mine," I said, disliking him more and more as the minutes went by. "Why did you call your fans 'followers'?"

I expected a glib reply, but Akira didn't respond. At least not with words. I caught a glimpse of pure sadness in his eyes. It was such a raw, unguarded emotion, I couldn't help feeling sorry for him. But it only lasted a moment.

"My cameras have motion detectors," he said, turning his attention back to Sanjay. "They send me a video of what sets them off."

"You saw Hiro?" Sanjay asked. "You saw his face?" The desperation in his eyes was clear. He didn't want his friend to be guilty.

Akira pulled up a video on his cell phone and held it out for us to see.

"The ninja," I whispered. I looked more closely, but almost as soon as his face appeared on the screen, it was blacked out by a hand and the blackness of spray paint.

"It's the same man," Sanjay said.

"I can't tell for sure," I said, shaking my head. "Can you play it again?"

Akira obliged. Even with only one good hand, he had extraordinary dexterity in handling the phone and maneuvering his fingers over the screen.

"I agree it's the same guy," I said. "But we can't see his face in the video, just as we couldn't see it earlier today."

Sanjay fidgeted with his hat. "I can't tell if I've talked myself into it looking like Hiro or if it really does."

"I got the closest look," I said. "Does anyone have a photo of him?"

"I do," Yako said.

I gave a start as I saw her standing next to me holding a tray with four cups and a tea kettle. The tea set looked like it belonged in a museum, but that wasn't what had startled me. I hadn't seen or heard her approach.

"Why do you have a photo of that traitor?" Akira asked.

Yako ignored him and picked up a hefty hardback book from a narrow oak bookshelf with fox bookends. She flipped through the pages as both men tapped their feet nervously.

"Here," she said, holding up the image of a modern magic show poster.

I shook my head. "It's been airbrushed. I can't tell."

"I wish I could send the police to arrest him," Akira said. "They'd be able to prove it's him."

"But with the police presence," I said, "your fans would learn the location of your workshop."

"She's quick," Akira said, looking at me but speaking to Sanjay. "And with that small body, she'd fit nicely in false panels. Why isn't she your assistant?"

"Yes, well, Jaya loves her job as an historian," Sanjay mumbled.

"Is that tea? I'd love some."

Yako smiled and scooped a light green powder into the small handle-less mugs and whisked as she added a small amount of hot water. The powder and water formed a paste, which dissolved in hot water as she filled the mugs the rest of the way.

Akira didn't thank Yako for the tea. He lounged against a wooden desk like a man without a care in the world as he sipped, but his face told another story. Like Sanjay, he seemed more worried about the sabotage than he was letting on.

"The question," he said, "is what we do about the traitor Hiro. This has gone too far. As a nonbeliever he'll ruin everything. We need to strike before he does."

I didn't like where this conversation was going.

Sanjay must have read my expression, because he motioned for me to calm down. He stepped away from us, out of Akira's view.

"It's not necessary," Yako said.

I felt my phone buzz from my jacket pocket. Glancing at the screen, I saw a text message from Sanjay. *He doesn't believe what he's saying. It's a performance. P.S. Delete this text. P.P.S. Not kidding. Delete this.*

Akira was a damn good performer in that case. I deleted the text and slipped the phone back into my pocket.

"I suppose you're right," Akira said. "I should be generous. It's not surprising Hiro failed. I'm the one with the *kitsune.*"

"And your fox spirit led you to the real Indian Rope Trick," I said.

Akira nodded, an arrogant smirk hovering on his lips. He handed me a glossy magazine opened to a full-page photograph of himself and Yako. This wasn't the magic show poster, but a press photograph. I couldn't read the Japanese writing, but it looked as if the two of them were inside a museum. From the cramped cases visible around them, it was a small one. A weathered old book was in Akira's hands. No, it wasn't a book. The text on the pages was handwritten. This was the diary he'd been talking about.

"Is that German?" I asked, squinting at the photograph.

"Dutch," Yako said. "It was the writings of a Dutchman who lived here during the Edo period, when Japan was closed to foreigners."

"Why wasn't the Dutchman beheaded?" Sanjay asked. "I thought that's what they did with foreigners then."

"The Dutchman of Dejima was a great man," Akira said, pointing to the poster for the show that hung on the wall behind him. It was similar to the one we'd seen at the train station, Akira in the center with three smaller figures hovering around him: a European sailor carrying a Dutch flag, a woman whose reflection was a fox, and an Indian man conjuring a rope to the sky.

"Actually," I said, "the Dutch East India Company was the only European foreign trading power allowed access during that time through the artificial island of Dejima. He didn't need to be anyone special to be granted access."

Akira frowned. I'd known more about the subject than he thought I would.

"The man wrote of traveling to India before Japan," Yako said, "and it was there he witnessed the Indian Rope Trick. He wrote down its secrets in this book."

"Did the museum realize what it had?" I asked. It wasn't uncommon for museums, especially small ones, to be overwhelmed and take years to catalogue their collections.

Akira's frown deepened.

"The museum," Yako said, "honors the tradition of cooking. Those were the pages they displayed."

"Really?" Sanjay said. "There's a museum dedicated to cooking?"

Yako laughed. "Kyoto is filled with hundreds of small museums, celebrating subjects such as tea, textiles, children's dolls. We honor our history."

"That's enough history." Akira snapped the magazine shut and tucked it into a drawer.

I resisted the urge to grab it back. I wasn't done looking at the intriguing photograph. Why didn't he want me to see it? It was clearly a staged photograph meant for the public. Was he worried that as a trained historian I'd notice it was fake? Akira had gone all out for this illusion, but there was no danger that I'd challenge the photo. I didn't speak eighteenth century Dutch and knew nothing about the paper of the time.

"Is it the trick itself that's a miracle," I asked, "or is the miracle the way you found this historical trick lost to history?"

"You don't believe me?" Akira sneered. "I hope Houdini-san told you what happens to people who don't believe. If not, you should ask him. It is unwise to doubt me."

"Yes, well," Sanjay said, tossing his bowler hat onto his head, "it's been great, Akira. I just saw that I missed an important call, so I need to leave. I'll see you tomorrow. And I'll tell you if anything strange happens on my end."

Sanjay hooked his hand around my elbow and steered me toward the door.

"One moment," Akira said.

We turned around at the door.

"Tomorrow," Akira said, "I will show you the secret of the Indian Rope Trick."

For once, Sanjay was speechless.

"Meet me at the performance site at noon," Akira said to Sanjay. "My *kitsune* wishes you to be part of the illusion. The great Hindi Houdini will be performing the Indian Rope Trick with me."

I pushed the inner door open and pulled Sanjay along with me. After the second door slammed behind us, I could still faintly make out Akira's voice bellowing at Yako in Japanese. By the time we were a few steps away, I could no longer hear Akira. If not for the fox knocker, I wouldn't have been able to determine which unmarked door led to the world of the magician and his fox spirit.

CHAPTER 12

"Thanks for faking a phone call," I said once we were a few paces down the sidewalk. "That guy is creepy. I can see why you were eager to jump at a chance to leave. Maybe you were right and you should go home."

"Are you kidding?" Sanjay grinned at me. "I'm going to be part of the headlining act now."

"The *impossible* act."

"You were right that I was being too hasty." Sanjay tapped the screen of his phone. "But I wasn't faking it. I missed two calls from Sébastien."

"Hang on a second. You're going to be part of an impossible illusion just a few days before performing, and that makes you *want* to stay? And why didn't you warn me about Akira?"

"I tried! Really, I did." Sanjay shoved his phone back into his pocket and led us farther away from Akira's unmarked door. "But now that you've met him, you can see there were too many things to warn you about. Which one should I have picked? The fact that he says he enslaves a spirit by keeping her strange ball hostage, or that he is so secretive he won't even let his guard down around you because you didn't sign that damn nondisclosure agreement—you really should have told me Fish-man was with you on that phone call, or I never would have brought it up. He can't forget he's a lawyer even when he's not working."

"He's never not working," I muttered.

"And then there's the gruesome accident that nearly killed Akira. His complete transformation from pop performer to harnessing miracles. And don't forget his ominous assistant, with her foxlike movements." Sanjay shuddered.

"I'd hardly call her ominous."

"Didn't you notice?"

"Notice what? Oh, that gorgeous red hair of hers does seem rather supernatural, since I have no idea how she controls it. I'll give you that. She was a natural to play the part of a mythological fox on stage."

"Not her hair." Sanjay stopped underneath a paper lantern hanging outside a sweets shop. I wondered if he was as peckish as I was, but he didn't turn into the shop. Instead, he faced me with a grim expression on his face. "When she walks across a squeaky floor, it doesn't squeak."

I thought back on how she'd snuck up on us with the tea. "You're freaked out by her because she's a good magician's assistant," I said. "You're starting to believe Akira's persona, and we're getting away from the point. You and I hung out for hours the night before you left San Francisco. Hours. All you did was talk about yourself. None of this."

He blinked innocently at me. "But I had to figure out what I was going to perform and practice. And you're always such a good sport as my guinea pig."

"Come on," I said. "I'm starving. Let's go find something to eat for dinner."

"Let me listen to Sébastien's messages first."

Sanjay listened to the messages and shook his head.

"He's still stuck in Nantes?" I asked.

"I don't know what magic he worked to get around his flight delay, but apparently he landed at Kansai earlier this afternoon, and he's already through customs. His last message says he's on the way to his hotel." Sanjay pulled a palm-size piece of paper from his pocket and scribbled the name of a hotel with a pen that appeared as if from thin air.

"He's not staying at the same one we are?"

Sanjay shook his head. "He wanted to stay in a *Ryokan*, a traditional Japanese inn. I'm going to meet him there. Do you want to come?"

I took a moment before answering. I was torn in too many directions. I was dying to get in touch with Professor Nakamura to look for our missing ship. But I also wanted to see Sébastien. And eat. And find out more about Akira and the sabotaged magic act. And make sure Sanjay was all right. I could combine everything except for Professor Nakamura. So going to the *Ryokan* won out.

"I'm coming," I said. "On the way, you can fill in the rest of the details Akira wasn't telling me. Like what's the deal with his accident? Was it sabotage as well?"

"I don't think so," Sanjay said.

I waited for him to elaborate, but he didn't.

"What happened?" I prompted.

"You don't want to know."

"I have an internet connection. With a few taps into a search engine—"

"Seriously, Jaya. Don't look it up."

"If there's any possibility that was sabotage as well, we should know. I know you're afraid—"

Sanjay took my hand in his, stopping me from using my phone. "For once, Jaya, will you please listen to me?"

His eyes were filled with such pleading, I couldn't refuse. I slipped my phone back into my bag. I'd look it up later. "Fine. At least explain to me what you know Akira is going to do with this famous illusion. Tamarind found the history of the Indian Rope Trick before I left. It makes for a good story, but I hadn't heard of it before. It's not nearly as famous as sawing a woman in half. How can it be the most famous illusion in the world?"

The night air was crisp. Sanjay flipped up his jacket collar as we began walking. "It's not."

"We read—"

"It's known as 'the world's greatest illusion.' There's a difference. This one is the most difficult, since nobody knows how to do it. It's the Holy Grail to magicians. Something one *wants* to believe, and that's been documented many times in history, but that the realist inside you suspects doesn't actually exist."

"But somehow Akira is going to perform it and rope you into it."

"A pun? Really? You've been hanging around Tamarind too much."

We turned from the small alley-like street and found ourselves on a broader road, next to a brightly lit lantern outside a small restaurant.

It was the height of autumn, and the plastic food replicas in the window showed sweet potatoes and other colorful squashes I didn't know the names of.

"Can we stop here to pick up takeout food on the way to meet Sébastien?"

"I'm guessing Sébastien won't turn down a good meal."

"Then let's get going. You can tell me all about the trick while we walk."

Sanjay's face lit up. I never asked him about magic history. Pleased that overreacting to the sabotage hadn't caused a lasting effect, I stepped off the sidewalk to cross the street, not looking where I was going. Sanjay wrapped his arm around my waist and pulled me backward. It was a swift move worthy of one of his shows. As my feet landed on the curb, a bicyclist whizzed by—in the exact spot where I'd been moments before. The movement was so fast and so close to me that I felt the wind on my face. My heart pounded in my chest.

"Your curiosity," Sanjay said, "is going to kill you one of these days."

"That was jet lag."

"You were too focused on me as I was about to tell the story."

I wriggled out of Sanjay's arm and looked more carefully at the street this time. My heart continued to flutter. I wasn't sure if it was the danger of nearly being knocked down in the street, or the danger of how it felt to have Sanjay's strong arms around me. What was the matter with me?

A taxi pulled up a few feet away from us, and a man and woman stepped out of the back. Sanjay and I looked at each other, then motioned to the driver, who nodded. Sanjay looked up Sébastien's *Ryokan* on his phone and showed it to the driver, who nodded again.

We arrived within minutes, so I didn't get to hear the story of the Indian Rope Trick from Sanjay. I did get to see a tiny car maneuver through even tinier winding roads that led through a section of town from another century. If we hadn't been sitting inside a Toyota taxi with a computer screen in the backseat showing us advertisements in Japanese, I could have believed it was two hundred years earlier.

"I don't know if I could stay at one of these places," Sanjay said as the taxi slowed and turned into an unobtrusive driveway. "Beautiful setting, but I hear they don't even have beds—"

He broke off as we exited the cab in front of the simple wood-framed building that housed the *Ryokan.*

"Beds?" I repeated. "How can they not have beds?"

Sanjay ignored me. I followed his gaze. Sébastien sat on a bench outside the wood-paneled lobby, a small man with a close-cropped beard and an enormous presence standing next to him.

"Why does that man look vaguely familiar?" I asked.

"That," Sanjay said, "is Hiro Matsumoto. My former friend who might have just tried to kill Akira by sabotaging his equipment."

CHAPTER 13

"Sébastien is with the saboteur?" I whispered.

"Sanjay! Jaya!" Sébastien called out. The elderly Frenchman must have visited Japan before, because his "shout" was several decibels lower than his usual gregarious voice. He stood and walked over to us, Hiro following behind. The look on Hiro's own face was unreadable. Confusion? Anger?

Sébastien's hair had been the same wild white mane when I met the ninety-year-old earlier that year, but the lines on his face hadn't been this pronounced. It was clear he hadn't recovered from our exploits at Mont Saint Michel. I was happy to catch up with my dear friend, but whenever I noticed a twinge of his frailty, I was reminded of how he had risked his life for me. Some of my worst moments ever had been spent trapped in a dungeon with the icy water, our only escape through the quicksand. The man who'd tried to kill me had perished under those treacherous waters, but none of us had left the ancient monastery completely unscathed.

I embraced Sébastien in a warm hug. His body was thinner than before. I stepped back and looked over his gaunt frame, hidden by a wool coat and scarf. It was my fault he'd fallen ill with pneumonia and lost so much weight. I glanced at Sanjay and Hiro, who stood apart, glaring at each other.

When Hiro saw me looking at him, his manners took over, and he bowed in greeting as Sébastien introduced us.

Hiro Matsumoto stood several inches taller than me, but was a smaller man than Akira. I placed him in his late thirties or early forties, though he might have been older. The firm physique he maintained to perform illusions could have disguised his age. His neatly trimmed beard and full head of hair were jet black. He wore glasses with silver frames so thin they were nearly invisible.

"We heard what happened," Sébastien said. "Akira called Hiro while we were on our way here. They spoke in Japanese, but I heard screaming coming from the other end of the line. *Alors,* I asked Hiro to tell me what was going on. Hiro didn't sabotage his colleague's studio, Sanjay, and you have no reason to doubt your friend."

"I mean you no harm, Houdini-san," Hiro said, bowing. "You should know this, my friend. I also mean Akira no physical harm. But beware. He's a dangerous man."

"Dangerous?" I asked.

Hiro adjusted his glasses. He looked as if he was searching for words to answer my question, but Sanjay spoke first.

"*With* him," Sanjay said. "I'm working with him, not for him."

Hiro muffled what I guessed was a scoff. He was too polite to express his feelings openly. "Akira is treating you as an equal, then?"

"I didn't know you and Sébastien were friends," Sanjay said. His voice and posture were stiff, and it didn't escape me that he'd avoided Hiro's question.

"The magic community is a small one, Houdini-san," Hiro said. He spoke English with only a faint Japanese accent, similar to Akira. "Likeminded performers find each other. I have always had the greatest of respect for Renaud-san."

"Please, old friend," Sébastien said. "After all this time, call me Sébastien."

Hiro smiled and bowed his head. "It was a great honor to meet Sébastien-san when he came to Japan to teach a workshop on the mechanical properties of magic."

"I appreciate the impulse to stick up for your friend," Sanjay said to Sébastien, continuing to ignore Hiro, "but your loyalty is misguided. We saw him on video."

"*Our* friend," Sébastien corrected, shaking his head. "You dismiss your friends so readily?"

"I saw—"

"It's impossible," Sébastien said. "Akira said the break-in happened this afternoon, no?"

Sanjay nodded.

"It must have been misdirection," Sébastien said. "Another magician wishing to cast suspicion on Hiro by disguising himself to look similar."

"We didn't actually see enough of his face to identify him for certain," I said, watching Sanjay's glare turn toward me. "And don't you dare kick my shin, Sanjay."

Hiro laughed. Sanjay scowled at him.

"I know Hiro well enough to know what he looks like," Sanjay growled. "I didn't want to believe it at first either, but how can you be so sure?"

"Didn't I say?" Sébastien answered. "Hiro was with me."

Sanjay groaned. "Really?"

"I'm afraid so." Sébastien squeezed Sanjay's shoulder. "Have faith in your friends, Sanjay."

"Hiro," Sanjay said, a tinge of red spreading across his olive complexion. "I'm sorry. I don't know what to say."

"Say you'll cease working with Akira."

Sanjay opened and closed his mouth. I knew he'd regret whatever came out when he opened it again.

"Who, then," I cut in, "is the ninja saboteur?"

"You're certain the thief sabotaged Akira's equipment?" Hiro asked. "Not simply breaking an apparatus in his haste to get out?"

Sanjay swallowed hard as he nodded. "I saw it. We all did. It was no accident."

"Then this is more serious than a magician trying to take a peek at his secrets," Sébastien said.

"Could we go somewhere warmer to discuss this?" I said.

"*Je suis désolé*," Sébastien said. "How thoughtless of me." He shrugged out of his thick gray coat, but I put a hand on his arm to stop him from being gallant.

"How about simply going inside," I suggested.

"The staff of the *Ryokan* will feel obliged to provide tea service for all four of us," Hiro said. "Besides, I think we could all use a real drink." He smiled and adjusted his glasses.

"And food," I added. "We can get drinks with a meal. I'm starving. And you can tell me more about this impossible Indian Rope Trick

Sanjay is performing in a few days."

Hiro and Sébastien stared at me, their eyes wide.

"No," Sébastien said to Sanjay. "You're performing the trick with him? Please tell me it's not true."

"What's the matter?" I asked. Unlike me, they didn't know Sanjay had been added at the very last second.

"The reason more magicians haven't tried it," Sébastien said, "is because they fear for their lives."

Sanjay glared at me before turning to Sébastien with a carefree smile. "We're not going to do anything dangerous. Akira thought it would be more of a spectacle to have The Hindi Houdini as part of the act. He's a master at marketing."

"And manipulation," Hiro said. "The interview he gave this week makes sense now. He said you're the descendant of a powerful *fakir* who performed the Indian Rope Trick centuries ago in India."

"What?" The smile on Sanjay's face disappeared.

"Because the great Indian magician's blood flows through your veins, Akira and his followers will be able to harness your power to perform the illusion."

"That's ridiculous," Sanjay sputtered. "Why don't I know anything about this?"

"Presumably because the interview was in Japanese," I said. I was again struck by the use of the word "followers" to describe Akira's fans.

"You're not helping," Sanjay said. "How could he say that? The Dutchman of Dejima's diary is the supernatural ploy. His *kitsune* supposedly led him to a mystical diary, so that's the prop they created and are playing up."

"You're in the posters," Sébastien said. "The Indian *fakir*."

"No." Sanjay shook his head. "Well, yes. But I'm not the emphasis. Yako is always his assistant, so her image is there in the sidelines too, with her reflection showing she's a fox spirit. The main figure behind Akira is the historical Dutch trader who was supposed to have seen the Indian Rope Trick and wrote about it in his diary."

"What part does Akira wish you to play?" Hiro asked.

"I'll find out tomorrow," Sanjay said. "He's showing me the secret of the illusion then."

"Hiro," I said, "why did you call Akira's fans 'followers'?"

"They call themselves that," he said. "It's a perilous path, worshiping a man who claims to perform miracles. He hasn't asked them to do anything yet, but what might he do?"

"Akira tells his followers they must *believe* for a trick to work," Sébastien said. "They behave like a cult."

"It's why Akira is dangerous. To them, he's not simply an entertainer. His powers are real. Houdini-san is now poised to make him more powerful in their eyes."

"I hope you know what you're doing, my boy," Sébastien said. "I hope you know what you're doing."

"I can handle Akira," Sanjay said. "I'd feel better if I knew who the saboteur was."

"The man dressed as *shinobi*," Hiro said. "It's an interesting affectation to disguise himself as a ninja."

"It makes sense," I said. "It provides a full disguise."

"So do many things. Why a ninja? It strikes me as something a foreigner would think of, since they're well-known outside of Japan—though not as their true Japanese name, *shinobi*."

"I don't know..." Sanjay said. He scratched his neck uncomfortably.

"I'm going to say what you're all thinking." Hiro paused and adjusted his glasses. "I'm the only person who has a reason to sabotage his act."

Sébastien raised his bushy white eyebrows. "But you didn't do it."

"Houdini-san doesn't appear to share your confidence. He believes I've found a way to be in two places at once. That perhaps I performed the sabotage at àn earlier time and used misdirection to make Akira believe it was done this afternoon."

"No," Sanjay said. "I know you didn't do it. I believe you *could have* figured out a way to cleverly commit sabotage if you'd wanted to, but I know you wouldn't stoop so low. I'm sorry I doubted you before."

"Why did you say you were the only person who had a reason to sabotage Akira's act?" I asked. "Surely someone as high profile as Akira has other detractors."

"None as adamant as I. When I was a young man, still at school, a tragedy befell my family. My sister died. More accurately, she was killed."

"I'm so sorry," I said.

"You may have heard of the poison gas attacks in the Tokyo subway. Two decades ago, sarin was released in subway trains across the city, killing several innocent people. My older sister had recently moved to Tokyo against my parents' wishes. She was riding the subway to work that day." He closed his eyes. "A cult was behind the attacks. Their followers."

We stood in silence in front of the *Ryokan*. A cult had killed Hiro's sister, and he saw the same cult-like devotion in Akira's followers.

"I'm sorry," Hiro said. "Please forgive me if I don't accompany you to drinks and dinner after all."

He walked toward an old Subaru in the parking lot. Sanjay chased after him.

"Nice to see our Sanjay growing up and learning how to apologize," Sébastien said.

"It's good to see you," I said, watching as the headlights from a taxi pulling up to the inn illuminated Sébastien's regal profile.

"*Toi aussi, ma belle.*" He took my hand in his, and I rested my head on his shoulder.

I'd never known any of my grandparents. My parents were each the black sheep of their families. My father had gone to India to find himself and found my mother instead. She went against her family's wishes and married him, so I never knew her family when I was a small child in India. After she died, my dad decided to raise me and Mahilan in Berkeley, the city of his heart, instead of the small town where he was raised. By the time Mahilan and I were old enough to want to reach out to his parents, they'd passed away.

Sébastien didn't have biological children, but the performers he'd helped teach the craft of traditional magic thought of him as an honorary grandfather. I felt the same.

Sanjay appeared back at our side, shaking his head. "I couldn't convince him to come to dinner," he said.

"Tomorrow," Sébastien said. "My flight is catching up with me."

I stood on my tip-toes and kissed him on the cheek before he went inside.

"Where to?" Sanjay asked.

My phone rang and I grinned when I saw who it was. "I'm so glad you called back," I said.

"Jones *sensei*," the caller said. "I'm so glad to have finally reached you. We have much to discuss. Are you free this evening?"

Sanjay frowned at me.

"Sorry," I mouthed to him. I had a date with a missing ship.

CHAPTER 14

"*Kanpai*," Professor Nakamura said. We clinked glasses of Sapporo and settled into the cushions. I was used to sitting on the floor to play my tabla, so I was right at home. We were gathered around a low table at a traditional style restaurant, with our shoes left at the front of the establishment as we sat on a *zabuton* cushion.

I'd met Professor Nakamura at a history conference a couple of years before, when I was fresh out of graduate school. I remembered him as older than the man in front of me, but it was only my frame of reference. When we'd met, he'd already been teaching for years. I guessed he was about ten years older than me, in his early forties. He had stylishly cut hair he'd dyed with rich brown highlights. Or perhaps it wasn't dyed. He might have been of mixed ancestry, like me.

Unlike Hiro, the professor had never offered the use of his first name. I didn't remember if it had been in the program at the history convention where we'd met years before, but his university website only listed the first initial A. I knew it wasn't a power trip, since he addressed me equally formally. His classically cut dark gray suit, worn with well-polished patent leather shoes that he'd left at the door, rounded out his decorous style.

"Thank you for treating me to dinner," I said, hoping he knew what he was getting into. He'd insisted, but now that we were here, the restaurant looked expensive, and I was ravenous. Even thoughts of finding our missing ship couldn't stop my stomach from insisting I slow down and eat.

"It's my honor, Jones *sensei*. You answered my humble request with more dedication than I could have hoped for. If your research bears out, you might end up with a worthy research paper."

"Co-authored by you, of course," I said. "But regardless of what we find, it was a great idea, helping your students see that real historical research is messy. The eighteenth century is a great period of Dutch colonial history to explore, since the VOC was in decline. It's as good as a soap opera." Without personal stories that bring history to life, none of us would have been lured into studying history.

The professor grinned. "It wasn't exactly my idea. It was my students'. Because of the *Indo no Triku* magic show."

I blinked at him.

"Forgive me," he continued. "I was thinking of the Japanese on the posters. In English, it's Indian Rope Trick. You must have seen the posters around Kyoto. They're everywhere. The story of this magic show comes from an eighteenth-century explorer, a Dutchman who witnessed this fabled illusion in India before he came to Japan. My students don't care about the history, just the performer, Akira. I don't much care for his type of spectacle, but he's given me an opportunity to get my students truly interested in history. I'll teach them the true history of Dutch traders in Japan after they watch the televised illusion. They'll all be watching. Akira is quite famous here in Japan."

"I know," I said.

I told him about my friend being the opening act, and Professor Nakamura told me about the Japanese education system in which rigorous study takes place in high school, but college is the time for slacking off. By the time our food arrived, I felt like we were old friends. But as interesting as the conversation was, I wanted to get to the missing ship we might have discovered.

"What kind of fish is that?" I asked, pointing at a piece of sushi on the long ceramic dish in the center of the table in hopes of changing the conversation. "Tuna?"

"Sanma. An autumn fish. You might know it as Pacific saury." He smiled. "But I don't think you're interested in local seafood. Shall we discuss our ship?"

"Definitely." I took a bite of the salty fish and reached into my messenger bag. I'd taken a photo of the page of the book I'd found in San Francisco.

"A painting," he said, dropping his chopsticks onto his plate and accepting the photo. "Iconic evidence. I should have thought of it." He pushed his plate aside to study it more carefully.

"Iconic evidence" was a fancy term historians used to refer to works of art. Inspired by beauty and the deep pockets of patrons, artists have always created representations of the world, but ones that are generally taken less seriously than official documents.

The irony was that works of art often revealed more of the truth about the world than administrative records. Artists could slyly include messages in their works of art, but there was something even simpler going on: good art survived the test of time far better than written documents. Families and bureaucrats might forget about the papers in a trunk in the attic or filed away with thousands of other papers, but they would hold on to a beautiful piece of art across generations. In the Netherlands, because trading ships contributed so greatly to the country's wealth in the sixteenth through eighteenth centuries, Dutch painters turned their attention to capturing the majesty of the ships in great detail. Many ships' recorded histories have been lost, but paintings of them survived.

When the professor looked up at me a minute later, he simply nodded and took a folded piece of paper from the inner pocket of his jacket.

"From Dejima," he said, handing me a page of Japanese characters, with his handwritten English translation in the margins. "The description of the ship matches your painting. The same strangely placed gun port, the same oversize oak timbers, even the same name."

"*New Batavia.*"

"You found it."

"No," I said. "*We* found it."

I felt giddy, and not because I'd finished my beer. I wished Lane had been there with me. He would have loved this hunt. Putting the missing pieces of history together.

"There's something more I need to look up," Professor Nakamura said.

"Can I help?" At least four VOC ships had been named *Batavia*, so I knew our research was far from over.

"Unless you read Japanese..."

I shook my head. "How long will your research take?"

"Perhaps you could meet me in my office tomorrow afternoon."

We clinked glasses. Now all that remained was to find our ship and prove we were right.

CHAPTER 15

I woke up to the shrill sound of the hotel room's phone. I covered my head with a pillow. The phone rang again. I pulled a second pillow over my head. The bed had four of them, so I was confident I could wait out the phone. But by the third ring, I was fully awake. I gave up and lifted the phone from its cradle and croaked a hello.

"Are you still in bed?" It was Sanjay's voice.

I considered hanging up. Professor Nakamura and I weren't meeting up again until the early afternoon. There was plenty of time for more sleep.

"We need to talk," he continued.

"Talking will be here later. I need sleep."

"I'll meet you in the breakfast room in fifteen minutes."

"Didn't you hear me—?"

"Breakfast ends in twenty minutes."

I sat up. "Why didn't you say so? I'll see you downstairs in ten minutes."

Nine minutes later, we were seated next to the window of the hotel's main restaurant with a buffet breakfast on one side of us and a Japanese style rock garden on the other. The garden was bathed in a light mist. In the reflection of the window I saw creases across my face from nearly nine hours of solid sleep, but with warming green tea and a heaping pile of food in front of me, I didn't care.

"They have coffee too," Sanjay said. He was dressed in his performance tuxedo already.

"When in Rome." I took a bite of scrambled eggs. All right. I wasn't exactly eating a Japanese breakfast. There was a small table with an assortment of Japanese breakfast foods like rice, miso soup, fish, and pickled vegetables with seaweed, but the other half of the spread was Western, catering to the tourist clientele. I added honey and hot sauce to the eggs.

"As much as I appreciate you getting me up in time for breakfast," I said, "it sounded like you had an ulterior motive."

"I'm going to kill Akira."

"What did he do to offend you this morning?"

"That ridiculous interview about me being descended from some fictional mystical magician was so popular that he's giving more interviews saying the same thing—and more. My own supernatural powers will be revealed to the world on Friday. How am I supposed to argue with that? Even if I could set things straight with the media, I'd be contradicting him to his legion of followers."

"He's trying to drum up publicity for the show in a business where all publicity is good publicity, right? Sébastien won't hold it against you. I don't know about Hiro, though."

"I don't know if my friendship with Hiro will survive this week. You're not going to hold it against me too, are you?"

"It's your life. You can make choices your friends disagree with."

At the sound of *Dance Macabre*, Sanjay lifted his cell phone from God knows where. He frowned as he listened. "But—you're sure? Yes...We'll be there."

"What was that about?" I asked.

"Akira wants to meet earlier than planned to show me the Indian Rope Trick on site. And he wants you to come."

I tried not to roll my eyes. I wasn't sure if I succeeded. "I've got other plans. That puzzle of the missing Dutch East India Company ship I told you about."

"All right, but you're missing what might be your only chance to see the secrets of an impossible illusion..."

I glared across the table. Those who are closest to us know how to push our buttons. "I've got a little time. I'll come with you if you promise you won't let Akira rope me into the act."

Sanjay grinned and took a last sip of coffee.

It was only when our taxi passed the famous bamboo forest that I realized we were in the same part of town as the temple where I'd met Sanjay the previous day. In the misty rain and morning light, the scenery on the way to Arashiyama looked completely different than it had shortly before sunset on a clear day. Even the colorful leaves of the autumn trees took on a different appearance in the mist, which gave way to thicker fog as we drove closer to the mountain range. After too many twists and turns for me to keep track of, the driver stopped next to an empty field.

"We go on foot from here," Sanjay said.

A few dozen yards from the road, modern chain link fencing encircled an area of hilly open fields, looking incongruous in this historic district on the western outskirts of Kyoto. The chain link fence was at least twice as tall as me, with razor-sharp barbs on top.

"That's some serious security," I said.

"It's not even finished yet. The show isn't until Friday, four days away. There's more safety fencing being added tomorrow, since the hills are so steep around here. Come on, the entrance gate is this way."

After following the circling fence to the summit of the hill, we reached a gate with a set of metal chains wrapped around it.

"Akira," Sanjay called out. His voice echoed through the trees. "Looks like we got here first."

"No, he was already here when he called me. He must have locked himself inside in case any of his fans came by. Let me call him back so he knows we're here."

I pulled my coat around me. Small droplets of water collected on my shoulder. It felt more like we were in a cloud than full-blown rain, but it was still damp and chilly.

"He's not answering," Sanjay said. "Let's walk around the fence to see if we can tell where he is."

"I'll wait for you here," I said, pointing at my high heels. "I'm dressed to be on a college campus, not a muddy field. And who performs outdoors in November? What if it rains?"

"We've got a plan in place. Be right back."

The air around me was still. I felt goosebumps forming on my arms. There were no statues of Buddhist disciples in this empty hillside, yet I could have sworn someone was watching me. I whirled around, but saw no one.

Sanjay was already out of my range of sight. I knew he was nearby, but I didn't like the idea of him disappearing just then. Why had I been so concerned about a little bit of mud? I decided to follow Sanjay. Before I took a step, his voice cried out.

"Sanjay?" I ran forward, following the sound of his voice, but I didn't see him. The fog must have confused me. "Where are you?"

My heel caught in the earth, but I didn't want to go barefoot without a full field of vision. I kept trudging along. "Sanjay?" I called again.

Strong arms pulled me back, nearly knocking me off my feet. Before I could cry out, Sanjay spun me around.

"Careful," he whispered in a shaking voice. "You don't want to end up like..." He snapped his mouth shut, looking as if he was going to be sick. He pointed to a steep slope.

We were on another mound in the hillside, with the fence on one side and a valley on the other. Through the fog, I made out the figure of a person at the bottom of the slope. It was a strange place to take a nap, but it looked as if the person was lying on a boulder.

"Is that—?"

"Akira must have fallen," Sanjay said. "I've already called an ambulance. I hope they understood me."

"We need to go down and see if we can do anything to help before they arrive."

"Look at the rock, Jaya."

My breath caught. A dark red stain covered the boulder.

"A gash on the head doesn't mean someone is dead," I said. "He might be knocked out."

But as I made my way down the steep hillside, ignoring Sanjay's protests, I saw I was wrong.

Akira lay face down, his gloved hand outstretched on the boulder that had stopped his fall. He was dressed in his white tuxedo, now stained green and brown from rolling down the hillside. His black hair was matted with dark red. On his head was a wound nobody could have survived, even a man who performed miracles.

A high-pitched wail came from behind me. For a fraction of a second I wondered how the ambulance had arrived so quickly. But this wasn't the sound of an ambulance. It wasn't a manufactured sound. It was too raw. It sounded like the cry of a wounded animal. But it wasn't. It was that of a person.

I turned and saw Yako rushing down the hillside, a red cape billowing behind her. As she ran past me, I reached out to stop her from rushing to Akira's side. She didn't protest.

"Don't look," I said. "There's nothing we can do."

I followed my own advice and looked away from the terrible sight, but not before seeing something even worse. Next to Akira's body, a shiny silver object caught my eye. A *shuriken*—the ninja's throwing star.

CHAPTER 16

An ambulance arrived quickly. Yako explained to them that we didn't think Akira had fallen down the hillside by accident. They called the police and asked us to move away from the body but not to leave the field.

Yako stood apart from us, at the pinnacle of the hill, looking toward the mountain range while the wind swept her red cloak upward as if she were about to take flight.

The police arrived promptly as well, but not before giving me too much time alone with my thoughts. Our ninja had been here with Akira before he died. Sanjay and I had been wrong not to fear him. As Akira lay dying in the ravine, did he think of the fox spirit who was supposed to protect him, wishing his own myth had been true?

The police talked with us separately, beginning with Yako. A female officer spoke the best English, so she took the lead as she and her partner interviewed me and Sanjay. It only took a few minutes for me to answer their questions, but when they left me alone to talk with Sanjay, the minutes stretched on.

"Why did that take so long?" I asked when he was finally done. "Do they suspect you of being involved?"

"Don't worry. The detectives only wanted to know what I saw. They were nice. So polite. I'm not a suspect."

I wasn't so sure. From my experience in Japan so far, everyone was polite, even in situations where you wouldn't think people would be. Would Sanjay have picked up on the cultural nuances necessary for him to know the truth about what the police thought of him?

"Unless they told you otherwise, we're free to go. We should call

Sébastien."

"Not from here. Let's get out of here before the press arrives. We can tell him what's happened once we're gone."

We walked back to the road. Sanjay was right. With two police cars and an ambulance, the press would be here soon enough.

"Do you think one of them will drive us back to the hotel?" Sanjay asked me.

"I'd rather get you away from the police, not spend more time with them."

"I have my car," Yako said. "I can give you a ride."

I hadn't heard her approach. But why would I? We were outside on a field of dirt and grass.

"Thank you," I said, "but it's not necessary."

"What are you talking about, Jaya?" Sanjay said. "That's very kind of you to offer, Yako. If it's not any trouble, we'd be glad to accept."

"Please, call me Yoko." Her hands shook as she wound her long hair into a bun and put on a knit cap. Her face was tearstained and blotchy, so different from the poised performer I'd met the day before. "Yoko Ryu is my real name. In my home prefecture, *Yako* is the regional word for *kitsune*. But now...I'm no longer Yako. Not with Akira gone."

"I'm so sorry for your loss," I said, wondering if Sanjay had accepted an offer from Akira's killer. She looked genuinely upset, but she was a performer.

Yoko nodded as the wind picked up. Her red hair escaped her hat and looked like falling autumn leaves as it bounced down to her waist. She didn't seem to notice. In her detached state, I'd never seen her look more like the *kitsune*.

The sound of thunder filled the air and seemed to shake her out of her stupor. "It isn't far."

We bundled up and followed her to her car. Yoko's stylish cape swayed in the gusts of wind. A designer purse bounced on her hip as she hurried to the car. What was so heavy in the small purse?

"Are you sure you're up for driving?" I asked once we were tucked inside the tiny Daihatsu. I'd climbed into the tiny back, giving Sanjay the slightly more spacious front seat.

Yoko's hands rested on the steering wheel. They were steadier than they'd been before, but she didn't start the car. "He always wished for time on his own to become his character. But he insisted on going places alone even after he knew he was being followed. If I'd gone with him—"

"You might be at the bottom of the ravine too," Sanjay said.

She smiled at him. "May I tell you a story?"

Sanjay glanced back at me. It wasn't just my take that she was acting strangely. Was it shock, or something more?

"I know you think I'm foolish to have put up with him for so long, but I'd like someone to understand. The detectives were polite. They looked at me with pity. I don't want pity." She gripped the steering wheel so hard her fingers turned white. "I want the truth to be known. And I want the truth to be found."

Yoko started the car. As she drove through the small winding roads of Kyoto, words spilled out of her.

The story began with what we knew. Akira Kimura was once in a J-pop boy band, reaching great celebrity at a young age. He was known to millions of screaming adolescent girls as Akira. That's when Yoko fell for him, while she was a teenager. Akira wasn't much older than her at the time.

When the boy band broke up, Akira missed fame. He wasn't a good lead singer, so he couldn't become a solo artist like the lead singer of Flash. He'd always had an interest in magic, practicing card tricks and other sleights of hand when traveling on long, boring flights or bus rides. He knew he was good at magic, and he thought his fans would follow him over to being a stage magician. He even spoke English well, from all the traveling they did and the singing style of J-pop.

The three other members of the boy band went on to become an actor, a solo artist, and one who was tired of living in the spotlight and wanted to settle down with a family. The actor and solo musician found success, but Akira bombed. For his first world tour, many of his former fans came to see him. But as soon as they realized there was no music and nothing sexy about his technically proficient magic show, they didn't want more.

He'd studied computer science and engineering in college and was great at creating modern illusions. Why did nobody care about Akira Kimura, he wondered? He possessed such talent that magicians couldn't figure out the secrets of his latest show. They wracked their brains, to no avail. Yet still, the public didn't care about his puzzling illusions. After the initial interest, they quickly moved on. He wondered what he was missing.

Akira knew he needed to do something to stand out. He couldn't get by on what he'd once been. After his producer told him that he needed to do something flashy and over-the-top, Akira planned a dangerous stunt. But Akira's producer had a background in music rather than magic, so the stunt they planned ended up being far too risky. Akira was nearly killed.

"What was the stunt?" I asked her.

Sanjay shook his head. It was the trick he hadn't wanted me to hear about.

"A water escape," Yoko said. "He was to be escaping from an old building along the coast that was underwater during high tide. The mechanism swelled with water, and he did not escape immediately, as his producer thought he had. His hand...it was crushed when, half-drowned, he had to claw his way out through the wood and stone."

She shuddered. I joined in. It was almost exactly how I'd nearly met my fate on the coast of France. That's why Sanjay hadn't wanted me to look up the details.

Akira went away from his home of Tokyo to convalesce, Yoko continued, but in all honesty, he didn't need a full year to recover. His pride was wounded more than his body, because he had been humiliated in front of millions on live television.

Akira was out of the hospital and recovering in a small house outside of Kyoto. Yoko discovered where he was and went to visit him. She wasn't planning to stay, but her devotion to Akira was very attractive to him, so the selfish young man invited her to stay with him. Neither of them realized that first day that his invitation would last until death parted them.

With Yoko by his side, he figured out what he was missing: the passion behind the illusion. It was a mechanical puzzle, no more interesting than how a car engine works. Most people don't care to figure out why their car takes them from point A to point B. Akira Kimura was a car engine. Impressive if you cared to open the hood and take a look. But nobody cared enough to look under the hood of his act.

But how could Akira reinvent himself after his near-death experience? He had effectively lost his hand—but what if he claimed that in exchange, he'd been granted magical powers? Yoko would pretend to be his *kitsune*. Yoko was dead from that point on, and Yako was born in her place.

Akira made his comeback performance with her as his onstage assistant. Akira claimed she was a nine-tailed *Yako* whose star ball he possessed, enabling him to control her. Their act was a hit.

"He did not truly believe I was a *kitsune*," she said. "We were an act. Not real. None of it was real. But the people. They loved Akira. He gave them what they wanted. His followers...they believed he traveled to the farthest reaches of Japan, guided by his *kitsune*. They believed I led him to monasteries and temples and libraries, as he sought ancient knowledge to perform his miracles. So you see, it's my fault."

"It's not your fault," Sanjay said. "You weren't the one who killed him."

I hoped he was right.

"No," Yoko said, "but I made it possible. People believed our ancient knowledge was real. It wasn't, yet I let them believe. The killer's only reward was a worthless prop."

"A prop?" I asked.

"The Dutchman of Dejima's diary doesn't reveal the secret of the Indian Rope Trick. It was only part of the illusion of our act. But the person who killed Akira didn't know that."

"He was killed over the diary?" Sanjay asked.

"This is what the police were asking me about," Yoko said. "You see, the Dutchman of Dejima's diary is missing. Stolen by the killer."

CHAPTER 17

If Yoko was telling us the truth about the diary, Akira's murderer had killed for what amounted to nothing. If they'd been after the secrets of the trick and realized they didn't get them after all, what would their next move be?

Yoko dropped us off at our hotel. If she had murderous intentions towards us, she was saving them for another day.

"That was foolish," I said to Sanjay as we watched her car pull away. "We can't trust her."

"She's not the ninja. There's no chance."

"She's an illusionist, Sanjay."

"You got closer to the ninja than I did. Do you really think it could have been her?"

"No," I admitted. "The ninja was a small man, and I doubt she could have hidden her curves so well or gotten that hair of hers under the head covering."

"I'm so sorry I dragged you into this."

"You didn't. You told me not to come, remember?" I led the way into the lobby.

Sanjay attempted to smile, but failed. "We should call Sébastien and—" He broke off as we walked past the hotel bar.

"And I need to call Professor Nakamura to reschedule." I berated myself for feeling disappointed that my own quest was on hold. A man was dead, and I was thinking of a ship with a crew that had lived more than two centuries ago.

Sanjay swore. It wasn't at me. I followed his gaze. On the television above the bar, a video showed the police officer who'd interviewed us.

"The press was certainly quick to get there," I said.

Sanjay stared at the screen. The volume was low, but he couldn't have understood it even if it was turned up. "I have an idea. Meet me back here in an hour. I want to call both Sébastien and Hiro."

"You need an hour for that?"

"Just meet me back here."

I left a message for Professor Nakamura, then tried to watch the news in my room to learn more, but the only stations with news were Japanese-language channels. The English-language stations didn't seem to care about a celebrity who was only famous in Asia, and online translations of Japanese news articles were lacking.

My feet tapped furiously. I had to get up and do something. Sitting still, I couldn't get the image of Akira's lifeless body out of my mind. I slipped into my running gear and headed out.

Across the street from the hotel, a museum showcased billboards in both Japanese and English for the *netsuke* exhibit the hotel clerk had mentioned. I shivered as my eyes came to rest on a close-up photograph of a lacquered wood fox. It was no ordinary fox, for it stood upright and was dressed in a kimono. A *kitsune*. Crowds of people were in line for the exhibit.

A block from the hotel I ran past a Buddhist temple. A fierce stone face looked down on me from the tiled rooftop. Crossing the street, I passed a set of stone steps leading upward toward an open-air Shinto shrine. Lanterns shone at the top of the stairs, beckoning to me. I bounded up the stairs and found myself nearly alone in a plaza. Red lanterns lined a path to an ornate wooden gate, which in turn led to additional smaller structures. Stone altars were open at all hours for people to pray. I wondered if Hiro had come to places like this to deal with the tragic death of his sister, and if Akira's loved ones would do the same.

As I turned to leave the shrine, I paused at the top of the stone steps. The street below me looked familiar. I'd never before been to Kyoto, though, and I hadn't taken a taxi in this direction. Then it hit me: the houses on the street below looked nearly identical to the

Sunset neighborhood near the ocean in San Francisco. I instinctively reached for my phone, before stopping myself. I normally listened to bhangra music when I went running in San Francisco, but there was no way I was putting on headphones in an unfamiliar city, especially after a man I knew had been murdered.

I left the phone in my running belt and kept going. I got less than a block before stopping again, this time in front of a shop of treasures. A mannequin wearing an ornate silk kimono in luminous indigo, modern guitars next to musical instruments I didn't recognize, and an assortment of jewelry were on display beyond the thick glass window. Posters with Japanese writing showed smiling models holding paper tickets and Yen. I thought at first the printed tickets and money were advertising a lottery of some kind, before realizing this was a pawn shop. I'd been gone for ten minutes and only gotten two blocks. If I let myself continue to get distracted at every turn, I wouldn't clear my head or get back in time to meet Sanjay.

I turned in the direction of the eastern hills, where I hoped the sidewalks would be less crowded. As I ran into the hills, I saw I was only partially right. The winding roads that cut through the trees were filled with hidden temples and shrines, as well as shops and restaurants. I turned onto a deserted path, before realizing my blunder. I was in a secluded stretch of a path. Without the sound of my footfalls, and the sound of my breath no longer as loud in my ears, the exciting sites around me felt empty and quiet. Too quiet.

A figure in black darted by. I turned, but he was gone. Had I just seen the ninja?

After hurrying back to the hotel, I had ten minutes before I was due to meet Sanjay. The lavender soap in the shower calmed me and convinced me it was only an overly active imagination that had caused me to think I'd seen a ninja. Lots of people dressed in black in Japan.

I turned off the ultramodern shower and dressed in my extra pair of fitted jeans without grass stains, a dark gray turtleneck instead of a black sweater, and boots instead of heels. I was a different person than the one who'd seen a dead body that morning.

When I showed up in the lobby, Sanjay was already there. He'd changed as well. Instead of his black tux, he was dressed in a black dress shirt and jeans.

"Hiro has forgiven me," he said. "Sometimes the Japanese sense of honor works in one's favor after all. Have you been watching the news in your room?"

"I tried, but it's all in Japanese. Oh, no...has something else happened?"

"I didn't mean to worry you. I meant that Hiro has regular Japanese cable TV at his house. He'll translate the news for us."

"That was the idea you had."

Sanjay nodded. "I told them both that the magic show diary, which doesn't actually contain any secrets, was stolen. They're worried about what it means too."

"What the ninja will do once he realizes he killed for a prop with no secrets."

CHAPTER 18

We didn't want to show up at Hiro's house empty handed, so we decided to stop at a supermarket to pick up easy food and drinks to bring for lunch. The hotel concierge suggested a nearby *konbini*. I'd noticed the convenience store and was skeptical, but after walking past the large magazine section, a large area of freshly prepared food appeared. I selected an assortment of *onigiri* rice balls wrapped in seaweed, steamed edamame, and several bags of potato chips. Sanjay picked out drinks, both alcoholic and not. He wanted to be prepared. We didn't know what the day ahead would hold.

When Sanjay and I arrived at the address Hiro had given us, we found Sébastien sitting on the front porch. He stood and gave me a hug.

"*Je suis désolé,*" he said. "I'm so sorry you were the ones to find Akira. I can't believe it. Sanjay said it couldn't have been an accident, that the ninja stole a prop for the show and left his throwing star behind."

I nodded, but felt a lump rising in my throat as I thought of speaking about what we'd seen earlier. "Why are you outside?" I asked instead, looking around. "Where's Hiro?"

Hiro's home was a single-story house nestled into a lush hillside on the outskirts of Kyoto. After walking up the path that led to the house, I could see no other residences. Here, we had a view of trees, both evergreens and those losing their leaves with such beautiful colors that people from all over the world flocked to Kyoto to see this autumn spectacle. I knew temples were nestled in the hills on the other side of the house, hidden by nature.

"Detectives are speaking with him at the police station," Sébastien said. "He expected to be back by now, but..."

"You didn't tell them he has you as an alibi?" Sanjay asked.

"Nobody has asked me. I'm hopeful they're only speaking with him as a formality, as a magician publicly known to disagree with Akira's methods."

Sanjay and Sébastien both reached for their cell phones.

"*Bon,*" Sébastien said, slipping the phone back into his pocket. "Hiro is on his way now. We can relax. How about opening some of the chips I see in the bag you're holding? Any of them except pizza-flavored."

"How about the one with the talking potato on the cover? I don't know what flavor it is, but I liked the cartoon potato."

"I don't know how you two can think about food," Sanjay said with a scowl. "And Jaya, one day you're going to accidentally eat something truly terrible."

"So what? Isn't it better to try new things, even if it means messing up?"

Sanjay paced across the path in front of the house, flipping his hat in his hands. He never went anywhere without it. I was half convinced it had a boomerang homing device. "This bottle of sake looks much more appealing. I can't stop thinking about—"

"It will get better," Sébastien said. "I promise."

"You don't know that. You didn't see him. And how am I supposed to feel with someone out there who was willing to kill over an illusion?"

"One of the perks of being ninety years old is that people are supposed to take my advice. And for good reason. I've seen many things in my lifetime, Sanjay. There have always been bad people along with the good. I've lived through several wars. I toured the world, where people both spat on me and asked for my autograph. I sat by Christo's side as he died. Is life always agreeable? No. But I can promise you the sick feeling in the pit of your stomach will lift."

Sanjay kept pacing across the winding stone path. I noticed the exterior of the house and the garden weren't well tended. I didn't know Hiro well, but it wasn't what I expected. His beard was perfectly trimmed and his clothing impeccably pressed.

"Why don't you show us some magic while we wait for Hiro,"

Sébastien suggested.

Sanjay stopped pacing. He didn't verbally accept, but the edges of his lips curled into a smile. He waved his hand over the bowler hat. A moment later, a thin rope rose into the air. I knew he must have been controlling it with an invisible thread or wire, but I saw neither, and the rope didn't move with his hand. He snapped his fingers and the rope fell.

"Jaya and I could read your mind," Sanjay said.

"Or not," I said. I'd once stepped in as a last-minute replacement as Sanjay's assistant at a charity show. "I don't remember my part. How about some shadow magic?" Sanjay's style of magic used vintage techniques like magic lanterns in the background to add a mysterious element to the backdrop of his performances. I didn't expect him to have his props with him, so I wasn't sure if he'd be up for the challenge outside Hiro's house. But he came through.

Hiro appeared on the path ten minutes later, as Sanjay was making shadows dance across the path.

"A mere formality, I hope," Sébastien said.

"Unfortunately," Hiro said, "the police have discovered the lawsuit Akira filed against me."

Hiro, Sanjay, and I sat on *tatami* mats around a table with tea Hiro had made to warm us up and the food and drinks Sanjay and I brought. Sébastien reclined on a cushioned armchair Hiro had moved from elsewhere in the house.

Hiro adjusted his glasses and took a deep breath before speaking. "The lawsuit was several years ago. I had been trying to debunk Akira's miracles."

"Like Houdini," Sanjay murmured.

"*Hai.* I believed I had sufficient proof Akira was a fraud, but when I couldn't prove it, my words were used against me. Akira filed a suit and prevailed. I was embarrassed, so I don't often speak of it. Japan has a strict code of honor. Our laws against slander and defamation are very strict as well. It comes from our history. Samurai practiced *seppuku*, a ritual form of suicide involving a sword to redeem lost honor by an honorable death. Our sense of honor has continued. I should never have said publicly that Akira was a fraud—without better proof. My anguish over my sister's death prevented me from seeing clearly."

"You got sued for saying something to the press without facts to back it up?" I asked. "And Akira *won?*"

"Akira was able to prove that my claims hurt his business. All I wanted to do was show his followers he wasn't a true miracle-worker, only an entertainer like Houdini-san and myself."

"And our ninja spy was trying to find out his secrets," I said. "The police think you might have been at it again."

"Even Houdini-san believed I might stoop to sabotage to ruin Akira."

"Only because he poisoned my mind against you," Sanjay said. "I'm sorry I fell for it."

"I know, my friend. But how can I hope the police won't think the same thing? Especially when a prop from Akira's show was stolen, and it supposedly contained secrets from his act. The only reason I'm here now is because there's no evidence linking me to the crime scene, because I'm innocent."

"What did they tell you?" I asked.

"Not much. I expect reporters will have learned more than I did." He turned on the television in the corner of the room.

The aftermath of Akira's death was on the first channel he turned to. The mysterious death of a celebrity who claimed supernatural powers had captured the attention of the public in a big way.

Sanjay and I took our laptops out, but continued to find that the press outside of Asia weren't spending much time on the death of a Japanese celebrity, and there wasn't much news in English available online. The short reports we did find in English were either obituaries or didn't tell us anything more than what we already knew. The photos his followers were posting on fan sites showed such a level of hysterical grief that I was secretly glad I couldn't read the words that accompanied the images.

The soft sounds of the television news filled the air. I told myself we weren't speaking much because we were all focused on learning what we could, but I suspected the real reason was the uncomfortable topic that hung in the air no matter where we went. A murderer was out there. If the police suspected Hiro, would they work hard to find the real killer?

"Listen to this," I said as I read one of the English-language obituaries. "The man described here is nothing like the man I met. Did you know he gave large amounts of money to animal shelters and funded magic classes at orphanages? I'm surprised it doesn't say he spent his free time rescuing baby kittens."

"The press coverage is incredible," Sanjay said, his eyes glued to the screen of his computer. "It's like he's royalty. He would have loved this."

"I wonder..." Hiro said softly. He looked out the window that gave a view of the lush hillside filled with hidden temples. Nodding to himself, as if the trees had spoken to him, he turned his attention from nature to technology. His fingers danced on the screen of his phone. He was so absorbed he didn't notice me watching him intently. Nor did he see my own intake of breath as he gasped.

The background hum of the television was enough that the others didn't notice Hiro's reaction. He shook himself, and then seemed to realize that he wasn't alone.

I caught his eye. "You don't think he's really dead."

Hiro's phone disappeared from his hand. I swear I didn't see him put it in his pocket. I needed to stop associating with so many magicians.

"It is not my idea, Jaya-san," Hiro said. "There is already speculation among his fans that his *kitsune* protected him—that he will soon be resurrected. The supposed sighting of butterflies at the scene has given them hope. This is the danger I spoke of—"

"I get it," Sanjay said, slamming his laptop shut. "I screwed up by working for a guy who pretends he performs miracles. But you don't actually believe he's going to be resurrected—"

"No," Hiro said. "Yet this raises another possibility."

"You're not suggesting—" I began.

Hiro nodded. "Akira's 'death' could be a stunt."

CHAPTER 19

Sanjay swore. "A stunt to fake his death would explain Akira's secretive behavior...And why he didn't insist on showing me the Indian Rope Trick until today...But hang on. If he knew we were never going to perform the Indian Rope Trick together, why bother going to the effort of making up the whole story behind the act?"

"All the more reason to do so," I said.

"Jaya-san is correct," Hiro said. "In death, Akira's life will be examined more carefully. If I created such an unfortunate stunt, I would be meticulous in my preparations."

Sanjay swore again. At least that's what I think he did. He'd switched to Punjabi.

"C'est impossible." Sébastien shook his head. "Have you all gone mad? Akira didn't fake his own death."

"Hiro and Jaya make a strong case." Sanjay picked up his bowler hat from the *tatami* mat.

"He didn't simply disappear," Sébastien said. "You saw his body."

"There are times," Sanjay said, "when what we see is not to be believed." With one deft flip, a beautiful origami crane floated toward the floor from the seemingly empty hat. Before it touched the bamboo floor mat, the paper crane disappeared. I knew better than to ask how he'd accomplished it.

Hiro clicked his tongue. "Houdini-san, you're an impressive magician, but you've been brainwashed to believe Akira's mystical claims. I thought you were past that."

"You," Sanjay growled at Hiro, "are the one who suggested he's not really dead."

"No," Hiro said. "I simply wondered if some of his followers had the idea. And they do. They believe he possessed magical powers after his near-death experience, as he claimed. An interesting complication."

"Misdirection," Sanjay snapped. "I didn't mean there was a supernatural explanation. I meant this could be misdirection in an elaborate stunt. Akira didn't brainwash me into believing he's immortal. He didn't need to. I signed his damn nondisclosure agreement. But"—he paused and paced the length of two *tatami* mats— "we didn't get close to the body. Someone else could have been murdered in his place."

"Like a stunt double?" I asked.

"God knows what sort of Frankenstein he could have kept hidden in that workshop of his. Someone could have been living there, getting plastic surgery to look like him."

"You realize that means you're suggesting Akira himself is a murderer," I pointed out.

"I would be very careful with such an accusation, Houdini-san," Hiro said. "I know what he is capable of."

"Or fake blood, along with making his heart appear to have stopped," Sanjay said.

"Does that really exist outside of fiction?" I asked.

"Yes," Sanjay and Hiro said.

I gaped at them.

"Placing a rubber ball under an armpit makes the pulse disappear," Sanjay said.

"Doctors are more sophisticated than that," I said.

"I agree it's far-fetched. Especially after seeing him…"

I walked over to Sébastien. "You've been unusually quiet. Are you all right?"

"I was waiting for you young people to calm down and come to your senses."

"This isn't a sensible situation," Sanjay snapped.

"Akira is dead." Sébastien didn't raise his voice. If anything, it was barely above a whisper. But he commanded the room. "Listen to each other. *Truly listen* to what you're saying. You young people have such fanciful ideas. It is as if you believe you are in a James Bond movie. I cannot believe the whole police force in a country such as this could be bribed. Nor do I believe the police are buffoons. They will study the body. They will follow the evidence. Hiro, do you dispute this?"

"You are correct, Sébastien-san." Hiro gave a slight bow. "I do not believe this would be possible. I was simply looking at all possibilities. And—"

"I heard my name," Sanjay said, his eyes snapping to the television.

Hiro shook his head. "They said *Hou*. Law. Nothing to do with you. And not even pronounced like Houdini."

"Oh." Sanjay took a bit of a potato chip of indeterminate flavor and grimaced. "I thought they were simply mispronouncing my name."

"Sébastien-san is correct," Hiro said. "We mustn't let irrational ideas cloud our judgment."

"*Arigato*," Sébastien said.

"Have you been back to Japan since you toured here when you were performing?" I asked.

Sébastien smiled. "You paid attention to the photographs on my walls in Nantes."

"How could I not? There were such stories there."

"When I was performing with Christo, *many* decades ago, we toured here. Christo and I did two tours in Japan in the '70s and '80s. I haven't been back since."

Sébastien Renaud had been a stage performer only briefly, much preferring to be involved in magic behind the scenes. He and his partner, Christo, had toured the world for a few years, learning that they hated the spotlight, because it exposed their personal life as well. They retired to the French countryside, where Sébastien amused himself building mechanical apparatuses from the Golden Age of magic. He'd replicated the famous chess-playing Turk automation, rigged an elaborate doorbell that caused mechanical birds to slide across his roof and alert him to a visitor, and his favorite—an automaton butler named Jeeves. Personally, Jeeves creeped me out. Sitting on a wheelchair, the legless butler moved on his own throughout Sébastien's house, carrying items to Sébastien. I'd never gotten a straight answer from Sébastien about just how much Jeeves could do.

Though Sébastien had outlived Christo, he was far from alone.

Such a skilled illusion-builder couldn't be forgotten. He was sought out by younger magicians who asked for his help constructing illusions for their shows. He had a studio at the *Les Machines de l'Île* in Nantes, France, the Jules Verne-inspired mechanical theme park, and his own magical barn studio in his home outside the city.

"Though I haven't been back in almost thirty years," Sébastien continued, "that's how I know Hiro."

I looked at Hiro, trying again to guess his age. He couldn't have been older than his mid-forties now, so he couldn't have been a magician at that time.

"I was a young boy," Hiro said, "and I loved magic."

"Once he became a magician himself," Sébastien said, "he got in touch with me. He remembered the show so well! It almost made me regret giving up the stage. Almost." He winked at me.

"It was one of the defining moments of my life," Hiro said, bowing his head. "At the time, much modern magic was being performed in Japan, as it is now, but not many people were performing classic magic, creating a true sense of wonder and honoring our ancestors. Renaud-san showed me the magic that was possible."

Sébastien waved away the praise. "Hiro is now a well-known magician here in Japan."

"Was," Hiro corrected. "I *was*, long ago."

A twig snapped outside the window. Both Sanjay and I jumped.

"Foxes live in the hills," Hiro said. "*Kitsune.*"

"Really?" I ran to the window. I'd never seen a real fox before.

He gave a sad laugh. "Before Akira's act, I used to appreciate their wild beauty."

"Because of Yoko?"

"Who?"

"Yako," I said. "She told us her real name is Yoko."

"It's unfortunate that such a rare talent would choose to work for Akira. She understands *Edo Tezuma*—traditional Japanese magic. That's true magic. Not Akira's false magic. His *kitsune* ruined any beauty foxes once held for me."

We stood in silence for a few moments, watching the trees outside sway in the wind, only the sound of the Japanese-language news station on in the background.

"I heard my name again," Sanjay said.

I'd never doubted the healthiness of Sanjay's ego, but in this case I heard it too.

"I heard *Houdini* as well," I said. "But maybe they were simply talking about the original."

"No, it was our Houdini-san," Hiro confirmed. He listened for a few more moments, then translated what was said in the news clip.

"Houdini-san," he said. "They are reporting that The Hindi Houdini alone, as the descendant of a great Indian *fakir*, was in the confidence of Akira's secrets. It seems they're drawing conclusions from the interviews he gave shortly before his death."

It's what I'd been afraid of.

"That means if the killer stole the fake diary for the secrets of the illusion," I said, "and realizes they're not there, he thinks Sanjay is the one person who can tell him what he wants to know. Sanjay could be the killer's next target."

CHAPTER 20

"But I don't know anything!" Sanjay insisted. He had been nervously running his hands through his hair. It now stood on end like a mad scientist, his thick black hair rivaling Sébastien's white bouffant.

"Calm down, my boy," Sébastien said.

"I will not calm down," Sanjay seethed, pacing in his checkered socks.

"No," Hiro said, "you shouldn't."

In response to that unexpected statement, Sanjay stopped pacing.

"The murderer is a person who wishes to obtain the secret of the Indian Rope Trick for some reason," Hiro continued, "and he's willing to kill for it. He believes you possess this knowledge, Houdini-san. You must be on high alert. The opposite of calm. Until the police solve this terrible crime, perhaps you should leave Japan."

"That is not a bad idea," Sébastien said.

"I'm sorry I doubted you in the first place, Sanjay," I said. "Leaving sounds like the right decision."

Sanjay began to gather his things.

"You're leaving this minute?" I said. "I didn't mean it had be right now. We can look up flights—"

"I want to be alone. I need time to think."

"Are you sure?" I asked.

"Definitely." He crouched to put his shoes on in the entryway.

"Okay." I knew that look, and it wasn't one to argue with. I sat back down on the soft floor.

"You aren't coming, Jaya?"

"I thought you said you wanted to be alone."

"I didn't mean you. You don't count as being another person."

"Thanks. I think."

Sanjay wanted to walk to clear his head. The sun hung low in the sky, but there was still plenty of light.

"Unless the police are forcing you to stay in the country," I said as we walked down the winding road that led from Hiro's house to the train station, "it sounds like a good idea for you to leave Japan. The show is off now anyway, so there's nothing keeping you here. Besides, it's cold." I rubbed my hands together.

"Umm..."

"Umm, *what?* Oh, no. Did the police forbid you to leave? Did they tell you something you haven't told me?"

"Oh, God no. But I'm not leaving. The show isn't canceled."

I stopped walking and stared in stunned silence at Sanjay. "Yesterday you were ready to leave Japan. When it was only sabotage you were dealing with. Not murder."

"I overreacted. You were right."

"No, I was wrong. It's not overreacting to get out of a killer's way."

"The thing is...there's this small matter of my contract."

"Your contract?"

"The contract I signed holds me to performing."

"You were happy to break it yesterday."

"Yesterday," Sanjay said, "I wasn't famous in Japan. Everything is different now."

"You think they won't let you break the contract now?"

"They have the right to charge me a high cost if I break it. Money I don't have."

"Very funny."

"I'm serious."

I watched his expression, looking for any sign he was joking. "You're not kidding?"

"Why do you think I took this gig?" he said softly.

"Because your theater burned down and you didn't know what to do next."

"Everything I had was tied up in the theater. The items themselves were insured, but not my income from the summer season that was supposed to happen. I haven't worked since then."

"But your shows demand high ticket prices and have sold out months in advance for as long as I've known you."

"Do you have any idea how expensive it is to have a loft in SOMA?"

The South of Market neighborhood of San Francisco was one of its priciest. And Sanjay's apartment was a grand one.

I stared at the person I knew I could tell anything to, who had held back more from me than I knew. "You never told me you were struggling. I mean, you always fly first class. Who does that?"

"First class is comfortable. I could easily afford it. I *wasn't* struggling. I had a good contract for a great cut of the profits at the theater, so everything was fine—better than fine. As long as the money kept coming."

"What about your savings?"

He shook his head. "I'm The Hindi Houdini. Why would I need savings?"

I groaned. Sanjay was immature in so many ways, but I had no idea this was one of them. But it made sense. Sanjay had grown up with money in California's Silicon Valley, an hour's drive south of San Francisco. With his upper middle class upbringing, he'd never seen money as a scarcity. Even when he dropped out of law school to become a magician and had a hard time making ends meet for a few years, he always had the safety net of his parents in case everything fell apart. That experience of living close to people who had so little made him committed to helping local homeless charities, which he helped through charity magic shows, but he had never internalized it. It was a stage in his life he knew he'd emerge from, and he had.

It was so different from my own childhood. In Berkeley, my dad taught music to make ends meet. A single dad teaching sitar kept a roof over our heads, but our clothes were from thrift stores, and our old VW didn't run half the time, since he gave away most of his extra money to charity. Mahilan, being three years older than me, had felt the insecurity more than I had. That's why the financial stability of being a lawyer was so important to him. We had a welcoming, if not stable, community of friends. I remember more potluck meals with our dad's hippie friends than meals at our house.

"My assistant professor income isn't much," I said, "but I've gotten finders fees from those treasures—"

"I'm not going to take your money."

I knew he'd never go to his parents either. Or, more accurately, that even if he swallowed his pride and asked them for money, they most likely wouldn't give it. They hadn't been on the best of terms since Sanjay left law school to become a magician.

"You can pay me back once you get on your feet. It's really not a problem."

"I won't be able to get future funding if I break a contract. That's not how things are done."

"But there are extenuating circumstances."

"This was the show that was going to save my career. It still is."

I gaped at Sanjay and felt myself seething. "That's the real reason you want to stay! To revive your career. The contract's just an excuse—"

"It's true, though. And it's also true that yesterday most people in Japan had never heard my name, but today..."

"Honestly, Sanjay. Your life is more important than—"

Sanjay pulled me into a hug. "Thanks for caring," he said into my hair. The feeling of his hands around me was more comforting than was good for me.

We'd reached the train station. We continued inside and tagged our Pasmo cards.

"You should go back to the hotel," Sanjay said. "I need to talk with Yoko about how to coordinate my performance with whatever she's going to do. She performs interludes of traditional Japanese magic to entertain the audience between Akira's splashier illusions, so we've got a lot to work with."

I stopped myself from strangling Sanjay. "You already talked with her, didn't you? After she dropped us off."

Sanjay shrugged. "You thought I needed a whole hour to call Hiro and Sébastien? I talked to the producers and then Yoko. They want to make it like a memorial concert, with equal billing between his *kitsune* and The Hindi Houdini."

"When were you going to tell me?"

"I thought if I told you earlier, you'd tell Sébastien and Hiro. They'd think it was in poor taste."

"It *is*." I pulled Sanjay aside as a crowd of people exited the station. "More importantly, you can't trust Yoko. It could have been misdirection that the prop was stolen, to throw the police off the scent."

"You saw how upset she was. I don't think she did it. But I'll be careful. Don't worry."

"Don't worry? A killer ninja thinks you know Akira's secrets, you're performing with one of the suspects, and how are you going to pull off a big enough act to be a headliner without your magic equipment?"

"Japanese audiences haven't seen my illusions before, so even the smaller ones I was planning for the opening act will play well. I only need one big illusion. I'll figure it out. But I need to get started. That's why I need to get to Yoko." He looked at the electronic signage scrolling overhead. "My train will be here in one minute, and yours in three."

"What aren't you telling me?" I asked. He bounded up the stairs to the platform and I followed. The hum of an approaching train made me speak more loudly. The train was approaching the station at the exact moment the schedule said it would.

"Weren't you listening to Yoko as she drove us back to the hotel? She was in love with him."

"That wasn't love," I said as the train came to a stop. "That was misplaced devotion."

"Are those two things really so different?" The door of the train car slid open in near silence and Sanjay stepped inside.

"Yes," I answered, but the door of the train had already slid shut. I stood watching it disappear into the distance.

It was my fault Sanjay was stepping into the lion's den. He'd known something was terribly wrong after the attempted sabotage. He'd wanted to leave then, but I'd foolishly talked him out of it.

I'd given Sanjay time for his ego to squash his survival instincts. Because of me, my overly confident best friend was juggling staying clear of a killer and performing a new act in front of millions of people on live television. He was walking a dangerous tightrope. And I had to keep my eyes wide open so he wouldn't fall.

CHAPTER 21

I didn't board the train. I was in no mood to be confined to the hotel. I exited the station, and fifteen minutes later I was standing outside Hiro's door. He opened it before I could knock.

"You missed Renaud-san," he said. "He was tired. I called a taxi for him."

"It's you I'm here to see."

A look of surprise flashed across Hiro's face, but he bowed and welcomed me inside.

"I need your help," I said as I removed my boots and left them in the entryway. "Actually, it's Sanjay who does. I know you're still angry with him for going to work for Akira, but I need you to hear me out."

"Angry is a strong word," he said.

"You're not denying it."

Hiro avoided my gaze and picked up a green dragon from the top of a low bookshelf. "It is unfortunate Houdini-san became involved with him. Akira was a dangerous man. I didn't hide my feelings. But that doesn't prevent me from being friends with Sanjay. How can I help?"

"Sanjay is going on with the show. He can't get out of his contract." There was no reason to tell him Sanjay's questionable, stronger motivation. "He's too confident to know it, but he needs your and Sébastien's help to succeed."

"Help with a performance based on Akira's false miracles?"

"It's only a few days away, and now he's co-headlining. He can't do it alone."

"I'm sorry, that's something I can't be part of."

"Don't give me an answer right now. Think it over. Please."

"If you knew as much as I do about Akira, you'd understand."

"Then why don't you tell me. I don't care if you're rude. What do you really want to say about Akira and his act?"

Hiro laughed. "American openness. Tell me, Jaya-san, how long do you have?"

He stepped out of the main room and returned with two oversize photo albums. He knelt and opened them on the low table. I sat cross-legged next to Hiro as he turned the pages. The albums were filled with clippings of Akira's supposed miracle performances. It was the type of thing a serious fan might have put together, except for the notes in the margins.

"The evidence you collected to debunk his claims?" I asked.

Hiro nodded. "I thought if I studied his work closely, I could show how he deceived people. I saved many recordings of his televised performances."

Hiro retrieved a tiny laptop computer and played a recording that showed Akira walking across a river. It wasn't a shallow river—his feet floated only an inch beneath the surface. I shivered not only for how convincing it looked, but because I was watching a man who'd been full of life the day before and was now dead.

The illusion was being filmed by at least two cameras, maybe more. But the setting wasn't an illusion. This was a real river, with real people watching from both a nearby bridge and the riverbank. As the camera angle changed, one figure in the crowd caught my eye. Bright red hair circled her face, nine ponytails swaying in the wind as if they had a mind of their own. Yoko stood silently while the other women on the bridge squealed and clapped.

"A common trick," Hiro said. "Many magicians perform it."

"Then why attack Akira for it?"

"Because most magicians don't claim quite seriously they are performing a miracle that's enabled by their *kitsune*. And this is the worst part: He says he requires the audience *to believe* in order for the miracle to succeed. It's not so different from what the cult did to convince their members to murder innocent people."

I gasped as a motorboat crossed Akira's path on the river, passing only a few feet in front of him. Water splashed onto his shins. Akira faltered, and for a moment it looked as if he would fall. His injured left hand remained in the pocket of a thin black jacket, which must have made it harder to balance. For nearly half a minute, as waves lapped around him, he stood still on top of the water, regaining his balance. As the waves subsided, I noticed him moving his hand. His fingers moved rhythmically around a glass ball. His *kitsune's* spirit ball. He stepped forward on the water, stepping across the path the boat had crossed moments before.

"It's amazing he does so much even with his injured hand," I said.

"Isn't it? He was a great magician. A great showman. Look at those theatrics." There was no jealousy in Hiro's voice or expression. "I wish he hadn't felt the need to deceive people."

"This is the performance that led to the lawsuit?"

Hiro switched off the video. "I was arrogant. I knew how I would have achieved the illusion. But magicians have many ways of creating the same trick. When I publicly revealed how I believed Akira had achieved his illusion without a miracle, he showed how my solution was wrong. He claimed I had slandered his reputation."

I didn't believe I'd witnessed a miracle, but I couldn't fathom how else he could have achieved walking on water on that river with real boats in the water with him.

"I was wrong about his method," Hiro continued, "so my claims were disproven. I dishonored myself by revealing a secret of magicians and was found guilty of dishonoring Akira in a way that harmed his career. The irony is that his career recovered, but mine never did. I can't blame Akira entirely. I was never as successful."

"Do you have videos of your own performances?" I asked. "I'd love to see them."

He bowed his head modestly. "I had skill, but it wasn't what the people wanted."

"Why not?"

"I'll show you."

On the screen, Hiro appeared in what I imagined was a traditional costume, a flowing white coat that was a cross between a kimono and a suit. He was alone on a stage and held only two closed fans in his hands. He flicked the wood-and-paper fans open. Along with the fans, a paper butterfly appeared. It hovered above the fans, and I could have sworn the creature was flying on its own.

I pressed pause. "Do you still perform this?"

"I haven't in quite some time."

"But you can?"

Hiro didn't answer immediately, but finally nodded.

"I'd love to see it. In person, I mean."

Hiro silently left the room. He returned several minutes later, dressed in the same flowing white costume I'd seen on the screen. He carried a fan in each hand. "Come," he said, beckoning me to follow him.

He led me to a back room of the house that was nearly empty. Without speaking, he pointed to where I should sit, then flicked open the fans. Before I saw where it came from, a paper butterfly floated in the air in front of him.

Soon, the floating mother butterfly was joined by smaller paper butterflies. More and more of them, floating in mid-air. Hiro smiled at my intake of breath. With one last motion, the butterflies flew high above the impromptu stage and floated down to Hiro's feet, unmoving.

"That was beautiful," I said.

"Thank you," Hiro said, closing the fans. "Most people don't have interest in such things."

"Because it's not a spectacle?"

"It was an art for another time. This day belongs to magicians like Akira."

"I don't believe that. I don't know when I've ever seen something so wondrous."

"Some people appreciate it. I spent many hours perfecting this for my sister, hoping she would be one of them. She was one of the people who didn't die immediately from the poison gas attack." His voice cracking slightly as he spoke. "The gas had that effect on many people, who lingered for days or longer, in agony that didn't bring death. I was selfishly happy I got to see my sister before she died, but I could see she wished she had died right away. I needed to help her. I already had an interest in magic, having seen Renaud-san perform as a younger boy. In hopes of making my sister well again, I practiced my act of butterfly magic many times, whenever I wasn't in the hospital with her. I wished to show to her this difficult yet bewitching paper magic in perfect form, to prove to her there was beautiful magic in this world that counteracts the evil that cults and false prophets do."

Hiro paused and closed his eyes. "Because I was still a boy in my parents' view, they didn't tell me how close to death my sister was. They didn't tell me I didn't have much time. Before I could perform butterfly magic for her, she died. Instead of witnessing my floating paper butterflies in life, I honored her with origami cranes in death."

He spun around, and a folded paper crane appeared in his hand. He closed his palm, and when he opened it, the origami figure had disappeared. "That's enough death for today."

"I don't want Sanjay to be next," I said. It was a low blow, but I needed to find a way to get him to help Sanjay. "His style of magic is a combination of classic and modern, so I can see why he wanted to perform in Japan. His shadow magic reminds me of your paper magic. Still, I don't know how he's going to perform a headlining act on his own in a foreign country."

"I'm sorry," he said. "Sébastien-san will help him, but I cannot."

I'd stayed at Hiro's house far later than I'd intended. It was close to midnight, so Hiro called me a taxi. When I was a few blocks from the hotel, the taxi pulled to the side of the road as a blaring police car rushed by.

When the taxi pulled into the now-familiar circular driveway, I learned where the police car had been headed. To my hotel.

I ran inside. In spite of the late hour, the lobby was filled with a dozen people milling about. Gossiping guests, mostly European, and looking like they were having the time of their lives finding an emergency at the hotel after they'd returned from bar-hopping.

But no Sanjay. I needed to find Sanjay.

"*Sumimasen*," I said to the doorman. "Do you know what's happened?"

"No need to worry, miss."

"But what's—"

"Miss Jones," a hotel manager said, stepping out from behind the counter and rushing up to me. "We have been looking for you."

My heart flipped. "What's happened?"

She spoke in Japanese into an ear piece before turning back to me. "One moment. He'll be down shortly."

"He? Who do you mean? What's going on?"

"Reason is fine."

"Reason?" Had everyone gone mad?

"Yes, reason." The manager smiled and gave a slight bow. "He is with the police."

"*Arigato*," I said, thanking the crazy woman and heading for the guests. Maybe they'd know more.

Before I could reach the other guests, Sanjay stepped out of the elevator. I realized the manager had been saying "Rai-san," not "reason." Rai was Sanjay's last name, pronounced "Ray."

It was Sanjay, but he wasn't his usual self. His hair was disheveled, the sleeves of his white dress shirt rolled up unevenly. He held his bowler hat in one hand. A red flower petal peeked out from the brim.

"Thank God," he said when he saw me. "When I couldn't reach you in your room..." He enveloped me in a hug. I felt his body shaking.

"What's happened?" I asked, unable to tell which of us was shaking more. "Why won't anyone tell me what's going on?"

"Akira's killer," Sanjay said, gulping as if he'd come up for air from one of his underwater escapes. "He tried to kill me. He nearly succeeded."

CHAPTER 22

I stood next to a floor-to-ceiling window overlooking a serene rock garden. Diffuse spotlights illuminated patches of the carefully coaxed pebbles. To apologize for Sanjay experiencing a break-in, they'd upgraded him to the best room in the hotel, a suite overlooking their Zen rock garden.

"A random burglary," Sanjay said. "That's what the hotel says. But this was no random burglary."

"That would be too much of a coincidence."

"It's not just that." He showed me a photograph he'd taken on his phone.

My legs didn't feel steady. I needed to sit down.

"The killer went for me," Sanjay said. "Or rather, where they *thought* I was."

I pulled my eyes from the horrifying photo. A pillow and bed sheets that had been ripped apart by a knife.

"How did you get away?" I asked.

"Do you need to sit down?"

"No, I'm fine." I gripped the back of the armchair. I needed to steady myself, but I couldn't imagine sitting still.

Sanjay couldn't either. He strode back and forth, subconsciously twirling his hat in his hands.

"My mind was so amped up after practicing my routine," he said. "I couldn't sleep. I went to the twenty-four-hour hotel bar to get a drink to relax."

"You weren't in bed when the attack happened?"

"I always sleep with an extra pillow next to me. I've been made aware of the fact that in the dark, it looks rather like another person. You can see the pillow that was slashed was in the middle of the bed. The killer was coming for me. It was only my insomnia that saved me. After that, he tore up the place in anger."

"He?"

"One of the guests heard him yelling angrily."

"So it's definitely a man," I murmured. "Not Yoko. But why kill you? Don't they need you alive? If they wanted to know the secret of the Indian Rope Trick, it would be more likely they'd want to torture—" I cut myself off as Sanjay's eyes bulged.

"If I'm the only person who Akira supposedly confided in," he said, "the only motive I can think of is that the person doesn't want anyone to perform the Indian Rope Trick."

"But why would they not want it performed? It doesn't make sense."

Sanjay flipped the bowler hat in his hands so quickly it became a blur. The rote movement appeared to be helping him calm down. "I don't know. Hiro has no reason to stop the trick from being performed by someone who doesn't claim it's supernatural. Not that I know what the secret is."

"A competitor," I suggested.

"It would look awfully suspicious if someone all of a sudden started performing the trick right after Akira was killed over it. Nobody is that foolish."

"Surely Yoko is going to perform it," I said.

Sanjay shook his head. "She doesn't know the whole illusion. It's one of the things we discussed last night. Akira kept her in the dark about a lot."

"We still shouldn't trust her. She could have a male accomplice. One of the people working on the show."

"Which is why you should go home."

"Only if you're coming with me." I felt a pang of regret as I thought about my missing Dutch ship. But Sanjay's life was far more important.

"I told you why I can't—"

"If it's fame you want, what about going back to India? They loved you there."

"India didn't love me."

"You escaped from the Ganges just fine. I thought it was a great success."

"The people loved me, it's true. But the country itself didn't. Do you remember how sick I got? No, you didn't know me yet. But you do know the food in India is way too spicy for me. When you look like me, nobody believes you only want mild food."

I couldn't help laughing. And I couldn't stop. I laughed so hard I began to hiccup. Sanjay had faced the most dangerous situations with ease but couldn't fathom adapting to spicy food. I was afraid Sanjay would explode, but he tossed his hat onto the bed, ran his hands through his disheveled hair, and joined me. As soon as he started laughing he couldn't stop either.

"Tea or mini bar?" Sanjay asked, wiping a tear from his eye.

I hiccupped. "We should probably stick to tea."

While waiting for the electric kettle to boil, I held my breath to stop my hiccups and looked out at the stone garden. Though the lights were soft, they cast enough shadows to make me nervous. I drew the curtains.

"I've escaped from a coffin in the Ganges," Sanjay said, "and I can't even count how many other dangerous stunts. I've been wracking my brain around why I'm so thrown by this."

"Someone just tried to kill you. You're allowed to be afraid."

Sanjay waved off the suggestion. "That's not it. I mean, of course that's the trigger. But I mean the underlying reason. What's different about today from all those other escapes? I've been thinking about it all night, and I think I know the answer. It's the fact that I was in control then. In those other potentially dangerous situations, I was in control of my own fate. It's the same reason I overreacted to Akira's equipment being sabotaged."

Sanjay was right. We weren't in control of our own destinies right now. And I hated it.

The kettle whistled. We both turned to look at it, but neither of us made a move toward it. Instead, I took Sanjay's hands in mine. "We could leave. Your life is more important than your career."

"He could follow us to San Francisco. I'd always be looking over my shoulder."

"Give some credit to the Japanese police. They'll figure out who killed Akira."

Sanjay turned to look at me. "Running away isn't like you, Jaya. When have you ever run from danger in your life?"

"Not for myself. But this isn't about me. I can't bear the thought of anything happening to you."

He squeezed my arm.

"You're shaking," I said.

"No, I'm not. You're shaking."

"No, it's you. Damn, you're right. It's me too. When I thought about the possibility that you—"

Before I knew what was happening, Sanjay had pulled me to him. But it wasn't for a brotherly hug. He wrapped a strong hand against the back of my head and brought my lips to his. He wasn't drugged this time. He knew what he was doing.

And what he was doing was kissing me.

Passionately.

It was everything I remembered and more. My whole body responded. Euphorically, at first, but then the high turned to a low. I needed him, but I also needed to push him away. My arms didn't listen. Had I subconsciously wanted this? Is that why I had told myself I wanted to be on my own? My stomach was filled with butterflies, but also a knife of guilt.

What was I doing? This wasn't part of my plan. This so wasn't part of my plan.

CHAPTER 23

I don't know how long we would have stayed locked in a passionate embrace if not for the interruption.

A firm hand rapped on the door. We broke apart. Even though the person on the other side of the door couldn't see us, my cheeks flushed. I felt like I'd been caught doing something forbidden. Because I had been. This was forbidden by myself.

Sanjay didn't speak, but blinked at me, wide-eyed. Another knock sounded, drawing his gaze to the door. He looked out the peephole before opening the door. It was the police. They apologized for the late hour, but explained they were done with the inspection of Sanjay's room and needed more details from him. They were taking the disturbance seriously, so they didn't want to wait until morning.

It was the break I needed to come to my senses.

"Talk to them," I said. "I'll see you tomorrow."

Before I walked out the door, Sanjay stopped me. With a lopsided grin, he pulled a flower out of his hat. At least he tried to. Instead of a fully formed flower, a mangled white handkerchief appeared. He gaped at the crushed piece of fabric. He tried once more. This time, a confused paper rabbit materialized. It looked confused because it only had one ear.

I laughed and shook my head. "Try to get some sleep."

I stumbled down the hallway, not wanting to know what my hair looked like or how red my face must have been.

I felt unfaithful to Lane, even though we weren't together and I was officially single. Still, the semantics of the word "officially" made me cringe. I felt like a bigger fraud than Akira. I was lying to myself if I thought this was anything less than a betrayal.

I'd let it happen. And part of me didn't regret it.

But I knew a bigger part of me did. Sébastien was right that Lane and I had something special. He filled an empty space in me that I hadn't known I was missing until I found him: the spot reserved for the person who understands you completely, baggage and all.

My feelings for Sanjay weren't so straightforward. I could be myself around him in a way I couldn't be with anyone else. But he didn't understand me in the way Lane did. And although I had belatedly realized Sanjay's charms, I wasn't attracted to him in the same lose-sight-of-the-rest-of-the-world way as I was with Lane.

After everything Sanjay and I had been through together, we loved each other. Of that I was certain. That kiss was an extension of a panicked worry about someone I loved. I never would have acted on my confused feelings if it hadn't been for that.

I reached the elevators but walked past them to the stairwell. The walk up four flights of stairs would do me good.

Sébastien had once told me Sanjay was in love with me. I hadn't believed it. But what if he was right? Was this more than acting out of character because of a near-death experience? I needed to tell Sanjay I was sorry. If Sébastien had been right, this would need to be the biggest apology I'd ever given.

It was the worst possible time to have realized it, but I knew, then, that as deeply as I loved Sanjay and didn't want him hurt—by me or anyone else—I was completely in love with Lane.

Why hadn't I had the good sense to tell Lane exactly how I felt? Why had I thought I needed to figure out my own issues before I could be with him? Would there ever be a time I'd figure myself out, or had I doomed myself to spending my life alone? Why had I pushed him away, even when he was back in San Francisco?

I let myself into my room and bolted the door behind me. I pushed the sole chair underneath the door handle for good measure, then stood with my phone in my hand. It was after two o'clock in the morning in Japan, making it shortly after eight a.m. the previous day in San Francisco. I felt myself flush with embarrassment as I looked at the photo of Lane that popped up when I tapped on his phone number. Horn-rimmed glasses askew, a smile hovering on his lips as he raised one graceful hand to straighten his glasses. A face I'd confess anything to. Even if it would crush him. This was a bad time to talk to him.

I was wrong, that much was clear.

Now I had to figure out a way to tell Sanjay.

Except I couldn't find Sanjay at the hotel the next morning.

And I admit I waited a while before going to look for him downstairs, unsure of how I would feel when I saw him.

He wasn't in the breakfast room, so I went to his room. After knocking on his door a second time, to make sure he hadn't just been in the shower, I asked the front desk staff if they'd seen him leave.

One of the clerks said a note was waiting for me. It had been there when their shift began.

Left early to practice with Sébastien, the note read. *Co-headlining means more practice. I'll be with him all day. Call you later.*

I knew he needed to practice. But with a killer after him, I didn't like it. Sébastien had many talents, and was the most fit ninety-year-old I'd known, but after his bout of pneumonia he was much more frail than he used to be. Sanjay would be single-mindedly focused on practicing, so he wouldn't notice anything amiss. I wished Hiro hadn't been so stubborn.

I went to the buffet breakfast, but I could barely eat. I downed three cups of coffee, which I desperately needed after barely sleeping. But after one half-eaten piece of toast that got soggy as I obsessively checked my phone, I gave up trying to eat.

From the lobby, I called Sanjay. His phone went to voicemail. I figured he was being frugal by keeping his phone off in Japan, so I called Sébastien.

"What do you mean he's not with you?" Sébastien said.

"Why would he be with me?" I was immediately defensive. What had Sanjay told him? I forced myself to calm down. That's when I realized the tone in Sébastien's voice. *Worry.*

A tickle of fear washed over me.

"Sébastien, have you heard from Sanjay at all today?"

"No."

My tickle of fear turned into a full-blown stranglehold. "But Sanjay told me he was spending the day with you."

"*Merde.* I'll be right there."

CHAPTER 24

While I waited for Sébastien to arrive, I asked at the front desk to see if any of the staff remembered Sanjay dropping off the note for me in person. None of them did. As they'd already told me, they were the day shift, and the note was there when they'd arrived.

The note, written on the hotel's stationary, looked like Sanjay's handwriting, but how could I be sure he'd written it of his own will, and not under duress? Or whether he'd written it at all. Sanjay and I didn't usually correspond by printed letter. A close approximation to his general style of handwriting could have fooled me.

The doorman was friends with one of the night clerks, so he called him. The night clerk didn't remember anyone dropping off a note. This wasn't good.

I convinced a nervous hotel staff manager to open Sanjay's room for me. I promised he could look on as I made sure my friend hadn't fallen ill.

The manager wiped beads of sweat from his forehead as I looked everywhere in Sanjay's suite for him. He was nowhere in sight. Neither was his bowler hat or his black Converse sneakers.

Okay. Things were finally looking up. An abductor wouldn't have thought to take his bowler hat. Would they? It looked like he'd left of his own accord. Probably. I thanked the relieved manager and tried to tip him, but he refused to accept it.

I waited for Sébastien in the hotel lobby.

I sat facing the sliding doors that led to the entrance, watching tourists and business travelers from across the world come and go. Everyone who was on their own looked suspicious to me. Why was the lean Australian man carrying an umbrella with such a sharp tip? Oh, it was rainy outside. Why were the elderly Japanese man's eyes darting around the lobby suspiciously? Oh, he was meeting his wife, who arrived moments later. In the ten minutes I spent in the lobby, I'd convinced myself we were dealing with a skillful kidnapper who knew how to imitate Sanjay's handwriting and who'd think to take his beloved hat, so when I saw the silhouette of a wild-haired man in the back of an arriving taxi, I leapt up to meet it.

"Should we call the police?" I asked Sébastien, beating the doorman to the car and pulling open the door.

Sébastien accepted my arm and climbed out. "And tell them what, my dear girl? That a grown man, who left a note that he was going out, isn't answering his phone? If they believed he was missing, he would probably become a suspect"—he lowered his voice—"in Akira's untimely death."

"But after what—" I groaned. "You don't know what happened last night."

He clung to the door of the taxi. "*Non.* What has happened?"

"His room was ransacked. Sanjay is safe, at least he was, but the man had a knife—"

"We have no time to waste, then." Instead of closing the taxi door, he climbed back inside.

"Where are we going?"

"To see a field fox."

I got into the cab.

"Address, please," the driver said.

Sébastien and I looked at each other. "Do you know the address?" I asked.

"No. I assumed you did."

"Please take us to the Gion neighborhood," I said to the driver.

"*Hai.*"

"Neither of you thought to call me after the burglary?" Sébastien asked.

"It was late. And we were, uh, busy. Then this morning, I thought you two were together, so he would have told you."

"*Ne t'inquiète pas.*"

"We think it was an attempt on his life," I said as the taxi pulled onto the road. "And it was a man. So it's not Yoko. Oh. Why are we going to see her?"

"Yesterday," Sébastien said, "Sanjay told me Yoko and the rest of the crew wished to practice some illusions with him today, and he wished me to go with him. Yet he mentioned a foolhardy agreement I would need to sign."

"You didn't sign it either?"

"A ridiculous invention. Though part of me wonders if I should have signed it so I could protect him."

"I'm surprised you didn't." I thought of gallant Sébastien offering to sacrifice himself for Sanjay, as he had done for me the previous year. The kindhearted old magician would have done it, I had no doubt. His life partner had died many years ago, and while he still lived life to the fullest, he was a brave soul who would risk his life for those he cared about, believing he'd be reunited with Christo after all these years.

"I told him it was a bad idea to go at all, even with me accompanying him. His life is worth more than the price of a contract, no?"

"He went there *alone*?" I gripped the seat of the cab. "That's where he is? When we don't know if Yoko is in league with a murderer?"

"I thought I'd talked sense into the boy. He agreed not to go. That's what he told me. Yet he declined my offer to spend the day with an old man who could help him come up with even better illusions for the Friday performance. He said he knew what he was performing like the back of his hand, so was spending the day with you to give himself a mental break."

"He hasn't been in touch with me at all since last night," I said. I felt my cheeks flushing. I coughed to cover it up and handed Sébastien the note.

"I can't say I know what his writing looks like," Sébastien said, tracing the lines of handwriting with his finger.

"I can't swear to it either."

We sat in silence for a few moments, and that's when I noticed it. The video screen in the back of the taxi was playing a music video. A familiar face caught my attention. Akira. This was his old boy band, Flash. His handsome face, ten years younger, lit up the screen as a jangly beat filled the cab. I clicked off the screen.

The amenable driver circled the neighborhood for fifteen minutes, meticulously covering each street in a widening circle, until I saw something I recognized: a Starbucks located next to a traditional Japanese sweets shop that had stood on the same spot since the medieval era.

"There," I said, pointing. "I can get us to the magic studio from here."

The driver maneuvered into a narrow spot on the side of the road and let us out. He wouldn't accept a tip, but Sébastien used sleight of hand to leave one anyway.

I looked longingly at the coffee house. The coffee at the hotel had been weaker than the espresso drinks I was used to at home. I mentally kicked myself. Sanjay was more important than coffee.

"What's your plan?" Sébastien asked me.

"This was your idea."

"But you have a plan. I can see it in your face."

"If Sanjay isn't there and Yoko doesn't want to talk to us, you can feign distress."

Sébastien wheezed. He steadied himself on a signpost.

I rushed to his side. "Are you all right? Sébastien? Sébastien?"

CHAPTER 25

Sébastien winked at me and stood up straight. "I'm as fit as I was in my seventies. Only testing to make sure my acting abilities are what they once were. I fooled them at Mont Saint Michel, did I not?"

"Don't do that to me."

I led the way to the studio. I only got lost three times before I found the hidden door with the brass fox knocker.

The door of the magic workshop was locked, but it clicked open a few seconds after we knocked. Yoko greeted us at the second doorway. Her red hair was tied in a single bun that rested on the back of her neck, but at least half of it hung in frizzy tendrils that had escaped. I guessed it wasn't a purposefully playful look, but the hair was acting in solidarity with her haggard face. Her hair wasn't what surprised me. Instead of being dressed in a costume, she wore jeans and a Hello Kitty sweatshirt.

"*Konichiwa*, my dear," Sébastien said from the doorway.

"*Ohayōgozaimasu*," Yoko said, bowing politely.

"Sanjay asked us to meet him here for a coffee break," I lied.

Yoko gave me a strange look. It might have been confusion, but she covered the emotion so quickly that I couldn't tell for sure. Was she blocking the doorway on purpose?

"I asked Houdini-san to meet me here hours ago," she said, ushering us inside. So much for the theory she was trying to keep us out. "This afternoon we're meeting with the television crew who are filming us in three days. We need to practice together first. Houdini-san called me to make an excuse."

"He called you?" My heart pounded.

Yoko showed me her phone. My heart sank. It was a text message, not a voicemail: *Sorry can't make it until later.*

"I wondered," Yoko said, "if he was deciding if he should return home to America."

"He's committed to performing," I said. I was certain that was true. What I was less sure of was whether it was Sanjay himself who'd sent the text message. I told myself to breathe.

"Is there really nothing to be done about the financial backers?" Sébastien asked. "Why is the show going on? With one murder and another attempted murder, why not cancel?"

Yoko gasped. "Attempted murder?"

"Someone attacked Sanjay," I said. "Or at least they tried to. And now he's missing. He might have been taken against his will."

"You believe Houdini-san has been kidnapped?" she asked. She gripped the edges of her oversize sweatshirt.

"It's possible," I said.

"Yet when you arrived you said...Ah, I understand." A sad smile spread across Yoko's face. "You do not trust me."

"We do," Sébastien said kindly.

Yoko bowed. "You would be foolish to trust me."

At my sharp intake of breath, she caught my eye as she straightened.

"I was the person closest to Akira," Yoko said. "Even with his thousands of followers, he had no one else. He was a difficult man, and you're intelligent people. You naturally wonder if I was involved. I don't resent it. But I know you must wonder if I harmed Akira or Houdini-san."

I showed her the note Sanjay had left for me.

"One moment." Yoko disappeared behind a set of bamboo and paper screens that divided sections of the warehouse.

At least I had previously thought the folding screens were made of paper. But Yoko's form behind them cast no shadow. She emerged a moment later holding a piece of paper.

"This is Houdini-san's handwriting," Yoko said, comparing the two pieces of paper. "He wrote instructions for the crew who are helping with the performance."

"Sanjay wrote the instructions on paper?" I asked. That didn't seem like him.

"The written English of the crew is better than their spoken English," Yoko said, comparing the two notes. "Yes, this is his handwriting."

I looked over her shoulder. "It is," I agreed. "That means Sanjay lied to us all."

CHAPTER 26

"I'm going to kill Sanjay when I find him," I said.

"He could have been under duress," Sébastien said.

"I know him better than anyone. He would have left me a clue in his note."

"I've always wanted to visit Fushimi Inari," Sébastien replied.

I studied Sébastien's face. Was he being serious?

The two of us had left Yoko to salvage her show and were sitting in the coffee house drinking strong, sugary coffees and eating pumpkin pie. I'd skipped breakfast, and now that I was fairly confident Sanjay hadn't been kidnapped, I needed food along with more caffeine. Unfortunately the tiny slivers of pie hardly counted as slices, and the coffees were suspiciously child-sized. I wasn't cut out for Japanese portions.

"I'm not in the mood for playing tourist," I said. "Sanjay has gone off God knows where, and there's a killer on the loose." I didn't add that I'd also betrayed the man I loved with another man I loved in a different way, and I was about to break the heart of my best friend— after I strangled him for lying to me.

"When you've lived as long as I have," Sébastien said, "you learn a few things. One of them is that when you believe there is absolutely nothing you can do, you're usually wrong."

"Why do you think he's gone to this shrine?" I asked. "There's nothing we can do to find Sanjay when he doesn't want to be found."

"You misunderstand me," Sébastien said. "I don't believe he's there. I believe that neither of us is thinking clearly. Only once we clear our heads will we be able to catch a glimmer of the truth. What better place to do that than one of the wonders of the world?"

The road leading to the fabled vermillion *torii* gates of Fushimi Inari was lined with street vendors selling hot food in addition to souvenirs, many of which were cuddly stuffed foxes. This shrine was built to honor Inari, the Shinto god of rice—whose messengers were foxes.

I kissed Sébastien on the cheek. "You knew," I said. "You were hoping it would make our subconscious minds get to work."

Sébastien shrugged.

I stopped to buy *inarizushi,* fried tofu wrapped around sweet sushi rice, before we continued to the shrine. The road was still wet from rain that had fallen during the night, but it was holding off for now. We'd borrowed two tall umbrellas from the hotel. I offered to carry Sébastien's, but he used it as a walking stick.

Where the hillside road of vendors ended, concrete steps led to the entry gates of the shrine. Carvings of stone foxes sat on columns, looking down on us as we stepped through the first gates. Colorful illustrated signs showed us the winding upward path, flanked the whole way by thousands of *torii* gates, leading to the uppermost part of the shrine at the peak of the mountain. The traditional Japanese gates were meant to mark the transition from worldly presence to the sacred.

I couldn't read the Japanese writing that adorned each bright red-orange post we walked past, but that didn't detract from the wonder of the place. The gates were placed so close to each other that they nearly formed a roof over our heads as we ascended the winding path up the mountain.

"This shrine has stood here since the eighth century," Sébastien said. "Almost fourteen hundred years. It's the largest Inari shrine in Japan—which is saying something, considering that there are at least three thousand others. In addition to being the god of rice, he—or she, depending upon the portrayal—is also the patron god of fertility, tea, sake, sword-smiths, and merchants."

"She certainly gets around," I said, marveling at the tall gates that stretched up the mountain in front of us.

"Even if it were only this one shrine," Sébastien said, "I would be in awe of Inari's power."

"If the climbing is too much for you at any time," I said as we began our ascent, "just let me know."

As we walked in the midst of tourists and worshipers, I hoped my subconscious would get to work. Was it my fault Sanjay had gone off the grid? Although I wasn't arrogant enough to think I could do the police's job for them, now that Sanjay had been attacked, I wanted to be doing more to figure out how to protect him. Sébastien appeared to be lost in thought as well.

"I can see the wheels of your mind spinning," I said.

"If I were a young man who still wished to be a performer, I'd have loved to stage a performance here. So many possibilities with these gates...Good thing Sanjay isn't here, or he'd probably get in trouble trying to do it himself."

"He has to turn up at some point," I said.

Sébastien didn't answer.

"Why aren't you reassuring me?" I asked.

"I didn't think that was the type of conversation we were having."

"What kind of conversation are we having?"

"Letting our minds wander to find the truth." Sébastien stopped and rested his hands on the curved handle of the umbrella. His eyes were wide.

"Are you all right?" I asked.

"I'm fine. But I can see it in your face—you're not. Sanjay ruined things, didn't he? He waited too long, until your heart belonged to another."

I looked away, focusing on the ornate Japanese calligraphy on the wooden gate pillars. "You're a mind reader now?"

"Sanjay was nearly killed last night," Sébastien said. "Afterward, you were both 'too busy' to think to call an old man who cares about you and should have been informed. You're both single young people. And this morning, Sanjay has disappeared of his own free will."

I didn't speak.

"So it's true..." he said. "Now I understand what's going on. He needs time to process what happened."

"Nothing much happened," I said. "But nothing *at all* should have happened. I'm technically single, but..."

"Your heart belongs to another."

"You really think it's my fault he's disappeared?" I groaned.

"What is it?"

"Right before I left, he failed when he tried to perform two simple magic tricks. He was more upset than he needed to be."

"I love the dear boy, but parts of his intellect appear to be stuck at the age of thirteen rather than thirty. To his credit, he's also one of the most talented performers of any age I've ever met. Give him time."

"But the more time he has, the worse things will be. I need to tell him it was a mistake, and I owe it to him to do it in person."

Sébastien hooked his elbow through mine. "Sanjay was safe when he was in touch with you and Yoko this morning, but the fact remains someone wishes to kill him as they did Akira. I don't like him being alone now. Let's put our heads together and figure out what we can do."

"We know Akira figured out a way to perform an illusion that's reminiscent of the world-famous Indian Rope Trick," I said as we climbed. "Akira was a master manipulator who pretended to possess a *kitsune* who led him to the solutions of ancient mysteries that he performed as miracles."

We reached a clearing near a lake, where you could take a break from the path. It looked like a sub-shrine. Dozens of stone foxes surrounded us, from the size of my hand to nearly as tall as me. Here, in spite of the crowds of tourists and worshipers passing on the nearby path, I felt as if we were alone.

"He was a good showman," Sébastien said, joining me in the clearing. "I didn't agree with how he lied to the public, but he was wonderful at what he did. Staging the finding of a Dutchman's diary that contained the supernatural secrets of the Indian Rope Trick was a brilliant touch. The posters for the show capitalized on it."

"The Dutchman of Dejima, the *kitsune*, and The Hindi Houdini," I said, remembering the poster of Akira surrounded by the three. "The ninja saboteur killer has to be a magician who wanted the secret, but why? It's not like he could perform it, even if the secret had been there. It could have been jealousy, or someone wishing to stop his fraud, or pure malice. There's no way to know."

"We have too many possible motives. I hope the police find forensic evidence."

"Before the performance on Friday."

"Three days," Sébastien murmured. "I wish to find him, if only to help prepare him for this performance."

We continued onward in silence for quite some time. I was getting tired, but Sébastien showed no signs of slowing down.

"Keep up, Jaya." Sébastien bounded around a crest, using the tip of the umbrella to propel him upward.

"These are new boots." I hurried to catch up. "I haven't broken them in yet." I'd had to buy a new pair after losing one when running through a garden of stone monsters in Italy.

"I turn ninety-one soon," he said, stopping on level ground and smiling at me. "Perhaps I should get myself one of these for a present." He stepped off the path into a clearing, twirled the umbrella in his hand, then tossed it into the air. It flipped in full circles above his head, and he caught it perfectly.

Two women passing by clapped and bowed with smiles on their faces before continuing on.

"Show-off," I said as we walked on.

"Occasionally, I have a fleeting idea that I should return to the stage—"

"Why don't you?"

Sébastien laughed. "Because I hated it. I also know I'm not as fit as I tell myself. Not only for the stage. I know enough to realize I'm not going to make it to the top of this mountain."

"That's where you're wrong," I said. "While we've been walking slowly, we've made it nearly to the top."

After one more turn, I saw it. We'd reached the top of the mountain. All of Kyoto lay before us. The sky was half dark clouds and half blue sky. Which way would it turn?

My phone buzzed. I wanted to ignore it, but with everything going on I knew that would be foolish.

It was a text message from Sanjay.

Meet me at this address, the text read. *He struck again.*

CHAPTER 27

"It could be a trap," I said as we hurried down the winding path beneath the *torii* gates. "It was a text message, not a voicemail."

Sébastien raised a bushy white eyebrow at me. "He only needed time away to think."

"Do we really know that?" I tried to raise an eyebrow back at him, but it was an expression I'd never been especially good at.

Sébastien sighed. "We'll approach carefully."

The address Sanjay had given us led to a modern apartment building.

Safety in numbers, I thought to myself as we walked along the concrete path connecting apartments. I knew which door before I came to the number Sanjay had given us. The door handle had been smashed.

I knocked on the door, and a familiar face opened it. Yoko.

She gave a start when she saw us standing in her open doorway.

"I thought you were the lock-maker," she said.

"Locksmith," Sébastien corrected gently.

A noise sounded from inside the apartment. Behind Yoko, an elderly woman wearing a kimono was preparing tea. Sanjay wasn't in sight.

Yoko smiled weakly. She held a small porcelain fox figurine in her hands. "If you're looking for Houdini-san, he left when the police did."

"You've seen him? In person?"

"I was with him all afternoon. He arrived late, as he said he would. There was something wrong with him, though. During practice, he repeatedly dropped his hat..." She shook her head. "I told him you were looking for him. He didn't call you?"

"No," I growled. So Sanjay had been screening calls. He'd ignored mine but had gone to see Yoko? I had no right to feel jealous, but I did.

My irrational jealousy faded away as Yoko shifted her body and I saw the full extent of what lay beyond. Her apartment had been trashed. I looked more closely at the fox figurine she held in her hands. It had been broken in half. The head was separate from the body, and the tail was nowhere to be seen.

The woman behind Yoko said something to her in Japanese. Yoko flushed and invited us in. Sébastien stepped out of his shoes and walked inside. I lingered for a moment. Should I be going after Sanjay?

Sébastien caught my eye. "If he doesn't want to be found..."

Yoko set the broken fox on a low wooden bureau with other broken objects, all neatly arranged with the broken pieces of each object in its own separate pile. She was beginning to put the things back in place. The ceramic bear looked especially forlorn, his smile subverted into a broken frown.

Was it misdirection? Had she ransacked her own apartment to throw suspicion off of herself? She looked truly distraught, but she acted on the stage for a living.

Sébastien tried to assist the woman making tea, but she swatted him away and insisted he sit down.

"Akira and Houdini-san," Yoko said, "and now this." A tear rolled down her cheek. Without makeup and with her hair tucked partially under a cap, she looked both older and younger. "Why?"

"What happened, exactly?" Sébastien asked.

Over the tea Yoko's neighbor served from her cast iron teapot and traditional chestnut sweets from her kitchen counter, we learned that Yoko had returned home after practicing for the show with the camera crew to find the front door had been crudely forced open. She went to a neighbor's apartment and called the police, and also Sanjay, from there. She didn't enter until the police arrived and made sure the culprit wasn't still there. One of her neighbors had caught a glimpse of him.

"It was Oku-san who saw him," Yoko said, nodding towards the woman fixing us tea.

The woman looked up and spoke a few words to Yoko. The words struck Yoko as forcefully as if she'd been slapped. I didn't understand any of them except one: *gaijin*.

A foreigner.

"Not a Japanese person?" I asked. "How can she be certain?"

"I apologize for her rude language," Yoko said. She turned and said something in Japanese to the woman, who nodded decisively and spoke several sentences of rapid Japanese, while Yoko nodded.

"The man covered his face," Yoko translated. "He tried to disguise himself, but she insists he was a foreigner. She told all this to the police, but I must have been occupied with what's left of my belongings."

"Could you ask her if he was dressed in black?" I asked. "Like a ninja?"

The woman laughed when she heard the word "ninja." Yoko repeated my question.

"Yes," she translated. "He wore black, with cloth over the lower part of his face. But this man didn't look like a ninja. Besides, she says there are no ninjas left in Japan."

But dressed in black, could this be our ninja? The eyes of the man I'd seen for a fraction of a second on the surveillance video had looked Japanese, but had I only seen what I was expecting to see?

"You think it's the same man?" Yoko whispered.

"No harm came to you," Sébastien said. "That's the most important thing."

"I don't fear him. It was not like the attack on Houdini-san, they did not wish to harm me. Only my possessions. He came during the day, while I was gone and my apartment was empty. He must have been looking for notes on the illusion."

"It seems likely," Sébastien said. "Perhaps someone who cares more for you, who didn't wish to hurt you, but didn't mind hurting Akira and Sanjay..."

"But a foreigner? Who could it be?"

Sébastien raised an eyebrow at me. Was I supposed to know what he meant?

Yoko's neighbor could tell something was wrong. Yoko stood and spoke again to the woman, a hand on her arm, murmuring something that sounded comforting.

Sébastien leaned in to me and spoke quietly. "A foreigner who didn't wish to harm anyone..."

"What are you talking about?"

"There's someone who cares very much for you, who is respecting your wishes and staying away from you. But if he thinks you're in danger, it might be too much temptation. He might have come with the best intentions—"

"No," I said. "You can't mean who I think you do. You think the foreigner is Lane Peters?"

"Of course," Sébastien said. "Who else could it be?"

CHAPTER 28

"It's not Lane," I said. "That makes no sense. You think he's trying to chivalrously protect me by figuring out this mystery, here in Japan, without me knowing it's him?"

"Perhaps."

"He wouldn't hurt anyone."

"I agree."

"But you said—"

"I said he might be the foreigner. Not that he's a saboteur or killer. We might be looking for two different people. A killer and a protector."

"Maybe," I said. "But one of them isn't Lane Peters."

Yoko finished speaking with her neighbor, who smiled and bowed to us and walked to the door.

"*Arigato*," I said.

"*Doo itashimashite.*" She bowed again and left.

"Such a sloppy break-in," I said as I watched the door close. Unlike the entry into Akira's studio. So the person who forced their way into Yoko's apartment wasn't an expert on picking locks. Yet Akira's studio was even harder to get into. There was no way this was the work of Lane Peters, even on a quest to protect me if he'd somehow found out what was going on.

"Can we help you with anything?" Sébastien asked.

Yoko shook her head. "I wish I had never seen the diary."

"You mean after Akira created it," I said.

She gave me another of her otherworldly, unreadable looks. "All of our props are real, Jaya-san. It was the only way to protect ourselves against people who wished to destroy Akira's reputation, as Matsumoto-san did."

I nearly dropped the mug of tea in my hands.

"The Dutchman diary is *real*?" I said. "You told us it was fake."

"I said it was *a prop*," Yoko said, "and the Indian Rope Trick's secret was not inside." She spoke slowly and precisely.

"But the diary itself is real?" I said. "As in truly written by an eighteenth-century Dutch trader?"

"*Hai*," she spoke quickly, then again slower while enunciating her words. "It is always easiest to misdirect when the lie is close to the truth."

"So true," Sébastien murmured.

I stared at Yoko. She had always spoken as she spoke to us now, yet I was only truly hearing it for the first time. She spoke English more slowly than Japanese, as if she were struggling for words, because she was. Japanese students all studied English now, but it was always easier to read a foreign language than to speak it.

"Yoko," I said. "You told us the beginning of the story about how Akira transformed himself from a J-pop star to a successful magician who performed miracles. But you didn't tell us the whole story, did you?"

"There is always more to a story," Yoko said, a flash of *kitsune* mischief in her eyes.

"You're the one who found the diary, aren't you?" I said. "Everything in Akira's 'new' act was your creation. You're the brains behind the show."

"If you mean I created the illusions, *hai*. Yes, these were all my illusions."

"You have an amazing mind," Sébastien said. "I only wish you hadn't pretended—"

"You misunderstand, Renaud-san. I never wished Akira to pretend to perform miracles. I only wished him to return to the fame he deserved."

"But that's how he got it," I said.

"He never wanted his fans to become followers either. You believed him to be an unpleasant man, but that was only because he was unhappy that this is what his life had become. Everyone from schoolgirls to surgeons worshiped the *idea* of Akira, not the man he really was. He was different when I met him."

"Since you weren't really his assistant, how did you meet him?" I asked.

"He was convalescing after his near-death accident. I discovered where he was staying, even though it wasn't publicly reported."

"How?" Sébastien asked.

She smiled. "He'd cut off his long hair. Without it, nobody recognized him. Nobody except for me."

"Hadn't he gone away?"

"He hadn't left Kyoto, because it was his home, where he felt most comfortable. I saw him buying food. It was difficult for him, because his hand was bandaged, and he walked with a limp. The anger on his face made others stay away. But to me, he looked forlorn. I knew it was him, so I watched where he went. The next day, I brought him a small gift for his recovery—homemade tea. I also took with me the few props I needed to perform paper butterfly magic. It's a traditional type of magic. I have always loved traditional Japanese magic. *Edo Tezuma.* Akira loved *Yozuma*, Western magic. We came to an understanding."

Yoko explained how she'd dropped out of college to take care of Akira. She was the one who convinced Akira he couldn't hide forever. He was worth more to the world than to hide away. But Akira was adamant in his claim that he was ruined. He showed her his disfigured hand. It embarrassed him, because he'd been a heartthrob, and beyond his embarrassment, he knew he would no longer be able to perform card tricks or other sleights of hand. Yoko convinced him that was only a small sliver of magic, and not the most interesting one.

Akira agreed to work with Yoko, both because he enjoyed her adoration, and also because she came up with his hook that would win back the crowds. While they were talking that first day, Akira told Yoko he would sell his soul to a demon if he could have the use of his hand back and attain his old fame. To which Yoko replied, "Why not?" He laughed nervously, then heard out her plan.

Yoko confided to Akira that the nickname her childhood classmates had tormented her with was Yako, the malicious demon fox with a name similar to hers. She excused herself for a few minutes, then came back to face Akira, her thick red hair pulled into nine pony tales. "*Kitsune*," Akira said, his eyes tracing the outlines of her wild hair. The untamable hair, so unlike that of her classmates, which had always caused her embarrassment and grief. A warm smile spread across Yoko's face. She nodded, then ran outside. "Where are you going?" Akira called, following close behind. Yoko picked up a rounded pebble, no bigger than a fingernail, from the earth near the cabin. Wiping it on her blouse, she handed him the smooth gold-white rock. "The *kitsune* spirit ball," Akira said, taking the pebble in his good hand. "Now that I have it, I control you." Yoko nodded. She had always thought that Akira was much more intelligent than people gave him credit for. Akira tucked the pebble into his pocket. "What would you have me do?"

Yoko became not merely Akira's assistant, but also his researcher and stage manager. Her new duty, as she explained it, was to facilitate his renewed rise to fame. This was his new identity, she explained. Their act would be based on the fiction that he possessed the spirit ball of a *kitsune*. Yoko—or Yako as she would be called in their act—would lead Akira to ancient magic, and this was the magic he would perform.

In truth, Yoko had so many ideas for historical magic because she was a bookworm and had studied so much history and had no social life, outside of listening to Akira's J-pop band.

However, Akira took the story further than she had ever imagined—further than either of them had imagined. Akira embraced it wholeheartedly, because the more he did so, the more adoration he received. It was like a drug. He refused to admit to the press that this was an act and begged Yoko to keep the truth a secret.

Their first illusion had been a historical reenactment of a famous old Japanese trick, which the captured *kitsune* had led Akira to. Next was walking across water, as recorded by a religious man in historical records at a temple. All of their shows were outdoor performances that combined traditional Japanese *Edo Tezuma* magic with Western *Yozuma* magic, staged with crowds and televised with cameras, and to every appearance truly magical feats.

"For all of our performances," she concluded, "I would find real historical documents to make the magic seem all the more real."

Yoko hadn't purposefully misled us about the diary. It was us who had misinterpreted her words. The Dutchman of Dejima's diary was real.

Which meant we'd been looking at everything all wrong.

CHAPTER 29

"The cooking museum had a diary written by a man from the Netherlands," Yoko said. "Its owner witnessed the Indian Rope Trick in India, before traveling to Japan. The Dutch were the only Europeans who were allowed to trade with Japan during our period of isolation. You're familiar?"

"Yes, I know it," I said. "The *Sakoku* period of the Edo Era."

"This man, Casper Van Asch, sailed with the Dutch East India Company."

"The man and his diary were real," I repeated, mostly to myself. I still couldn't quite believe it. Casper Van Asch. The marketing materials for the magic show hadn't mentioned him by name. He was simply a Dutchman.

"*Hai*. Van Asch was an early—what is the word? 'Foodie'?—interested in recipes, both Dutch and Japanese. That's why a collector purchased his diary. It was then bequeathed to the cooking museum with the rest of his collection upon his death."

"The museum simply gave it to you?" Sébastien asked.

Yoko lowered her eyes. "It's a small museum. Akira gave them a generous donation in exchange for purchasing a diary that was of no interest to most patrons." She glanced up at us with flushed cheeks. "It was of no consequence, simply a small item in the collection. It was no longer on display. There was no harm—"

"There's no fault in buying the diary," Sébastien said.

Yoko nodded and gave a slight bow. "In addition to the money Akira paid to the museum, the publicity they received from having their museum appear in magazines was beneficial to them. They have more patrons now." She paused. "Why are you interested in the diary? As I said, it doesn't contain the secret of the most famous illusion of all time. That was my invention."

"Then why show it to the press photographers?" I asked.

"The diary was written primarily in Dutch, but there were many sections where Casper Van Ash also wrote basic Japanese kanji next to his words. It looked like he was learning the language, because he lived here many years. The page of the diary we used for the staged photos has a Japanese account of Van Ash witnessing the Indian Rope Trick in India. Not with that name, but the words describe watching a conjuror charm a boy to climb into the sky."

"Casper Van Asch really witnessed the impossible trick?" I said.

"*Hai*. This was real, and to the press we hinted that his story would continue if we turned the page—which we didn't do in front of cameras or reporters of any kind."

"Did you make a copy of the diary?" I asked.

The flicker of rage that shone in her eyes transformed her face. But only for a fraction of a second. The emotion seemed to emanate from a *kitsune*, though it disappeared as quickly as it had begun, and her words were calm. "Yes. It is part of our Japanese heritage. I insisted on it."

"Can I—"

She cut me off with a brisk shake of her head. "Akira kept the copy. He didn't want anyone to find it. He kept the original with him at all times. That's how I knew his killer had stolen it. He took it very seriously. This was the only way we could ensure nobody saw that the diary was fake. That it was only a prop."

I groaned inwardly at her word choice. How easy it was for translations to get things wrong. I'd seen this time and time again, beginning with when I was doing my own original research on British East India Company records during graduate school.

We'd all assumed "fake" meant a modern reproduction meant to fool us, but it could also refer to a true piece of history being used for a fraudulent purpose.

"You mentioned that only some of the Dutch was translated into Japanese," I said.

"*Hai.* Van Asch wasn't fluent. He made his own Japanese notes next to his Dutch, but not for all of it. The museum translated recipes of interest where his Japanese was poor."

A sharp banging made me jump. The broken door of Yoko's apartment swung open a few inches as knuckles rapped on the wood.

"The locksmith," Yoko said. "If you'll excuse me."

"Is there anything we can do for you before we leave?" Sébastien asked.

Yoko looked around her trashed apartment. Her eyes came to rest on a framed poster of her act with Akira, showing the miracle of him walking on water. The intruder had knocked it to the ground and smashed the glass covering. A spiderweb of fine cracks covered the surface. The image underneath was more lifelike than the Dutchman of Dejima poster, looking almost like a real photograph. The bridge above the river was the one I'd seen in the video Hiro had showed me. The whole scene was nearly identical to the performance I'd watched, except for one important difference. Underneath where Yoko stood on the bridge with her bright red fox-tail hair swirling around her face, her reflection was missing from the water—replaced with that of a fox.

"There is nothing," Yoko said, "that you or anyone else can do."

As Sébastien and I stood up to leave, my eyes swept over the wreckage of her apartment. My sadness for her transformed into surprise as my gaze came to rest on an object that had avoided the burglar's wrath: Akira's spirit ball.

I covered my involuntary gasp with a fit of coughing.

How did Yoko have Akira's spirit ball? Wouldn't he have had it with him when he died?

As Sébastien patted my back in an attempt to ease my "coughs," I tried to indicate to him with my eyes the gold-flecked glass ball that sat in a bowl of citrus fruits on the kitchen counter. His only response was to pat my back harder. He must have thought my eyes were bulging from my head because of my coughs.

I hoped I'd learned enough from Sanjay to pull off what I was about to do. As Yoko moved toward the sink to get me a glass of water, I palmed my cell phone in my hand, covered by a tissue, and raised both to my mouth. I faced the direction of the fruit bowl, and took a photograph of the spirit ball.

In Japanese mythology, a *kitsune*'s spirit ball would return to its rightful owner when its thief died. The spirit ball had returned to Yoko.

CHAPTER 30

The wind whipped my hair around my face as Sébastien and I stepped outside. Dark clouds gathered over the eastern hillside, but it wasn't raining where we were—yet.

"Did you see that?" I said. "The spirit ball."

"Is that what you were photographing?" Sébastien asked.

"You noticed?"

"You're no Hindi Houdini, my dear."

"Do you think Yoko saw me?"

"I doubt it. She was too distracted by the destruction of her worldly possessions and by you having a coughing fit without a surgical mask covering your mouth, while the horrified locksmith looked on." The look on Sébastien's face told me he thought this was hilarious.

"Why are you so calm? Don't you see what this means? Yoko has Akira's spirit ball. He always had it on him and would have had it with him when he was killed."

"There are a number of explanations I can think of," Sébastien said. "The easiest of which is that there are multiple spirit ball props."

"Oh." I looked at the clandestine photo I'd taken. It was too fuzzy to make out any identifying markings on the glass ball. Not that I knew any identifying markings.

Sébastien's eyes crinkled as he smiled at me. "You're losing sight of the far more interesting development."

"The diary is real."

It was too late in the day to visit the cooking museum where the diary had been found, but I could do so tomorrow. I wished I had

Tamarind at my side to help with a library search, or at the very least that I was in an English-speaking country with reference materials in a language I understood.

"It changes everything, Sébastien. This isn't about the modern secrets of an ancient illusion or even about Akira himself. It's about a secret from history. That means it's no longer clear why someone is after Sanjay and why they tried to kill him. Akira's killer already has the diary, and they can't think Sanjay knows or cares about history." Why was Sanjay pig-headedly ignoring me? He was in more danger than he knew.

Sébastien glanced at his phone. "This would blink at me if I had a missed call or text message, wouldn't it? Jaya? Are you listening? I was certain you were going to ask me when I purchased this ridiculous phone, which is smarter than I am."

"Sorry, what? Oh, yes. Your phone would blink if you had a message."

"Then Sanjay hasn't called me."

We walked briskly in silence back the way we'd come while Sébastien made a phone call. I had phone calls of my own to make. I tried Sanjay again. The phone went directly to voicemail. I squeezed the phone so tightly I was afraid I'd snap it in half. I was about to hang up in anger, but I was too worried to do that. Instead I left a brief message asking him to be careful because I'd found new information.

I desperately wanted to call Lane, but this wasn't the time. What could I say to him? But there was a far more practical call I could make. Dr. Nakamura. The professor studied the Dutch in Japan, so I might be able to get his help with Casper Van Asch's diary. My call went to voicemail, so I stopped walking to leave a message.

I caught up with Sébastien, who was hanging up his own call. I hadn't heard the conversation, but his face wore a grimace when he turned to look at me.

"I'm afraid we've made another faulty assumption today," he said. "That was Hiro. Sanjay was with him this morning before he met Yoko."

I groaned. "But Hiro was adamant about not wanting to help Sanjay because he was working for Akira."

"Hiro believed what he told you at the time. His feelings run deep when it comes to his dead sister. It's the one thing I've seen that makes him irrational. Hiro said you convinced him helping Sanjay was the right thing to do. He was even more concerned when he saw Sanjay."

"Why?"

"He kept flubbing the close-up magic that requires dexterity. Which is unlike him, even under stressful circumstances."

"Did you talk to Sanjay?"

Sébastien shook his head. "Hiro doesn't know where he is now either."

I mumbled something under my breath about wanting to strangle Sanjay, but my anger was quickly forgotten when I saw what was in front of us. A cozy cafe with replicas of bowls of noodle soups in the window. The vibrant blue brushstroke illustrations on the bowls and the imitation meals inside them looked equally sumptuous.

"I've barely eaten anything today," I said. "How about stopping here?"

"You ate pumpkin pie and then food from the vendor next to Fushimi Inari."

"Hours ago. Before we climbed a mountain."

"Fair enough. *Après vous,* my dear."

The small soba restaurant seated six people at the counter, directly in front of the chef, with four small tables squeezed into the cozy space. A monochromatic mural of ocean waves and ships covered one wall.

It was late in the afternoon, so it wasn't surprising that there was only one other customer in the restaurant, a fair-haired man in an expensive suit and more expensive Italian shoes. A foreigner. He spoke Japanese with the chef, and the two men laughed over a shared joke. Or maybe they were laughing over the man's poor Japanese. I had no way to tell. I knew rationally that he was far more likely to be a businessman, not a murderous mastermind who knew exactly which restaurant I'd select and had gotten there well enough ahead of us to have eaten most of a serving-size bowl of noodle soup...The idea was ridiculous. Wasn't it?

A waitress motioned that we could sit at any table we liked. I chose one with a view of the European. The tiny table had a wicker basket underneath it, which I'd learned was for purses. My messenger bag fit snugly inside. Once we were seated, the waitress brought us menus that included no English but had pictures of dishes, along with the moist hand wipes that were common at Japanese restaurants. Shortly after the waitress took our orders—two bowls of the regional specialty Nishin Soba, a noodle soup with sweet and salty herring—the European left.

"Either you were trying to forget about both Sanjay and Lane by checking out that handsome gentleman, or you were considering him as our larcenous killer *gaijin*."

"Is it so far-fetched?"

"Yes, it is. You're so distraught you aren't trusting your instincts. You're one of the cleverest people I've met in my long life, Jaya Anand Jones—and I've met many brilliant people. I know it's doubly difficult, because Sanjay is in danger and your feelings for him have become confused. And I planted the reasonable idea that the other man you love, and who loves you, is here in Japan to keep you safe. But you need to snap out of this. Stop second-guessing yourself."

The waitress set two steaming bowls of soup in front of us. The rich scent of the salty-sweet broth calmed me and focused my mind.

"This whole mess," I said slowly, "has something to do with what's in the Dutchman of Dejima's diary."

"What do you intend to do about it?" Sébastien dipped the wooden ladle spoon into his steaming bowl.

"We find out who Casper Van Asch was. We don't have his diary, but if it's worth killing over, there's got to be more information about him out there. How else would the killer know there was something worthwhile in it?"

"Go ahead," Sébastien said.

"Go ahead...and what?"

"I can tell you're eager to look him up. Under normal circumstances I oppose the habits of the kids these days. But these aren't normal circumstances. I won't think you're rude for using your phone while we eat."

I grinned and grabbed my phone. Five minutes later, my untouched soup had grown cold and I wanted to drop my useless phone into the bowl. I glared at the mural on the restaurant wall. The outlines of waves and ships swirled together, as if the ships were battling a fierce sea. Casper Van Asch would have battled similar storms on his voyages from the Netherlands to Japan.

"No luck?" Sébastien said.

"I should have known better than to get my hopes up. The internet is rarely the answer when it comes to history."

I set my phone on the table and picked up my spoon. The phone buzzed.

"Jones *sensei?*" said the voice on the other end of the line.

I hung up two minutes later with a smile on my face.

"I hope you don't want dessert," I said, "because there's someone who can help us."

CHAPTER 31

Sébastien and I found Dr. Nakamura in his office at the university. I wasn't sure I'd call it an office, though. It was a cubby hole no larger than a closet, even smaller than Lane's old graduate school office.

The office was more sparse than mine—which made sense since it was so tiny—but he had a few photographs on display, including one of himself with an older Japanese woman who looked very much like him. I smiled at the fact that he had a photo of his mom in his office. A single bookshelf lined the longest wall. It was filled with neatly-ordered rows of books in many languages in addition to Japanese.

He motioned for Sébastien to take his own desk chair. The office was only large enough to fit two chairs, one behind the desk for the professor and one next to the door for a student. Although the space was tiny, the office furniture was much more pleasant than the cheap squeaking chairs my university provided, which is why I'd added a bean bag to my own office for the squeak-averse.

"I don't mind standing," I said, giving the guest chair to Sébastien. "We're here on an urgent matter. Not what you and I were working on before. I'd like to learn about what you found at the library about our ship, but that will have to come later."

I remembered belatedly that it was customary to begin conversations in Japan with pleasantries before getting down to business, even with people you already knew. I hoped he wouldn't think me too rude and revise his opinion of me.

Instead, he smiled with what looked like relief, and a lock of hair fell across his forehead. "I'm glad to have the opportunity to return the favor so readily. And I'm sorry to tell you I haven't found out any more about the *New Batavia*. It's going to be a more involved research project, I'm afraid."

"That's okay. Right now, I'm hoping you can help me look up a man from the Netherlands who lived in Japan in the late 1700s. His name was Casper Van Asch. There's nothing about him online in English. But I thought here in Japan, where he lived..."

"I don't remember coming across the name in my research on the Dutch in Japan. Do you have additional information about him?"

"He would have lived in Dejima."

Professor Nakamura gave me a patient smile. "Of course. Where all the Dutch were granted permission to live. Any more details?"

I bit my lip. "Not really."

"Let me see what I can find."

He looked up the name Casper Van Asch in a library database on his computer but couldn't find any references to such a man living in Japan. He shook his head as he dug through the indexes of books that lined a shelf in his office.

"Nothing," he said. "At least not anything I can find with only a name. Why do you think this man was here in Japan?"

"Because of the Indian Rope Trick magic show," I said.

"Such a tragedy. That poor man..."

"He may have been killed over the diary they're using in the show—it's real. It belonged to Casper Van Asch."

Dr. Nakamura drew a deep breath. "A historical document in plain sight?"

The professor cringed as I explained how Yoko and Akira used real historical documents in their act to add to the magical aura of their shows. The feeling was mutual. Akira had carried a two-hundred-year-old diary in his pocket.

"What's this research you two were up to already?" Sébastien asked.

"Dr. Nakamura was looking at ship logs for intra-Asia travel, for trading ships that came through Dejima. He found one that had been lost for centuries."

"No, *sensei*. It was *you* who found the ship. I knew you would. I contacted you because you're a world-renowned expert on the British East India Company and its trade routes. I simply asked a question."

I knew it was his cultural norm of being overly polite, not that he was trying to flatter me in particular, but I admit it was a nice feeling. As an assistant professor, the lowest rung on the ladder in a competitive field, I appreciated hearing praise from a fellow historian.

"What ship?" Sébastien asked. "You located a lost ship? Don't tell me it's a sunken tr—"

"We didn't locate a ship," I explained. "We found the existence of one that people previously thought was another."

"I'm only sorry," Professor Nakamura said, "that I couldn't be more help with your quest to find Casper Van Asch."

CHAPTER 32

"Tu n'as rien à dire," Sébastien asked as we made our way out of the university building. "You don't need to say anything. I know it's a disappointment."

"I think it's this way," I said.

"No, we came from here. And even if we didn't, there's an English sign for the exit."

I laughed. I was used to finding my way around places where I didn't speak the language. I didn't speak any Indian languages fluently, since I'd left Goa as a young child and was raised by my American father. Getting around without fluency wasn't a difficult skill to master. The secret was staying comfortable, rather than following a natural instinct to freeze and retreat when confused.

What had it been like for men like Casper Van Asch, so far out of their comfort zones in far-off countries with customs and languages they'd had no opportunities to study before getting there? Far too often they felt morally superior, but Van Asch had tried to learn Japanese, and had written about the wonders he saw in other countries like India.

"Sébastien, I know what we need to do next."

"Besides finding Sanjay?"

"Yes. Give me just a minute." We stopped in the lobby of the modern building. I found the contact information I was after and typed an email from my phone. I hoped what I was asking didn't sound too crazy. At least I wouldn't have to wait long to find out. The person I was emailing was in a time zone nine hours behind me. It was morning there, and hopefully he'd be checking email soon.

As I waited to make sure the message went through, an email

popped up from the very person I'd emailed. That was too soon. I groaned. It was an out-of-office auto reply. I didn't bother opening it. I tucked the phone back into my bag.

"I thought I had an idea that would help," I said. "But I was wrong."

"What in this life," Sébastien said, "is ever truly certain?"

"Could you please stop being so French for a moment?"

That got a chuckle out of Sébastien, before he sobered as he glanced at his watch. "*Merde.* I'm late meeting Hiro."

"Can't you cancel? This is rather important."

"Hiro might have ideas about where Sanjay is."

"Good thinking. I suppose I could eat again."

"I would invite you, but we're not going to an early dinner."

"Oh, good, a drink sounds even better."

"You misunderstand. We're meeting in a bath house."

"Oh."

"*Je suit désolé.* Let me see you back to the hotel, and I'll check in with you later tonight."

The sun was setting when Sébastien dropped me at the hotel.

I shuffled through the lobby, feeling completely dejected. I almost didn't bother looking at my phone when I heard it buzzing from my bag.

"Flora," a man's voice said when I picked up the phone. "Is that you?"

"Sorry, I think you have the wrong number."

"You do a damn good American accent, lass." The thick Scottish accent was jovial. "And it was a bloody-good joke in your email. How did you fake the return address?"

"Professor Lamont?"

"Aye," he said hesitantly. "This isn't Flora?"

"I'm Dr. Jaya Jones, a professor of history in San Francisco. I'm the person who emailed you a little while ago to ask what you could tell me about Casper Van Asch and the Indian Rope Trick. I know my request sounded strange, but it's not a joke."

"Just like it wasn't a joke when Jonas called me Mr. *Arse.* He knew it was over the top, so you've picked the exact opposite, the simplest name you lot could think of. Jones."

I stared at the phone. "Uh, I assure you, I'm not kidding. My name is Jaya Anand Jones. I teach history at a university in San Francisco."

Professor Lamont was the world's foremost expert on the Indian Rope Trick. Tamarind had found his book before I left San Francisco. If Casper Van Asch had witnessed it as his diary claimed, this man would know about it. If I could convince him this wasn't a joke.

The man on the other end of the line was silent for a few seconds, and I was worried he'd hang up on me, until he began to apologize. He'd paused to look me up online.

"An apology isn't necessary," I said, cutting him off.

"It's not often two people call within a day of each other, asking about the same long-dead chap who was cut from the final draft of my book."

Two people?

"Someone *else* called you?" I croaked.

"I thought it was a joke. He said his name was Arse, after all. I don't know if you've been to Britain, but that's the name of a certain part of the anatomy."

It was a strange name for someone to make up, so I didn't blame him for thinking it was a joke. "I know," I said. "I used to live there when I was working on my dissertation."

"I'm sorry for thinking your message was part of a joke. Since you've got real research questions about my humble book, could you email them to me? I'm sorry to put you off, but I've actually just arrived in Japan today—"

"You did?"

"The Indian Rope Trick is being performed in Kyoto. It's a big deal to those of us interested in its history. Are you all right, lass?"

Twenty minutes later, I was sitting across from the Scottish professor at a small club thick with cigarette smoke.

"You came all the way to Japan to see the Indian Rope Trick?" I asked him.

"Why the surprise? You said you did too."

"My friend is in the show. The Hindi Houdini."

"Hadn't heard of him until now, but I'm looking forward to his performance."

I realized that to the public, they assumed since the show was going on, the Indian Rope Trick would be performed. I hoped Sanjay was working on putting on one hell of a performance.

"I also have an academic interest in the history of the illusion," I said. "I study India's colonial history, and a Dutch merchant named Casper Van Asch supposedly witnessed the illusion when he was in India."

"Well, I'm happy to help. You're much more forthcoming than the bloke who called me, whatever his real name was."

"What can you tell me about the man who called you?"

"Not much. I couldn't place his accent. It's Casper Van Asch you're after? I remember him well."

"You've heard of him?" I nearly spilled my Asahi beer. "He wasn't in your book."

"I love my job. I love my students. My wee office could have more light, but I love my life."

"Um..." Had the professor been at the club for a while? He wasn't smoking, so I wondered why he'd insisted on meeting in this venue.

"I didn't include Van Asch in my book because I didn't want his descendants to ruin my life."

"His family?"

"His descendants are still alive. I came across Casper Van Asch in secondhand accounts from East India Company men who knew him and heard his stories. I thought the family might have additional details. They didn't."

"Like his own diary?"

Professor Lamont laughed. "Wouldn't that be dead brilliant? Too good to be true, I'm afraid."

"Right...But what were you saying about the family? Why would they stop you from writing about a magic trick one of their long-dead ancestors saw?"

"Bloody mistake to go to the family. There was a wee bit o' controversy surrounding our man Casper. That's why I remember him. He was accused of theft, but died at sea before he could be brought up on charges. The family didn't want the Van Asch name sullied. They threatened legal action, so I didn't include him in the book. Bloody nuisance."

"You had details about what he stole?"

"That's what '*Arse*' asked about."

"And you told him."

"Sorry, lass. Casper Van Asch was rumored to have stolen a hoard of gold pagodas in India from the English company."

By pagodas, he didn't mean temples. Pagodas were the gold coins used for currency by south Indian dynasties that were later issued by foreign traders as well.

"How many?"

"That I couldn't tell you. And nobody could ever prove it was him. Before they could, his ship was blown off course and sank."

"When was this?" I asked, my voice shaking.

"Sorry about the smoke," he said, misinterpreting my shaky voice. "There's a chap performing *Edo Tezuma*, traditional Japanese magic, on the stage shortly. It's a style of magic with paper fans disguising things like masks on the performer's face that change instantly. I didn't want to miss it." He pulled a laptop out of a satchel hanging on the back of his chair. "Back to your question. Late eighteenth century. Looks like...1790."

1790. Exactly when the Dutch East India Company was in disarray. The employees were certain it was going to go bankrupt—which it did—so they were embezzling like crazy and pulling off brazen thefts to try not to die destitute themselves.

"The ship, called *Batavia*, went down somewhere off the coast of Indonesia," Professor Lamont continued. "Maybe his deeds cursed the expedition. Whatever the reason, Van Asch and his 'theoretical' stolen gold ended up at the bottom of the Indian Ocean."

"A Dutch merchant who was lost at sea," I murmured.

Only he wasn't lost at the bottom of a fierce sea. *Casper Van Asch was on a different ship with a similar name.* My research had given me the answer.

The Dutchman of Dejima had made his way back to Japan—where he could take advantage of the Dutch exception in Japan's isolationist policy to hide where people from other nationalities couldn't get to him.

"That's all I know," the Scotsman said, "but it didn't seem to bother the man who called me. I seemed to be confirming what he already knew."

Casper Van Asch was a fugitive. An outlaw running from the English. They were the ones he'd stolen from, and the only reason he wasn't brought to justice was because he was lost at sea and presumed dead. But the truth was that he'd made his way to Japan. A place where all other European countries had been banned, enforced by a punishment of death. The one place the English couldn't get to him.

This was much bigger than stealing a magician's illusion. The Dutchman of Dejima was not only real, but he had a treasure. And Akira's killer knew it.

CHAPTER 33

Night had fallen by the time I saw the row of bamboo trees in front of my hotel. The encroaching darkness left me feeling like I was running out of time. I couldn't pinpoint what exactly I was afraid of, but that didn't stop me from feeling as if things were closing in around me.

The Dutchman of Dejima was real. He'd stolen gold pagodas in India from the English. The English Company pressed them in Madras, now Chennai. The Dutch were farther down the coast, in Tuticorin, now Thoothukudi.

But where had Casper Van Asch's pagodas come from? And who was after them now? I knew what the English were up to in 1790, and it didn't involve a lost treasure that made them want to hunt down a Dutchman. The two rival companies weren't even based in the same parts of India.

I was filled with an overwhelming desire to see Lane. I at least needed to talk to him. Both to hear his voice, and also because this was exactly the type of problem he'd help me solve. Not because he had the answers, but because of the way our minds worked together. I didn't care that it was the middle of the night in San Francisco. I'd call him as soon as I reached the hotel room.

On the way to my room, I did a double-take in the lobby. It was someone I knew. Here. In Japan.

She stood at the reception desk, looking around the vast lobby, which had been decorated with autumn foliage leaves to reflect the change in nature occurring outside. Dressed in all black except for purple combat boots and blue hair, she was as wide-eyed as a star-struck fan. A backpack of plaid fabric rested on her back, looking rather out of place at the upscale hotel. Not that any of the staff would comment on that fact, even in their expressions. The reception clerk said "Ms. Ortega" twice before he could get her attention to hand her a room key. She accepted the key, but didn't accept the offer of assistance with her luggage. When she turned toward the elevators, she saw me.

"Tamarind?"

"Jaya! OMG, look at this place. Can you believe I'm here?"

"Not really." I couldn't. "How *are* you here?"

"Very funny." She laughed. I didn't chime in. "No. Seriously? You don't know? He didn't tell you? Sanjay called me yesterday morning. He said you needed me—" She broke off, leaned in toward me so much that I was afraid even with her solid frame that she'd topple over in the hefty backpack, and lowered her voice to a whisper. "Because of the m-u-r-d-e—"

"You don't have to spell it out. We're not surrounded by toddlers."

"Oh. Good point. Anyway, he said he had a plane ticket from San Francisco to Japan for me, which, really, how could I refuse that offer? Especially since the library is closed over Thanksgiving break. So here I am. It's terrible about the murder. And *Akira*. I still can't believe he's dead. It's tragic, but can you imagine the cult films that are going to be made about this? And I'm part of it! Oh, that sounded bad, didn't it? Too soon? Yeah, too soon. Oh, and this note is for you. Sanjay left it at the front desk along with the one for me."

"Meet your bodyguard," I read aloud.

Men.

"You don't really have to be my bodyguard," I said to Tamarind.

"I figured."

"You did? But you came—"

"It's *Japan*, Jaya. Japan." She said it with a straight face, but she couldn't hold it. She broke into a grin. "No, seriously. I didn't just come because it was a free trip to Japan. Though I'd be lying if I said that didn't make me jump at the chance. I get it there's more at stake. Strange things are afoot at the Circle K."

"The what—?"

"I gather Sanjay is the one in danger, not you. I thought we *both* could protect him. I figured he thought it wasn't manly to ask for help. Especially from a woman."

"I don't think that's it, actually." I couldn't believe Sanjay was so afraid to talk to me that he'd brought Tamarind over as a buffer. I was going to kill him. Right after I found a way to save his life.

"Where's Sanjay, anyway?" Tamarind asked, looking around the lobby.

"Practicing his act," I said.

"I seriously don't understand how he's going on with his performance."

"It's a long story. Are you hungry?"

"Ravenous. I don't see how airlines can call those tiny squares of food 'meals,' but whatever. It leaves more space in my stomach for real food. Can we go to a ninja restaurant?"

"I've heard of cat cafés, but not ninja restaurants."

"Ninja restaurants are just for tourists, but I'd still love to go to one. Ninjas do some sort of performance with throwing stars."

I felt my stomach tighten as I thought back to the ninja's *shuriken* next to Akira's body.

"I don't think I'm up for ninjas tonight," I said

"Spoilsport."

We dropped off Tamarind's bag in my room, which we'd be sharing, and headed out to dinner. It took a while to get out of the hotel, though. She kept stopping to examine everything from the automated toilet to the flyers on a rack in the lobby.

"The Indian Rope Trick," Tamarind said, picking up a flyer for the magic show. "I love how the use of English is sprinkled into Japanese entertainment just enough to be cool in Japan, and be understandable to us. The artist didn't do Sanjay justice, though."

I took the flyer from her hand. When I'd first seen it, I was drawn into the magical world it created, with the European trader who wished to witness the secrets of the world, Akira's over-the-top persona with his *kitsune*, and the powerful Indian conjuror. But now each element had a sinister meaning. The Dutchman was a thief, Akira was a dangerous fraud, and Sanjay was in danger because he was supposedly in Akira's confidence.

"We couldn't tell if it was supposed to be Sanjay in the poster," I said, "or an Indian *fakir* that the Dutchman of Dejima saw in India."

"It's totally Sanjay."

"How can you tell? He's not dressed in his signature tux and bowler hat."

"Those come-hither eyes. That's the one thing the artist got right. You can even see his luscious eyelashes."

I crumpled the flyer in the ball of my hand.

"Hey," Tamarind said. "I was going to keep that as a souvenir."

I unclenched my fist and tossed the ruined flyer into a discreet trashcan hidden next to an artful display of elegant branches with pink and white buds. I hadn't made the cursed poster disappear as magically as Sanjay could, but it would have to do.

CHAPTER 34

At a *yakitoriya* we selected for its lack of tourists, I got Tamarind up to speed. The restaurant didn't provide ninja entertainment, but we sat at the bar and watched as the chef, who didn't speak a word of English, grilled our food behind the low counter.

"By the time I'd been in Japan for three hours," I began, "I'd chased a spying ninja across Kyoto, been taken to a secret magic workshop, and seen the ninja spray paint a security camera before sabotaging the workshop."

"I'm so sorry for the ninja restaurant pressure. I had no idea about your ninja baggage. Put down the chopsticks, Jaya. I'm going to need a lot more details."

I told Tamarind everything. Spying, sabotage, and murder. A ninja and a foreigner. Hiro and his vendetta against Akira. Yoko being the brains behind Akira's act. A Dutch trader's real diary behind the Indian Rope Trick. The stolen diary and recovered *kitsune* spirit ball. The attempt on Sanjay's life. A burglary at Yoko's apartment. Sébastien thinking it was possible Lane was in Japan watching over me.

"So," I concluded, "the central prop of the show was a real historical document written by a Dutchman who lived in the eighteenth century. Before arriving in Japan, he witnessed the Indian Rope Trick in India and stole gold pagodas from the British."

Tamarind clasped her hands together. "The story behind the Indian Rope Trick illusion is real? So. Awesome. I mean, it sucks what it led to. But still. Awesome."

"I looked up the museum where the diary was found, and it opens at ten tomorrow morning, so we have time for breakfast before we head there—"

Tamarind looked at her beer. "I've only had one of these. Yet I'm hallucinating."

I blinked at Tamarind. "What did I say?"

"You're planning on going into the lion's den? The place where the diary someone killed over came from?"

"Of course I am. Sanjay is in danger. What am I supposed to do?"

"Walk your petite self to the police station."

"Tamarind Ortega, have you been replaced by a robot? The real Tamarind would never suggest going to the police."

"Resisting The Man is all well and good from the comfort of home, but we're in a foreign country that neither of us is familiar with. And this isn't like when you were blackmailed, or when the police didn't take you seriously. These guys know there was a murder. They're on it."

"But they don't know—hey, where are you going?"

"We're *both* going to the police station."

An hour later, we were sitting at the hotel bar.

"You can say it," Tamarind said. "Go ahead."

I twirled my cup of sake around the smooth counter of the bar. "Say what?"

"'I told you so.' You want to say it, don't you? Go ahead and get it out of your system."

"I really don't want to say it. I'd have been thrilled if the police took our advice seriously that they should approach the case by looking at a foreigner who lived nearly two hundred and fifty years ago. All I can hope is that their forensics will come up with something. That's how most cases get solved, isn't it?"

"I think you've been watching too much television," Tamarind said. "They were so polite, though, weren't they? Did you know the police don't even hardly use guns here? Instead they just roll petty criminals up in a futon and haul them down to the police station to cool off."

I smiled. "I'm counting on the police to do their jobs regarding the killer. All I want to do is figure out why someone wanted the diary, so we can get Sanjay *out* of that path."

"O.M.G."

"What?" I whipped my head around. There were a few other hotel guests in the bar, none of them close by, and none of whom I recognized.

"You want it."

"Um..."

"You want the treasure. The Dutchman of Dejima's treasure. I can see it in your eyes."

"You can?" I tucked my hair behind my ear.

"There's a sparkle."

"It's called 'bar lighting.'"

"I don't think so, Jaya," Tamarind said. "I don't think so."

Was she right? With my heart pounding, three thoughts ran through my mind:

Find the treasure. Save my best friend. Get back the guy I wronged.

CHAPTER 35

My phone rang as Tamarind and I finished our drinks. It was Sébastien. Since Sanjay hadn't reappeared by the time we got back to the hotel, I'd left a message for Sébastien to see if he knew any more.

"He's with me," Sébastien said. "He understands now that he shouldn't be alone. I offered to travel back to your hotel with him, but he wanted to come back to my inn."

That confirmed it. Sanjay was avoiding me. I glowered at the closest person to me. Tamarind's eyes grew wide.

"He stepped into the toilet for a minute," Sébastien continued, "so I wanted to call." He paused. "I'm worried about him."

"Me too," I said. Because I was about to kill him.

"He's having trouble focusing," Sébastien said, ignoring me. "He nearly broke one of his fingers today. I know there's a lot going on, but he's one of the most professional young magicians I've met over the years. Do you know what's—*mais alors*. I must run."

He clicked off.

"Why," Tamarind said, pushing her barstool backwards, "does it look like steam is about to come out of your ears?"

"That's weird," I said.

"You're going to have to be a bit more specific. Everything here is weird. In an oh-my-God-this-is-awesome way, I mean. Except for the murder. And sabotage. And theft..."

"Sébastien told me Sanjay was having trouble focusing. That's what Hiro and Yoko told me as well."

"I'd have trouble focusing if someone had recently tried to kill me."

"Sanjay has performed under the most stressful circumstances I can imagine."

Tamarind shrugged. "Maybe he's better when the pressure's on for real."

An hour later, we were still talking when Sébastien walked into the bar.

"I thought you'd still be awake," he said.

"You switched hotels?" I asked.

"No, but I wanted to see Sanjay safely home."

"Where is he?"

Sébastien paused before answering. "He went straight to his room. Said he was tired."

"I'll be right back," I said.

"Jaya, I don't know if now is the best—" Sébastien called after me.

"Hi, I'm Tamarind," I heard Tamarind introducing herself as I walked away.

I banged on Sanjay's door until he opened it.

"You're going to get us kicked out of the hotel," he said, looking both ways into the hallway. His thick black hair stood on end.

"What's going on, Sanjay?"

"I've lost it."

"Lost what?"

"My magic."

"What does that mean?"

"I'm sorry, Jaya, but I can't do this." He began to close the door.

I put my foot in the doorway. "Don't ignore me, Sanjay."

"I told you I can't do this."

"Can't do what? Act your age? Because you're acting like you're fifteen. Please talk to me."

"I've never—I've never gotten together with anyone I—with anyone I—" He cleared his throat and let me into the room.

He picked up his bowler hat from the bed and flipped his hat onto his head. It landed askew and fell onto the floor. In the years I'd known Sanjay, I'd never seen that happen. We both stared at the hat as if it had sprouted wings.

"That," Sanjay said, pointing at the hat, "is what I'm talking about.

My magic is gone. Broken. Being held ransom. *Something.* I can't do even the simplest of magic routines. I'm a mess."

"Is it because—"

"I need to get some sleep," Sanjay said, not looking at me. "I have a long day tomorrow. If I have any chance at pulling off this show, I have to."

I felt wretched. I was sabotaging Sanjay's magic career. We'd been so worried about a malicious man dressed as a ninja sabotaging his act—but with one kiss I'd done far more damage.

I slunk back to the bar.

Sébastien was looking haggard and bid us good night as soon as I arrived.

Once he was no longer in earshot, Tamarind grabbed my arm and leaned in close to me. "Jaya, I think I'm in love with a ninety-year-old gay Frenchman."

CHAPTER 36

"Honestly, Jaya," Tamarind said in the morning. "Why are you so tired? I thought you were a good traveler."

I'd been up for most of the night tossing and turning, thinking about Sanjay, a dead Dutchman, and stolen gold.

How could I have screwed up so badly with Sanjay? In an attempt to calm down enough to sleep, I'd reminded myself it could have been worse. It's not like I'd stolen a hoard of gold from a foreign power and had to live in exile for the rest of my life. How could Casper Van Asch have gotten away with stealing from the English and then ended up in Japan? Would they have let him into Japan with English coins during a time when they banned all European texts and scientific inventions and, for a time, even banished children who were half European?

But thinking about lost treasures to distract myself from Sanjay wasn't calming me down; it had the opposite effect. I didn't know what to do about my mingled guilt and desire over Sanjay and Lane, but I could take action in pursuing the treasure stolen in India and find out what had become of it.

After a few fitful hours of sleep, I'd been woken at dawn by a call from Sébastien, assuring me he would stick with Sanjay at all times. With that assurance, I'd gone back to sleep until Tamarind opened the curtains.

"Ten minutes," she said. "You have ten minutes to get ready or else you need to absolve me of my bodyguard responsibilities. My stomach is telling me I should have eaten eight hours ago."

I flung aside the covers. Sleep was a lost cause anyway. "I only need five."

*   *   *

"Oh. My. God." Tamarind eyed the Zen rock garden beyond the floor-to-ceiling glass windows as a hostess led us to a table in the hotel's breakfast room. "This is the most perfect thing ever. There's even fish for breakfast. I'm in heaven, Jaya. Heaven." She cleared her throat. "I mean, except for all the murderous stuff. I'll shut up now."

After breakfast, during which Tamarind pointed out all the seasonal vegetables in the buffet, from matsutake mushrooms to kabocha squash, and I drank copious amounts of coffee, we caught a cab to the small cooking museum.

We were greeted by an elderly ticket-taker who spoke no English. Tamarind spoke enough Japanese to convey that we wished to speak to someone about the diary Akira had found there.

"I'm impressed," I said to her as we waited for someone to speak to us.

She shrugged. "When you watch enough anime, you pick things up."

The young woman who greeted us in English had pink hair. She complimented Tamarind on her blue hair. She also asked us our ages and occupations. I was coming to understand that this wasn't nosy but considered polite in Japan; the idea was that you were getting to know the person you were speaking with. We learned this was her first curator job.

"You are American fans of Akira?" she asked.

"Big fans," Tamarind said before I could stop her. That hadn't been part of the plan.

The curator gave us a shy smile. "I was as well."

She led us to a room that contained glass-covered shelves of antique cookbooks and cooking implements. And along one wall, a curious shelf of playful miniature carvings of wood and ivory. I smiled at the sight of a two-inch wooden carving of a cat sticking its nose into the bowl of an irate cook. What skill it must have taken for an artist to convey the humorous scene so expertly in a small format. Each of the six miniature statues had a hole at the top, as if they'd once been affixed to something. The signage was only in Japanese, so I couldn't read about the carvings.

"*Netsuke*," she said, following my gaze. "These carvings were decorations on clothing, attached to the end of the rope used to tie kimonos."

"They're beautiful." I smiled at the shared sense of humor across time and cultures. I understood why *netsuke* captured people's imaginations and would be a high-profile exhibit at the larger museum near my hotel.

"Where is everyone?" Tamarind asked.

"We are only a small museum," she said. "Except for one room, we don't have many visitors aside from scholars. It's unfortunate our *netsuke* don't have the same famous history as other collections. People want a story. Such as a collection of *netsuke* crafted by a great artist but separated over the centuries after the artist was killed for trying to leave the country to see the world. All the pieces have been restored except for one wooden fox. Our *netsuke* have no such story."

"They're still stunning," I said.

"Akira discovering a magical diary here is our best story."

"We heard about that," Tamarind said as she examined a diorama of a medieval Japanese castle and village with the kitchens highlighted. "That's why we wanted to come see this place for ourselves."

"Yes, many people came after it was reported he visited our humble museum."

"How exactly did Akira come to find the diary here?" I asked.

She looked at me strangely.

"Of course my friend and I know it was his *kitsune* who led him here," Tamarind said. "Jaya was asking if you were the one to help him."

She smiled and shook her head. "Akira visited once. I met him, but did not assist him."

"Once?" I said. I wondered if the egotistical man went around with an entourage of press. How else had the carefully staged photos appeared?

"His assistant, Yako-san, came many times."

"Why did she want the diary?" I asked. "How did she know what it contained?"

"I'm not allowed to speak of the contents of the diary."

"Even though Akira is now dead?"

"*Hai.*" She bowed. "I'm sorry. We signed agreements."

"Surely you can tell us what was publicly known about the diary before Akira and his assistant acquired it," I said.

She stiffened. I could tell the curator was trying to remain polite, but it must have been obvious we weren't simply superfans of Akira. "I'll take you to the room you wish to see."

Tamarind raised an eyebrow at me as we followed. "The room?" she whispered.

We were led to a small room packed to the gills with young women. Five of them were crying. Two more were smiling and taking photos of themselves next to the exhibit. An exhibit featuring Akira. One wall of the room contained blowups of the magazine features that had been published that fall with Akira visiting the museum.

The museum curator clicked her tongue. She spoke a few harsh words to one of the crying women and snatched up the bundle of flowers the woman had left in front of the photos. Shaking her head, the curator walked off with the flowers.

"I guess they don't want to turn this place into a shrine," Tamarind said.

I pulled my eyes away from one of Akira's fans who wore foxlike contact lenses and contemplated the enlarged magazine spread Akira had showed us before he died, which showed him and Yoko reading the diary. The Dutch and Japanese writing on the page was visible, so I took a photograph. I needed to have it translated.

Next to the framed magazine spread was a photograph of Akira holding both the closed diary and his spirit ball in his good hand. Yoko stood next to him, her red hair divided into nine fox tails, looking as if it were being tossed by the wind even though it wouldn't have been possible for wind to blow through the museum. Since she wasn't truly a *kitsune.*

"That woman," Tamarind murmured, "has some amazing hair." She tucked her own blue hair behind her ear.

"Fake," the museum employee said, making Tamarind jump. I hadn't noticed her return to the room either.

"You scared the bejesus out of me," Tamarind said, her hand on her heart.

"The photo staging was fake." The curator crossed her arms. "No woman's hair can achieve this naturally."

"You didn't like her," Tamarind said.

"Yako-san was not good for Akira." From the wistful look in the curator's eyes, it was evident she wished she could have been the one by Akira's side.

I hesitated before speaking, but I was here for information and this woman was clearly a fan. "Have you heard the rumor about Akira not truly being dead?"

I heard Tamarind gasp beside me. I'd forgotten to tell her that crazy idea. Because it *was* crazy. I hoped.

"You speak of the news this morning?" the curator asked.

"What news?"

"You don't speak Japanese, do you?"

I shook my head as Tamarind gripped my arm.

"Akira's body," the curator said, "has disappeared."

CHAPTER 37

I pulled Tamarind out of the museum.

"I think I'm hyperventilating," Tamarind said. "How does a person know if they're hyperventilating?"

"You'd know."

We walked down the winding stone path that led back to the road. A thick cropping of tall trees with red and orange leaves lined the path, making it difficult to see more than a few yards in any direction. I thought of the lurking ninja. Where was he?

"I'm so hungry after being in that place," Tamarind said. "Is that a symptom of hyperventilation?"

"I'm hungry too, but we have more to do before lunch." I buttoned my jacket and wound my scarf around my neck.

"Are we going to the morgue?"

I gaped at her. "Of course not."

"But you heard what she said—"

"We don't know where the morgue is. We don't even know if it's true Akira's body has disappeared. And if it has, it's more likely it's been moved by the authorities for an autopsy or something. Not that Akira faked his death."

"Don't forget he could have come back to life. What? I don't really think that. But I'm sure that's what some people are saying."

"This is going to make Friday's performance even crazier..."

"You need to relax, Jaya. Did you see the exhibit on traditional pastries? There was a flyer that they're having a cooking class here in a few days. They're going to recreate some medieval recipes. How cool is that?"

"It's probably taught in Japanese."

"Oh. You're right. Anyway, if we're not tracking down the morgue lead, what takes precedence over lunch?"

"You saw the blown up image of the press photograph of Akira with the Dutchman of Dejima's diary. Do you see what that means?"

"Of course." Tamarind paused. "No. Not really. What does it mean?"

"The page of the very real diary was visible. For anyone to read."

"Oh. Oh!"

"We don't have the diary," I said, "but we can get that page translated."

"Good thinking. How can we get it translated?"

"I know someone who can help us." I tried calling Professor Nakamura, hoping he'd be up for helping one more time. His phone went directly to voicemail. Perhaps he was teaching a class. "I'll have to try him back later."

"You know what we need to figure this out? Food."

We picked up food from a street vendor. With teriyaki skewers in hand, we walked along a canal on a winding stone road called the Philosopher's Path and debated a plan of action.

"I don't trust what Yoko told us was on the page in the diary."

"What about the ninja you saw? I thought it was a guy, ruling her out."

"I'm almost positive the ninja I saw right when I arrived was a man."

"Only *almost* positive?"

"I'd been in transit without sleep. I wasn't at my best." I wasn't at my sharpest at this moment either. I led us toward an empty bench under a tree half-filled with bright golden leaves.

"Fair point."

"And the person who tried to kill Sanjay wasn't seen, but he was heard by a hotel guest who couldn't identify the nationality but said that the shout was deep like a man's voice. So I'm pretty sure Yoko isn't the killer."

"Misdirection?"

"You're worse than Sanjay. This is real life, not a magic act. The more likely explanation is that it was an angry man who was angry and couldn't help exclaiming."

"Don't forget the foreigner sighting."

I groaned and sat down on the wooden bench. In spite of what Sébastien had suggested, I knew it couldn't be Lane.

"Jaya, I know this week has been stressful for you. But I need to tell you something. I know it would be nice to summon a translator with one's mind, but you aren't going to conjure anyone by sitting on that pretty bench."

I rolled my eyes and polished off the last of my sweet and savory chicken, then pulled my phone from my bag.

On my phone, I zoomed in on the words Casper Van Asch had written in his diary in the page that was photographed, writing them down as best as I could in my pocket-size notebook. I then typed the words into an online translator.

"Damn," I said. "This program thinks he's writing about midgets. That can't be right."

"A code?" Tamarind suggested. "This teriyaki chicken is to die for. Do you remember which of those little vendors we got it from? Maybe I should go back for more sustenance while you crack it."

"More likely a bad computer translation."

"Dutch, right? I think I can help." Tamarind licked her fingers. "Send me the photo."

Tamarind had a Dutch librarian acquaintance from grad school who owed her a favor. Or at least she thought she did. "Dammit," she said once she looked up her acquaintance. "She's Danish, not Dutch."

"Who are you texting, then?"

"She still owes me a favor. She goes to a bunch of European Union library conferences. I bet she knows someone."

"I'm sure Dr. Nakamura will call me back soon."

Outside of my pockets, my fingertips were losing feeling. I rubbed my hands together in the crisp air. No wonder the bench was empty. Nobody else wanted to sit still on this frosty day. The sky was free of clouds, but it was the coldest day since I'd arrived. After a group of Chinese tourists dressed appropriately in warm coats passed by us on the Philosopher's Path, we stood up to follow suit. I suggested we walk in the direction of the university, in hopes we could catch the professor.

Tamarind's phone pinged. "Bingo. Janet knows a librarian she thinks will help us."

"Also ask if the Dutch librarian has anything on Casper Van Asch at her library."

"Sexist much? It might be a *guy* librarian who Janet knows. Anyway, what's up with Sanjay? I know he has to practice and all, but why didn't he even come say hi last night?"

"Nerves. Oh, look at the beautiful miniature trees on this path. I bet it leads to a shrine." I was glad my face could have been red from the cold rather than embarrassment.

"But—"

"Oh, good," I said, saved by my phone. "Dr. Nakamura has time to see us."

"You're a woman of vision, Jones *sensei*," Dr. Nakamura said an hour later.

The three of us were squished into the professor's office, the photo of Akira's promotional still image blown up on his computer screen.

"It's a page of reminiscences," he translated. "A recipe for Japanese cured fish that reminded him of a recipe from home. Seeing a famous collection of *netsuke* figurines that moved him. What a sentimental chap! And here, this is why the great Akira selected this." He pointed at a section of Dutch text next to Japanese characters. I only recognized one word: *Indië*.

"When his ship took him to India," Professor Nakamura read, the excitement in his voice barely contained, "he remembered seeing an Indian street magician whose assistant climbed to the sky."

"Do you buy that?" Tamarind asked.

"Buy what?"

"That Nakamura fellow's groveling."

"That wasn't groveling. It's called being polite. I thought you knew about Japanese culture."

"You're biased because he thinks you're the greatest thing since sliced green tea bread."

"I'm not biased."

"Then you admit it's suspicious that he speaks both Dutch and Japanese and is obsessed with this Indian Rope Trick performance."

I stared at Tamarind. Could she be right? Was I letting his flattery obscure the truth? "He was the one who got in touch with me in the first place. Why would he do that?"

"Not that your ego needs someone else flattering you, but you really are an expert on finding treasures and stuff."

"He didn't ask for my help finding a treasure."

"Exactly." Tamarind crossed her arms and looked down at me.

"He asked for my help finding a missing ship. One we didn't even know was missing until I figured it out."

"Are you sure? He's a smart guy."

I wasn't feeling so smart myself. It was possible we'd gone to Akira's killer and showed him we were interested in the diary.

CHAPTER 38

I felt like I was the one hyperventilating now. I rushed out of the university building and took deep breaths of cold air. It wasn't as bright as it had been when we arrived. I looked up at the sky. Clouds were rolling in.

Dr. Nakamura had gotten in touch with me before I went to Japan. He didn't know I was coming here in person. He could have thought it safe to ask me some innocent questions without details, which would help him find Casper Van Asch's stolen gold without me knowing what he was after. And it had worked. I hadn't suspected a thing.

Tamarind patted me on the back. "I know exactly what you need."

"What?"

"A cat café."

Tamarind led us to a café not far from the university. I hadn't known what to expect, but I quickly saw that it wasn't simply a cat-themed coffee house, but spacious room where you could play with real cats. In a city where many people lived in apartments that didn't allow pets, I could see the appeal. I felt more relaxed within minutes of arriving.

While Tamarind frolicked with the cats, I sat on a squishy yellow cushion drinking a brightly colored juice of indeterminate origin.

Tamarind's phone pinged. "Sweet. Janet's Dutch librarian friend came through. Aris. Is that a guy or girl's name?"

"No idea."

"Whoever they are, they're about to reveal if the good professor is up to no good."

I admit I held my breath as Tamarind showed me the screen of her phone. I didn't exhale until I'd finished reading. I gave a giddy half-laugh, half-sigh of relief.

"The librarian's translation is nearly identical," I said. "Dr. Nakamura didn't lie to us."

Tamarind scrunched up her face. "I was so sure he was misleading us. But that doesn't mean he's not Akira's killer and now after Sanjay. It just means he's clever."

"Actually," I said, "now that I've had a few minutes to think more clearly, I see there's a much simpler reason why he's not the killer. He has an alibi: me."

"Shut. Up."

"At the exact moment I was chasing the ninja, Dr. Nakamura called me."

"He could have hit a button on his phone while running."

"He left me a voicemail message."

"Oh. That's pretty solid."

Tamarind's phone pinged again. She grabbed my arm. "He found Casper! Or she. Damn, I need to look up this name."

"Focus."

"Sheesh. Okay, let me read this note. Casper Van Asch died at sea. Aris found Casper V-A's name in their VOC files. What's VOC?"

"The Dutch East India Company is what the English called them. In Dutch, it's *Vereenigde Oost-Indische Compagnie.*"

"I'm so impressed right now."

I, however, was less impressed with myself. If a Dutch librarian had so easily found Casper Van Asch, why hadn't Dr. Nakamura and I been able to find him? I knew the answer. It was only someone in the Netherlands, looking up Dutch records in the country where Casper Van Asch was originally from, who had been able to find him. It's a common misconception in the modern world that anything can be found on the internet, when that's far from the truth. Still, something nagged at me. I felt as if the solution was just past my fingertips, circling like a wisp of smoke from the magic show.

Tamarind stood up and brushed cat hair from her black on black ensemble.

"You're done playing with cats?" I asked.

"There's a manga museum I need to visit while I'm in Kyoto. It's not far from here. I'm your bodyguard, so you need to come with me."

"I have a better idea. You go to the museum. I'd only hold you back. I won't be alone. I need to talk to Sanjay."

I found the brass fox knocker more quickly than before. Yoko buzzed me inside but wasn't happy I was interrupting their practice. Her arms were crossed over a red kimono. I didn't blame her. They only had two days left before the show, and Sanjay wasn't his usual amazing magician self.

"Ten minutes," I said. "I won't interrupt for longer than that. But I need to talk with Sanjay."

"He's behind the mirror with Renaud-san. Houdini-san! You have a visitor."

Sanjay's head floated in mid-air, turned sideways on his ear. He smiled when he saw me, and his full body appeared as he walked out from behind a mirror that I hadn't noticed was a mirror. How had they accomplished that?

"Can we talk in private for a minute?" I asked.

"We can use the cupboard," he suggested. "That's the name for that disguised entryway between doors."

We stepped into the dim cupboard hallway. In spite of the bad lighting, I could see the dark circles under Sanjay's eyes and a bandage wrapped around his pinky finger. He smiled and took my hands in his.

"This is my fault," I said. I would have pulled away from him if it hadn't been such a sad smile. "Your self-sabotage."

"I know." He sighed and let go of my hands.

"You do?"

"I wanted this for so long, but—"

"You have?" I thought back on how my brother had seen it, how even Sébastien had picked up on it, and how Juan said Sanjay only played the sitar badly when he was in front of me.

"Of course. But you've broken my magic mojo." He gave a sad laugh, then pulled me forward into his arms. He kissed me. I didn't kiss him back this time. As soon as he could tell I wasn't responding, he let go.

His face was a mix of frustration and sorrow.

"Sanjay, I—"

"This isn't the time for us, is it?"

I shook my head. "I love you, Sanjay. You're my best friend."

"The universe appears to be mocking me. I can't have it all. I can't have both you and magic."

"That's why you invited Tamarind here," I said. "So you'd have an excuse to ignore me while you figured it out."

"I should have known it wouldn't work." He ran a hand through his hair. "But give me a little credit. The main reason I maxed out a credit card to get her here is because none of us are safe. Don't you know what it would do to me if anything happened to you?"

"I don't want anything to happen to you either. I couldn't stand it if anything happened to you. Especially if it was my fault. If you're on stage and something goes wrong." I motioned to his injured finger. "So I'm making the decision for you. You're about to become a star. I'm not going to hold you back. Go back inside and create the world's greatest illusion."

CHAPTER 39

Only after the door had locked behind me did I realize I hadn't told Sanjay about the treasure. I thought about knocking, but Sanjay didn't need another distraction. I headed back to the hotel.

My shoes were off and my feet up on the bed when Tamarind walked in the door.

She frowned. "You're not supposed to be alone."

"I'm fine. How was the manga museum?

"A-manga-zing." She cringed. "That didn't work, did it?"

"Nope."

"You look like a complete bummer sitting around the house in a bathrobe."

"I'm in leggings and a t-shirt. In a hotel room." My hair might have been a tad ratty from being tucked into a hat to fight the autumn wind, but I didn't look that bad.

"Semantics. The point is the same. I'm seriously going to need to go into intervention mode if you don't snap out of this."

"Snap out of what?"

"I've never seen you this lovelorn. Call Lane already."

I pulled a pillow over my face. "That obvious?"

"There's something going on you're not telling me. But my spidey-sense is good enough to know it's about him. You keep looking at Lane's photo on your phone. I'm not arguing it's not a mighty fine photo..."

"Sanjay kissed me," I blurted out, still hidden safely under the pillow. I hadn't meant to do that.

"Shut. Up." Tamarind grabbed the pillow from my hands. I tried to hold on, but she was stronger.

"I kissed him back. It was right after someone tried to kill him. I wasn't thinking straight."

"You're single. How could you regret it? If he's a bad kisser, I'm a ninety-pound model."

"That's the problem. He wasn't. It was exhilarating. Exactly what I'd want my life to be like—if this were an alternate universe. Not one where I'm in love with Lane Peters."

"I knew it. I just knew it. L. O. V. E. Ain't it grand?"

"No. It's terrible."

"Well, yeah. Of course there are the terrible bits. Does he know?"

"Does who know what?"

"Do either of them know anything?"

"Before I talked to Sanjay just now, I talked to him last night when I left you with Sébastien at the bar. He said I made it impossible for him to focus, because he's never gotten together with someone he…"

"Loves? He said he loved you?"

"I don't know. Not exactly. He stopped himself."

Tamarind nodded sagely. "But he does. He can't deal. That's why he convinced me to come and tried to stay away from you until I got here. I'm a buffer. Have you not listened to him play sitar at the Tandoori Palace while you play tabla?"

I groaned. Even Tamarind had noticed what I'd only realized in the last day. I was the only clueless one. I'd always believed Sanjay was a terrible sitar player. How could I have known? Raj had always turned down his mic.

"Jaya, Jaya, Jaya." Tamarind shook her head. "Sanjay is only a bad sitar player when he plays in front of *you*. Do you really think he'd subject himself to the agony of not being perfect at something in public, if not for you?"

"I know. I didn't realize until this trip…"

My phone rang.

"Where are you?" Sébastien asked.

"At the hotel. Is everyone all right?"

"The hotel? Does that lovely friend of yours have you under lock and key? From my brief encounter with her, I believed her to be more adventurous than that."

"She is. We've discovered a lot today already. You didn't answer my question."

"Oh. Yes. Of course. Hiro and I haven't let Sanjay out of our sight. I wish you would have stayed to see me when you came by the workshop. I wanted to speak with you."

"What is it?" I asked, my body tensing.

Tamarind mouthed the word "speaker" and pantomimed pressing the speaker phone button on her phone.

"I don't like," Sébastien said, "that Sanjay and Yoko are supposed to be performing in two days with a killer still at large."

"I don't like it either, but Sanjay is stubborn."

Sébastien lowered his voice. "He's fine, but not his usual self. Which is another reason I'm uneasy."

I sucked in my breath. Even after we'd resolved things, he was still feeling the effects of our mistake. "He's okay, though?" I asked again.

"Yes, do we have a bad connection?" Sébastien shouted. "I already answered that he was fine."

I held the phone out from my ear. "No. The connection is fine. But I'd rather talk in person."

"That's why I'm calling. Yoko is frustrated the secret of the Indian Rope Trick died with Akira, and we've practiced all we can for now. I took the liberty of inviting us to Hiro's home. There we can talk safely among friends. We're stopping at the market, and Hiro is cooking dinner. You remember how to get there?"

"I do."

"*Bon.*"

I tossed the phone aside and opened my mouth to speak.

"A dinner party in Japan?" Tamarind said, clasping her hands together.

"You heard?"

"He was totally shouting at the end. A Japanese dinner party...I hope I have something appropriate to wear."

"I wouldn't really call it a dinner party—"

"Assuming you and Sanjay were going to screw up your relationship at some point," Tamarind said, "I'm glad you did it now.

Not only did it mean I got to come to Japan, but also to look after you. Because just look what happens to people when they go off on their own. Someone tries to kill them."

CHAPTER 40

We arrived at Hiro's home with a bottle of sake and a strange cake of indeterminate ingredients. Tamarind had wanted to bring two bottles of sake, but I insisted we keep clear heads.

As the taxi drove away, my cell phone pinged. I pulled it from the pocket of my messenger bag, and my breath caught. A text message from Lane.

I know you don't want to hear from me, but I saw the news about the magician Akira being killed. You still in Japan? Please let me know you're all right.

My body tingled, and it wasn't from the cold air surrounding me on the rickety porch. I wanted to call Lane back more than anything, but I was in a house filled with people including Sanjay. Instead, I texted him back that I was safe and wanted to talk later.

Midnight here, Lane wrote back. *Going to sleep now, but call and wake me anytime.*

Hiro's house was made in the Japanese style with thin sliding doors separating rooms rather than solid locking doors. There was no good place that would allow me any privacy. Talking to Lane would have to wait.

Inside, after Tamarind had gone through the laborious process of removing her purple combat boots, I introduced her to Hiro.

"*Shōji* screens," she said as she looked around the room in ecstasy. "You have a beautiful home. And that view..."

"Would you like to see the rest?" he asked.

While Hiro showed her around the house, I joined Sébastien.

My skin prickled as I looked around. "Where's Sanjay?" Was he really so uncomfortable around me now that he wasn't coming?

"At the police station," Sébastien said. "They needed to speak with him again about the hotel break-in."

"Everyone else is here. He went *alone*?"

Sébastien smiled. "Don't worry. Hiro and I went with him, and an officer promised someone would drive him here when they were done speaking with him."

I wasn't thrilled with the idea of him being on his own, but what could I do?

"Did you see the *oni* detail on his roof?" Tamarind asked as she stepped back into the main room. "It's like a gargoyle, but way more fierce. Hey, where's Sanjay?"

"He'll be here soon," Sébastien said.

"Should we fill them in without him?" Tamarind asked me.

"What Tamarind and I are about to tell you," I said, "doesn't leave this room."

"Pinky swear," Tamarind added.

"Even if it's someone you think you trust," I said.

"You're thinking of Yoko?" Sébastien asked.

"She did have Akira's spirit ball." I wished I'd gotten a clearer photograph.

Hiro choked. "She did?"

"It frightens you?" I asked. "I thought you didn't believe in Akira's miracles."

He shook his head. "You misunderstand my expression. I don't believe the spirit ball returned to its *kitsune*. I'm disappointed. Disappointed Yoko might be involved in Akira's death. It's unfortunate she became involved with Akira's fraud, but now that Renaud-san explained his illusions were of Yoko's creation, I'm disappointed that someone so talented threw her life away by committing murder."

"I don't think it's her," I said. "I can't see her impersonating a man or a foreigner. But maybe she had a partner. We don't know. So we can't trust anyone besides the four of us in this room, and Sanjay."

"Especially the *gaijin*," Tamarind said, pursing her lips as she looked from me to Hiro to Sébastien.

Hiro winced.

"What?" she said. "I'm a foreigner. I can use the word, right?"

"It's an offensive term to many," Hiro said. "In Japan, context is everything."

"Hmm..."

"Whoever the foreigner is," I said, "and whether or not he's a killer, the point is he wasn't after the secret of the Indian Rope Trick."

Hiro shook his head. "But Jaya-san—"

"That's what I wanted to tell you all in confidence. Not only was the Dutchman real, but Casper Van Asch stole a gold treasure in India that the English had a claim on. Japan was the perfect spot for a Dutchman like him to hide from the English."

"During our period of isolation," Hiro murmured.

"The Indian Rope Trick was mentioned on a page of his diary with several reminiscences. That's what confused everything."

"Because we thought the killer was after the secrets of the illusion," Tamarind added.

"Yoko selected the diary as a prop," I said, "because the Japanese translation described an Indian magician performing a feat that sounded like the Indian Rope Trick. But there were a lot of other reminiscences on the page. Something else there must have made the killer interested in the diary."

I was hoping Hiro could shed light on something from his perspective as a native of Japan, but he was as baffled as we were. He spoke Japanese and English, as well as basic French, but said he didn't read Dutch. So he couldn't check for any nuance the other translators might have missed.

"I don't know what anything here has to do with a treasure," Hiro said. "I wonder if this diary itself is a false lead. It has barely anything to do with the Indian Rope Trick at all."

"But it does," I said. "Both of the people who translated it for us confirmed it mentions it in Dutch as well as broken Japanese."

"He wrote of a boy climbing a thick piece of bamboo," Hiro said. "Not a rope."

Sébastien barked a laugh. "Splitting hairs, Hiro. There's no single 'Indian Rope Trick.' You know this. The illusion is a victim of its own fame."

"The Dutchman of Dejima described a feat of climbing bamboo," Hiro insisted. "It was a much more common magical performance in India. Climbing bamboo was a real illusion that required great skill but wasn't impossible."

"That theory of mass hypnosis is looking pretty good right about now, eh?" Tamarind said to me.

"Why does it matter?" I asked Hiro. "They selected it because it could conceivably describe the trick."

"I simply wonder if the diary is leading us down the wrong path. I don't wish to see Houdini-san hurt."

We bounced around more ideas, but I was distracted by Sanjay's absence.

"What's taking Sanjay so long to get here?" I said, looking out the large window that covered one wall of the living room. "The police couldn't think he was responsible in some way, could they?"

Sébastien and Hiro exchanged a look.

"What?" I said.

"Spill," Tamarind added, crossing her arms and glowering at them.

"It's a possibility," Sébastien said, "that occurred to us. Sanjay didn't tell me what they said to him."

"Because he was embarrassed he was going to be arrested?" I asked.

Sébastien gave a shrug. "If he's in police custody, he is safe, no?"

I gaped at him. "You think Sanjay was arrested? And all this time we've been discussing a man who's been dead for over two hundred years?"

"Unlikely," Hiro said hastily. "A most unlikely possibility."

Then why wasn't Sanjay here yet?

CHAPTER 41

When Sanjay finally arrived half an hour later, he entered with a flourish, as he always did, tossing his hat onto a coat hook—from several feet away. And it worked. He'd gotten his magic mojo back. Only then did he more humbly remove his shoes and jacket.

It was one of the most glaring differences between Sanjay and Lane. Sanjay wanted to stand out and be the focus of attention. He had a short attention span and always brought a topic back to himself. Lane wanted to understand the world and had learned how to blend in wherever he went—no small feat with his striking features. He'd once used that skill for a questionable purpose, but now used it to help make the world a better place. Lane had been forced to grow up too young, but Sanjay still had a lot of growing up to do.

"The police think Akira was killed by one of his crazed fans," Sanjay said, "and that the same person who killed Akira tried to attack me—and also stole his body."

"So his body was really stolen," I said.

"Immediately," he said.

"They told you that?"

Sanjay grinned. "No. But I recorded a snippet of their conversation with my phone and used an online translator."

Hiro clicked his tongue. "That wasn't wise, Houdini-san."

"Have they found something new?" Sébastien asked.

"Two things. First, nobody used a key card during the time the intruder was in my room. The police think I must have left my door ajar. They think I'm another American who didn't find it necessary to be careful while traveling here, because of Japan's reputation for being such a safe country. Can you believe that?"

"It's common," Hiro said. "I've seen tourists leave their bags at restaurant tables when they use the toilet, thinking nobody will take them."

"Does anyone?" I asked.

"No. I've never seen anyone's bag stolen."

"Anyway," Sanjay said, drawing out the word, "back to me. The person who was almost killed two nights ago."

"Go on," Sébastien said.

"The police think the intruder made his escape through my window. Before I moved rooms I was on the third floor. The window had a balcony and was jumping distance from the roof of a lower section of the hotel."

"He jumped onto a roof?" Tamarind said. "Like in the movies?"

"Apparently. They found footprints visible because of recent rains. It sounded like they were going to compare what they found at the scene of Akira's murder. But I don't know how quickly that'll happen. And I'm performing in front of a crowd of Akira's fans in two days."

"It's too dangerous, Houdini-san," Hiro said. "How can the police catch a crazed fan? It could be anyone. Are you sure you still wish to perform?"

"I've almost perfected my act."

"The Indian Rope Trick?" Tamarind asked.

He frowned. "Well, no."

"Why not?"

"It's impossible. But I'll be doing—"

"Jaya and I did our homework. We read an account of it."

"By all means," Sanjay said, bowing theatrically. "Maybe you can enlighten me."

"Jaya can do the honors."

"An Indian *fakir* would charm a rope rather than a cobra," I said. "Using his magic, he'd cause the rope to uncoil from a basket and stretch far into the sky. His assistant, a young boy, would climb the rope and disappear. The fakir shouts after the boy to come down, but the boy refuses, so the man climbs up to get him. Taking his sword. They fight above the crowd, and the boy's bloody limbs fall to the ground. The fakir reappears as he climbs down the rope and puts the bloody limbs into the basket, chants some magic, and the boy emerges from the basket unharmed. Ta da."

"That covers the technical specifications," Sanjay said.

"Then why are you frowning?"

"You missed the *magic* of the illusion," Sébastien said. "The spirit of the show. The reason it has captured imaginations for centuries. Perhaps thousands of years."

"I wasn't trying to perform," I said.

"Everything is a performance, Jaya." Sanjay flipped his bowler hat onto his head. I hadn't seen him grab it from the entryway. A small orange flower appeared in his hand in place of the hat, and he tucked it into the hat's side. "There are two reasons the illusion is so revered, neither of which you touched on."

I waited.

"See?" Sanjay said. "You're already waiting expectantly."

I scowled at him.

"The illusion," Sanjay continued, "was first documented at least as early as the ninth century. More than a *millennium* ago. It has a history that goes so far back modern technology *can't explain it.* It's from a time when the only way it would have been performed was with 'real' magic, or with an understanding of physics that was so far ahead of its time we still don't understand it." He paused and pressed his hands together. In his element, he was having fun now, his anger of a few minutes ago forgotten. "The illusion was always performed in an open field, where no trickery could be employed, and yet it was documented *countless* times. But whatever method Akira has figured out, he didn't tell me or Yoko."

"How was it done before?" I asked.

"Nobody knows," Sébastien said.

"Really," Sanjay said. "*Nobody.* That's the biggest allure of the trick."

"Invisible wires holding up the rope from nearby trees—"

Sanjay dismissed that with a wave of his hand. "The eyewitness accounts are clear. The illusion was always performed in wide-open spaces, where the fakir could more easily summon his otherworldly strength."

"A metal pole inside the rope, rather than wires," I suggested, "and the sun blinding the audience if it was performed at the right time."

Sanjay grinned. "Now you're thinking like a magician. I'm sure something like that was how it was done when it was actually seen. But since then audiences have become more savvy. It *shouldn't* have been possible to perform in its purest form—the one that involved being in the great wide open, with both men disappearing, with the bloody limbs falling down, and the boy appearing unharmed in the basket. Why are you shivering?"

"It's so gruesome. Magic. Like sawing a woman in half."

"We only give the people what they want. Anyway, all the great Western magicians used watered-down versions of it in their acts: Blackstone, Le Roy, Thurston. They performed their acts on stage, where it could more easily be faked, with the rope being held up by wires from above, and the stage lights blinding the crowd when the assistant disappeared into the rafters."

"We read it was mass hypnosis when it was performed outside," I said, "but that doesn't make sense."

Sanjay stopped and studied my face. "You didn't have as much time to do research as usual, did you?"

"No, why?"

"It's a hoax, Jaya. That's the second reason—and the most important one—why the Indian Rope Trick is so infamous."

"What do you mean *it's a hoax*? Isn't all magic a hoax? We're tricked into seeing what you want us to see."

"I mean it in the deceptive journalism sense. It was fake news. The rope trick wasn't a big deal until 1890, a little over a hundred years ago, when a hoax was perpetrated on the American people by the man who went on to become the Chief of the Secret Service, and it quickly spread across the world."

"Wasn't it in the *Chicago Tribune*?" Sébastien asked.

"That's the article I found," Tamarind said.

"But you only found the first one?" Sanjay said, a wicked smile on his face.

"We didn't have time to do more digging," I said.

Sanjay was laughing so hard I knew I'd missed something.

"What?"

"Leave it to you, Jaya, to fail to see the forest for the oldest tree. You went to an 'original source' rather than simply looking it up in an online encyclopedia."

"Do you know how much misinformation is online?"

"But also *context*. That article you read really did appear in the *Chicago Tribune* in 1890. But it was recanted after it became a worldwide sensation."

"The newspaper fell for a hoax?"

"They perpetrated it," Sanjay said. "The article was an undisputed eye-witness account of the illusion. Before that, there had been a few documented eye-witness accounts, but they were mostly from unreliable narrators, such as men from British East India Company who were overwhelmed by India and tended to exaggerate facts when they wrote home. But much more common was a different type of witness: the hundreds of people who had a 'friend' who'd witnessed the trick. All foreigners. Not a single Indian magician claimed responsibility. The *Tribune* article captured people's imaginations much more than its author imagined it would. It got out of control. The story was reprinted across Europe, and attention-seekers claimed to have witnessed the illusion firsthand. The story had been written by reporter John Wilkie, writing with the pseudonym 'Fred S. Ellmore.'" Sanjay paused. "Get it? *Fred Sell More*."

I groaned. I'd missed the reference. "Seriously?"

Sébastien chuckled.

"The publicity stunt story was retracted a few months later," Sanjay said, "once Wilkie and the paper realized the stunt had gotten out of hand. But, as you can imagine—"

"Nobody paid attention to the retraction," I said.

"Bingo."

It was an experience I knew well. After I'd played a part in finding a couple of historical items dubbed treasures, the press reported that I was actively requesting queries from people who had leads on other "treasures." It wasn't true, and the press retracted it, but in the age of the internet, the misquote was the one that spread. Earlier this summer, I'd been so overwhelmed by the correspondence that I'd missed an important email. I was still reeling from the series of events that email had set in motion.

"Hang on," I said. "You said the hoax was perpetrated by the director of the CIA?"

"Secret Service. But yes. John Wilkie was a young reporter at the time. That experience taught him a lot about what propaganda could do, and he became so great at it that he was tapped to lead the Secret Service a couple of decades later."

"The legacy of that Indian Rope Trick article endured," Sanjay continued. "In the early 1900s, several magicians offered rewards to anyone who could perform the illusion. The Magic Circle in London did as well. And a hundred years later, just a few years back, Penn & Teller performed a similar experiment. I just wish I knew what Akira had been planning. I wish—"

Tamarind screamed.

"A fox," Hiro said, stepping to her side at the window. "That's all it is. Foxes like it here. They like these woods."

Hiro turned on an outside light, and we heard the sound of a creature running into the woods.

But along with the sound, I caught a glimpse of a light.

"Is that a flashlight?" I whispered.

Hiro's breath caught. He moved quickly and turned out the lights inside the house. I looked through the trees, following the light. It was a man—covered from head to toe in black.

"It can't be," Hiro whispered. "The ninja is here."

The man in the woods must have noticed us turn out the house lights, because he turned off his own flashlight.

"Sanjay," Hiro barked, "let's follow him."

"Are you crazy?"

"Don't you want to know who it is?"

"Not like this."

"It's too late anyway," I said. "While you two have been arguing, you've given him plenty of time to get away."

Chapter 42

The party broke up shortly after the ninja sighting. Part of me wondered if he'd been a figment of our collective imaginations.

On the cab ride back to the hotel, Tamarind and I told Sanjay what he'd missed before his arrival about the treasure. He barely paid attention, though. His gaze was focused on the hills, perhaps looking for a lurking ninja.

Tamarind fell asleep quickly, making it easy to slip out of the room to call Lane in private. But…I wasn't sure where to go. I knew jiu-jitsu and could take care of myself, but that didn't make me act foolishly. There was no way I was leaving the hotel.

I ducked into the stairwell and called Lane with a video app on my phone. I wanted to see his face in addition to hearing his voice.

He answered on the second ring. An image of his tousled hair on a pillow filled the screen.

"I woke you," I said. It was just before six a.m. in San Francisco.

"I'm glad."

His smile made my insides melt. The smile evaporated quickly, though.

"You're all right?" he asked, sitting up and propping the phone on a bedside table.

"I'm fine." My heart beat frantically in my throat. I was not okay. I wasn't ready to be having this conversation.

"Sanjay and Sébastien?"

"They're fine." Short answers. That I could handle.

"Thank God. I can't read Japanese, and it's killing me that the English-language media isn't covering the story of Akira's murder much. From the little I've been able to follow, it looks like they haven't yet caught his killer."

"Unfortunately, that's true."

"Why didn't you—" He stopped, and took a moment to compose himself.

In the background on the screen, the uncontroversial floral art of a hotel room loomed behind him. Since he'd only recently returned to the Bay Area for his temporary job with the Asian Art Museum, he was staying at one of those extended-stay lodgings, a cross between a hotel and an apartment that catered to business travelers.

"Sorry," he said. "I have no right to expect you'd call me. It's not like we're together—"

"I want to change that."

"You..."

"I screwed up," I said. "Big time. I was wrong."

"I understood. I still do."

"I was wrong. I don't need to be on my own to figure out my life. I want to do it with you. I mean, if I didn't screw up too badly. If you'll have me back."

Even on the small phone screen, I could see the emotion in his eyes.

"Will you be home in time for Thanksgiving tomorrow?"

"I didn't know it was an important holiday to you."

"That's not what I meant. Your brother invited me over for Thanksgiving. I declined, of course, thinking you'd want me to stay away. But now—"

"Fish is hosting Thanksgiving dinner in Nadia's house?"

"You haven't talked to him?"

"No, I haven't."

"Maybe you'd better call your brother," Lane said.

"Nadia is going to kill him when she gets back."

"So, Thanksgiving?"

"I won't be back that soon. But soon." I hoped.

"When is your flight home?"

"I don't have one yet."

"What do you mean you don't have one yet? The show is off, so Sanjay won't be performing—"

"Why do you think the show has been canceled?"

"How can the show not be canceled? The headliner is dead." Lane picked up the phone from where it was resting. His face filled the screen. His hazel eyes held flecks of green and gold.

And anger.

"The murder has given the show that much more publicity," I said. "Sanjay couldn't get out of his contract." I didn't add that I didn't think he wanted to.

"And you," Lane said slowly, "won't leave without Sanjay."

"Why did you say it like that?"

"Say it like what?"

Was I reading too much into Lane's tone when he mentioned Sanjay? Surely he was just thinking of the fact he was worried that there'd been a murder.

"I'm not in any danger," I said.

He paused before speaking. "Why did you say that?"

"To reassure you."

"Why would you be in any danger? You don't have anything to do with Akira."

Damn. "Isn't that why you wanted me to call you?"

"Yes, but I'm not *rational* when it comes to you, Jones. I wanted to hear your voice, to know you were all right, even though I had no reason to think you weren't. A celebrity Sanjay was working with was killed by a crazed fan. Or so I thought. Is there something more going on?"

Lane, like me, knew better than to trust what the media reported.

There was so much I wanted to tell him. Instead the first thing out of my mouth was, "You're not rational when it comes to me?"

The edges of his lips turned up. "You haven't realized this yet?"

If he wasn't going to be rational, there was no way I should tell him about the attempt on Sanjay's life and everything else going on.

"I'm not in danger," I told him truthfully. Not only did I *not* have what the killer wanted, but I wasn't going to leave the hotel on my own.

"What aren't you telling me?"

"A bunch of things. I tried this regional Kyoto specialty called *Nishin* soba that's simultaneously sweet and salty, which you know is a combination I love. And there's this neighborhood of Kyoto where the houses look exactly like they do in the Sunset in San Francisco."

Lane's face grew darker on the screen as I spoke.

"Jones."

"And did you know that Japanese cell phones have a built-in feature that prevents you from turning off the sound it makes taking pictures, so you can't spy on people?"

"I'm hanging up now, Jaya. Call me back when you're ready to have a real conversation."

I sat in the nook of the staircase looking at the disconnected phone. He'd really hung up on me. Not that I blamed him.

Now all I had to do was figure out why the person interested in Casper Van Asch's treasure tried to kill Sanjay. At least I now knew what he was after. How hard could it be?

Chapter 43

"JJ," my brother said. "Do you have any idea what time it is?"

"Nadia will kill you if you host Thanksgiving dinner at her house. You're house-sitting, not making the place your own."

"She's back."

"What?"

"There was some tropical storm that cut her cruise short, so she and Jack arrived yesterday. You've reminded me I need to follow up with her about the paperwork from the cruise. They might be entitled to more than the tiny refund the company is offering. Most people jump to accept the first amount of money offered to them, but often if they accept it, they're agreeing to that amount."

"She's letting you stay with her?" That was nice of her, and unusual. Nadia loved having her own space. She was nosy with other people, but when it came to her own space, she wanted it left to herself.

"She gave me the key."

"You already had the key."

"To your place."

"You're staying in my attic apartment?"

"Don't worry, I know not to move your research papers. Though it's killing me not to be able to."

"Thanks," I grumbled. "Wait, my kitchenette isn't big enough to cook Thanksgiving dinner. Don't try to fit a turkey into that half-size oven. And I don't have enough chairs for a big dinner party."

"Relax, JJ. Tell me about Japan. How's Sanjay? Is that fellow he's performing with still doing whatever odd things had him so worried before you left?"

"Japan is, um, gorgeous."

"The fall leaves changing colors is spectacular, as I understand it. Have you gone to a tea ceremony yet?"

"Not yet. We've been busy."

"Right, getting ready for the show. You better not have signed away your rights."

"I haven't signed anything."

"Good."

"So, the deal with Thanksgiving, Fish?"

"Oh, right. I'm not at my best. I think you woke me from REM sleep. I've been sleeping in past six o'clock since moving up here. This San Francisco firm doesn't expect people to arrive at seven a.m. Can you believe it?"

"Bizarre."

"Nadia and Jack are hosting Thanksgiving dinner tomorrow. They decided since they can't be on their cruise, they'll bring the fun here. They insisted I come. Nadia even wanted to invite Lane, even after I told her you two weren't seeing each other. She didn't have his contact information, so I passed along the message. Oh, he told you. That's why you're calling."

"You sound disappointed."

"You didn't call me to chat about your trip."

"Fish, when have you ever called me while you're on vacation?"

"Of course I haven't. Why would I do that? Wait, you called Lane? I thought you broke up with him?"

"It was a rash decision."

"You're just now realizing that?"

"Very funny."

"I'm serious. Seeing the two of you together, it's like you're meant to be. Like me and Ava."

I was glad we weren't on a video chat, because otherwise he would have seen my face turn purple. Lane had convinced me not to tell my brother about his girlfriend's past as a thief. I didn't want to hurt Mahilan, and I believed Ava truly cared for him. Enough that she'd made up an excuse about taking care of her sick son to get out of his life. She hadn't officially ended things with him, though. I thought she was most likely trying to decide if she was going to sever ties or tell

Mahilan the whole truth and hope he could deal with it.

"I'm sorry it didn't work out like you'd hoped," I said.

"There's hope yet, JJ. There's hope yet. You're going to think this is silly, so I can't believe I'm about to tell you this."

"Fish, you can tell me anything."

"I think it's a sign."

"What's a sign?"

"Ava likes the name Jupiter."

"You can't be serious."

"I thought you liked that old family name. And who else has ever liked it besides the two of us? I'm telling you, it's a sign."

"You talked about having *kids* with her?"

"Well I haven't exactly broached the subject that directly."

"I'm fine with you naming a kid after Jupiter, or whomever you want to. But seriously, Fish. You're thinking of having a kid with Ava?"

I hated keeping secrets from my brother. But this was someone else's secret.

No, who was I kidding? I wasn't keeping Ava's past a secret for her. I was trying to give my brother the best chance of avoiding his heart being ripped in half. I hoped Ava would stay away from us forever. If she didn't, Mahilan would need to know the truth. And he'd learn I'd kept her secret. If it came to that, I hoped he'd forgive me for keeping it.

I was in an impossible situation. Mahilan needed to know the truth about the woman he loved, but it was a messy truth that involved illegal activities and deceit—and that implicated more people in our lives than Ava herself. Was it worse to tell my brother and potentially ruin several lives, or to keep a horrible secret?

"Who knows what the future holds, JJ."

"Happy Thanksgiving, Fish. Don't do anything crazy until I get home."

CHAPTER 44

When I woke up the next morning, Tamarind wasn't in her bed. The bathroom door was open, so I thought she must have gone down to breakfast without waking me. Except there was a problem with that theory. The hotel room door was bolted, and our chair was nestled firmly underneath the handle, where I'd left it after coming back to the room the previous night.

I tried not to panic. I slid open the closet doors. No Tamarind. I crouched down and looked under each bed. No Tamarind. The bathroom door was open, and she wasn't there either. I splashed water on my face, wondering if I was going crazy.

That's when I heard it.

When I listened carefully, I could hear her voice faintly. I followed the sound to the window. We didn't have a balcony, but she'd climbed outside the window to the fire escape.

I knocked on the glass and she jumped. She was holding her phone to her ear, and with her other hand she held up two fingers and mouthed "two minutes" to me.

Five minutes later, she stepped back inside. She peeled out of her fluffy black coat.

"Miles is the greatest guy. Ever. I'm forever in your debt for introducing us. Though, since I'm acting as your bodyguard here, do you suppose that balances the karmic scale?"

"You gave me a heart attack. I didn't think our window opened far enough to get out."

"I didn't either. But after Sanjay said his attacker had gotten out through the window, I looked at the hinge. If you remove one bolt, it opens wider. I should put that back in." She cracked the window and leaned out.

"I guess the chair under the door gave me a false sense of security." I was glad I had a friend with me.

Tamarind closed the window and shook her head. "It's not something anyone can access from the outside when the window is closed. So it's not like it's an oversight from hotel security. The guy in Sanjay's room would have had to push open the window from the inside, then remove the bolt."

"After realizing he screwed up and yelled loudly enough to be heard, you think he took the time to figure out he could remove a bolt from a window to get away?"

"No, he must've planned it."

"Meaning he could have gotten *in* that way too. Sanjay insisted he wasn't careless enough to leave his door ajar, and I believe him."

"But," Tamarind said, "that means the guy would have waited until he knew Sanjay had his window open, long before he snuck in."

My mouth felt dry. I'd been sitting exposed in the hotel stairway the previous night. "That means the intruder was probably a guest."

"I don't remember seeing anyone twisting an evil mustache," Tamarind said, "but how would we recognize the guest who's the killer?"

"It's at least worth telling the police."

"And you're sure Sanjay would have opened his window?" Tamarind asked.

"Sanjay runs hot."

"I bet he does." Tamarind licked her lips.

I crawled back under the covers.

Tamarind pulled the comforter aside. "I think you might need to accept this is one mystery you're not going to solve. We just need to keep you and Sanjay safe until he performs, then we can all go home."

"Why do you say that?"

"I was just talking it through with Miles. He's so much smarter than people give him credit for, you know. But neither of us could figure out any way for all of this to make sense."

"We're missing something."

"Sorry I worried you, J. Especially since you were sleeping so peacefully when I slipped out of the room. You had a smile on your face."

"I talked to Lane before I went to bed. I was being foolish before. I told him I wanted to be together."

"Rock on. Can we double date when we get home? No. Scratch that. Lane has cheekbones to die for. And that hair. Not as amazing as Sanjay's...but pretty damn close. Probably safest if I don't sit across the table from him when I'm with Miles."

"Noted."

"Miles is bummed I'm not going to be back by Thanksgiving."

"You still have time to make it if you leave later today."

"We came up with an even better plan. We're going to have a second Thanksgiving after I get home. You two should come. Oh, just make sure—"

"—that we don't seat Lane across from you."

CHAPTER 45

"So," Tamarind said, "what's the plan for today?"

"We need to tell Sanjay that we might have been wrong about just how premeditated the actions of this man can be, find out if he recognized anyone in the hotel, and tell him about the window."

"After breakfast, right?"

I dialed Sanjay's number and his phone went right to voicemail. Damn. I didn't think he was still ignoring me, but I couldn't be certain. I called Sébastien, who answered right away.

"What I wouldn't give for a cup of hot cocoa in front of a roaring fire," he said.

"Where are you?"

"Standing guard at the end of a road in Arashiyama."

"You're what?"

"It's complicated."

"Right. Are you with Sanjay?"

"That's a difficult question to answer."

"Do you care to explain that cryptic answer? No, never mind. I need to talk with you both in person. How do I reach you?"

I scribbled down directions.

"No breakfast?" Tamarind asked.

"We'll pick up coffee and pastries on our way. We should stop at the police station to tell them about the window as well."

"No fish breakfast for Tamarind," she mumbled to herself.

"Look, Jaya." Tamarind pointed out the taxi window. "On the path itself the word 'BAMBOO' is painted stretched out, just like a stalk of bamboo. They didn't have to add that detail, but it's perfect, isn't it? People here really take pride in their work."

I wasn't sure how we'd find the spot Sébastien had mentioned. The last thing he'd said to me was, "you'll have to go the last bit on foot." I needn't have worried. As soon as we approached the area, I knew where we had to go. At least a dozen serious-faced security guards milling about.

"That's a lot of security guards," Tamarind said.

"The magic show is tomorrow night. Today is their last big day to rehearse, so they're getting set up on the spot."

"What if it rains harder?" Tamarind said as she stepped out of the taxi into the mist. "The end of November doesn't seem like the best time of year for an outdoor show. Couldn't they do it inside?"

"The whole point is that Akira was an outdoor magician. He could perform anywhere."

"But Akira is dead. In spite of what some of his fans say."

Colorful leaves filled the autumn trees around us, glistening in the moisture from the light rain. Tamarind and I walked past a security guard to pass through a chain link fence surrounding a field—or at least we tried to. He stopped us at the gate. Until a familiar French-accented voice I recognized called out from beyond the fence that it was all right to let us pass. The guard bowed respectfully at Sébastien, but spoke into an earpiece before letting us through.

We found Sébastien sitting comfortably on a lawn chair at the edge of a bank of trees. He sat underneath a vinyl awning that swayed gently in the wind, with a blanket around his legs and a steaming paper cup in his gloved hands.

"They call this security these days?" I said.

"I'm an important cog in this security wheel." Sébastien winked at me. "I report if I see any onlookers getting through where they're not supposed to be. Miss Ortega, it's lovely to see you again."

"Likewise," Tamarind said. "Looks like they're taking good care of you."

"Where's Sanjay?" I asked.

"Beyond the crest of the hill. I'm not authorized to go farther than this, but nothing untoward should happen to him with so many people around."

"Still, I need to see him."

"We've got new information," Tamarind added.

Sébastien called out to one of the uniformed guards, a younger man who spoke perfect English. The guard ran to get Sanjay as if his life depended on it. Which it very well might have.

The guard returned less quickly, a few minutes later, his head lowered. He apologized that the rehearsal had just begun and should not be stopped.

"Tell Houdini-san there's a risk of sabotage," I said.

"Sabotage?" the man repeated, and was off again.

This time, Sanjay accompanied the guard. I spotted him by his bowler hat as it crested the hill.

"Sabotage?" he said as he reached me, his voice low.

"I don't know for sure it's sabotage," I said. "I needed to get your attention. Sorry. But they wouldn't let us through, and this is serious. The person who tried to kill you was probably a hotel guest, and he's been planning things a lot more cleverly than we thought."

I told Sanjay what we'd learned about the hotel window.

"That's awesome news," Sanjay said.

"Um..." Was Sanjay feeling all right? Maybe he'd finally snapped.

"If this was as premeditated as you think," Sanjay said, "it sounds like he *wasn't* really trying to kill me after all." He grinned. "He was waiting for me to leave, so he could look for something I had in my room, not trying to silence me about whatever he thinks I saw in the diary."

"Like a treasure map," Tamarind cried. "Something he thought would be inside the diary but wasn't."

"That's not a bad idea," I said. "He slashed your pillow and yelled because he was angry he didn't find it."

"I'd feel even better if I understood his end game," Sanjay said. "The secret of the Indian Rope Trick? The riches from sunken English gold? The world's greatest Dutch-Japanese mashup recipe? I just had a thought. If he didn't try to kill me, that would also explain why he trashed Yoko's apartment when she clearly wasn't there."

Yoko perked up at the mention of her name and came over.

"We were just talking about—" Tamarind began.

"Tamarind," Sanjay said sharply.

Her eyes grew wide and she had a coughing fit. I was glad Sanjay had cut her off. I didn't seriously suspect Yoko, but it was still foolish to talk about Casper Van Asch's English-stolen treasure in front of her.

"We were talking about how Tamarind is having allergies," I said. "Maybe you could suggest a good medicine she could buy here?"

"Medicines are more regulated here," Yoko said, "but I'd be happy to help if I can."

"I wanted to ask you something else," I said as she wrote Japanese characters on a sheet of paper for Tamarind. "I know you said Akira kept the only copies of the diary, and you didn't have any reason to translate the whole thing, but is there anything you can remember about what was in the rest of it?"

"I wish I'd never thought of the idea of using the diary. It's brought us all nothing but grief. Why does it matter now?"

"The performance is tomorrow," I said, "and we still don't understand why someone has been coming after us even though they must have the diary."

"I remember one thing clearly," Yoko said, "because it related to the Indian Rope Trick. Casper Van Asch really did see it performed in India."

Sanjay gasped.

"Yes," she said with a mischievous smile. "He's one of the few people who claims to have witnessed the trick, not someone who said their brother or friend saw it. What Van Asch-san saw was a version of the trick requiring great skill, which has been performed for as long as people have walked the earth. He saw a boy climbing a bamboo rod."

"A great feat," Sanjay said, "but not truly the Indian Rope Trick."

"Of course the page we photographed didn't contain such detail," Yoko said. "Only on the next page did it describe in detail what he witnessed."

Now it was my turn to gasp. "The bamboo wasn't mentioned on the page you photographed? Are you certain?"

"Yes," Yoko said. "We were careful. The page we released to the press alluded to rope, not bamboo. It was perfect."

I stared at Sanjay. "Hiro must have seen the rest of the diary."

"You believe Matsumoto-san could have killed Akira for the diary?" Yoko asked. "No. He's a man of great integrity. He couldn't have done such a thing."

"You know Hiro personally?"

"I hoped, once, we might have been able to perform together. He's one of the greatest magicians of our time. I understood his reasons for disapproving of Akira, and I was sorry it prevented me from working with him." She shook her head. "Regardless of his feelings, he wouldn't harm anyone. If he mentioned bamboo, perhaps he mistranslated the Dutch visible in the press photograph."

I knew that wasn't the case. Even someone who wasn't a formal translator would know the difference between woven rope and a bamboo stick. And both people who'd translated the page, Dr. Nakamura and the Dutch librarian, had come up with the same translation.

"Hiro lied," I said. "He covered for himself, trying to turn our attention away from the diary. But he knew about the bamboo."

I turned to Sanjay. His face was dark.

"I should have trusted you from the beginning," I said. "You thought the saboteur on the video was Hiro. You talked yourself out of it because you thought Akira was manipulating you."

A knot clenched in my stomach that I couldn't imagine ever going away. I thought of the evening I'd spent talking with Hiro and watching his beautiful butterfly magic performance.

Sanjay shook his head. "It can't be. You were right. I shouldn't have let my fear of sabotage get the better of me. I only thought it was Hiro on the fraction of a second of video because Akira has been poisoning my mind against him. And remember Hiro has an alibi. It couldn't have been him. He was with Sébastien."

We all turned to Sébastien. He was now standing, and his face was pale. He looked as ill as he had after nearly freezing to death in the icy waters of Mont Saint Michel.

"He doesn't," Sébastien said.

"What?" Sanjay and I said as one.

"Hiro," Sébastien said slowly, "doesn't have an alibi."

"But—" Sanjay sputtered.

"I'm sorry," Sébastien whispered. "I'm so very sorry."

CHAPTER 46

"Sébastien?" I said, incredulous. "You protected a killer? But why?"

"I didn't believe he was guilty," Sébastien said. "I was so certain." He shook his head. I'd never before seen him look like a helpless old man, but now he looked confused and far older than his ninety years.

"I saw no harm in saving Hiro's friendship with Sanjay," Sébastien continued. "It seemed the greater good. What harm was there in saying he was with me a couple of hours earlier than he was?"

"Sabotage, theft, and murder," Sanjay growled. "By not coming forward, you helped him do it. I thought of you as a mentor. A friend. You betrayed me."

"How could I have been wrong?" Sébastien whispered to himself.

Sanjay grabbed my hand and pulled me away. "Tamarind," he barked, "you stay with the old man. Make sure he doesn't call Hiro. And don't let anyone leave. I'm counting on you."

With Sanjay gripping my hand, we ran.

We didn't stop until we reached the train station five minutes later. Sanjay collapsed onto a bench.

"You could at least pretend to be winded," Sanjay said to me, attempting a smile.

"Where are we going?"

"I thought we could catch a taxi here."

"To Hiro's house?"

He nodded.

"Um, Sanjay?"

"Hmm?" He glanced around, presumably looking for the taxi stand.

"He's killed before. Unless you have a gun hidden inside your hat, this is a very bad idea."

My phone buzzed with a text message from Tamarind. *Yoko disappeared. I'm a bad bodyguard. Sorry.*

I showed Sanjay the text. He waved it off. "It's not Yoko I'm worried about."

"Then it's not your brain thinking for you right now. Even though Hiro no longer has an alibi, that doesn't mean he killed Akira. We still don't know want's going on. We can't trust Yoko."

Sanjay balled his hands into fists. "She's not the ninja who was spying on us. She wasn't the man on the video or in my room. And she wouldn't have destroyed her own apartment."

"Wouldn't she? Losing some possessions is a lot better than ending up in jail. They could be working together."

"If she wanted Akira dead," Sanjay said, "why would she convince a rival of his to do it for her? She worked closely with Akira. She had many more opportunities to kill him and steal the diary. And to have it look accidental."

"That point," I said, "I'll grant. It doesn't make sense."

"God, I don't know what to believe. About anything." He paused. "I don't suppose you have a time machine hiding in that massive bag of yours, so we can go back in time to last week, do you?"

"No, but I'll make sure we get through this one."

Sanjay accepted my hand, and we were off.

Fifteen minutes later, Hiro opened his front door to us.

"The police are on their way," Sanjay said. "They know we're here."

Hiro's Adam's apple bobbed up and down as he swallowed. "I was dreading this day. Though in many ways, it's a relief."

"It's true?" I said, my gaze falling from his face to his trembling hand. "I was hoping we were wrong..."

"How long do we have before the police arrive?" Hiro asked.

We'd called them from the taxi, shortly before arriving. That way we could ensure our safety. The police would know where we were and who they should blame if anything happened to us, but it would also give us time to talk with Hiro by ourselves. Sanjay was intent on performing the following day, so we at least had to figure out if Hiro was working on his own or with an accomplice.

"Not long," I said.

"No sudden movements," Sanjay said as Hiro's shoulders fell.

Hiro stopped and gave Sanjay a strange look. "You fear me?" His eyes grew wide. "You suspect me of killing Akira?"

"You're saying you didn't?" I said. "What were you acknowledging just now, if not murder?"

"Perhaps you should come inside."

CHAPTER 47

"It wasn't supposed to happen like this," Hiro said.

"Most things aren't," I said.

We stood in the main room of Hiro's house, with the view of the forest.

"Thank you for speaking with me," he said. "I appreciate—"

"We don't have time for pleasantries," Sanjay said. "Remember, the police are on their way."

Hiro nodded. Yet still he found it difficult to flout Japanese convention and launch into a difficult story. "I didn't ask Sébastien to lie for me and say I was with him when Akira's studio was searched. He volunteered."

"Why?" Sanjay asked.

"Akira called me. He was irate. He claimed I had sabotaged his equipment. I would never do that. Never. I didn't know why he would say that." Hiro's words became more agitated as he spoke.

"But you did break into his studio," I said, "didn't you?"

Hiro turned toward the window. My skin prickled. I suddenly felt incredibly exposed in front of the tall window. I walked across the room and drew the blinds. I didn't trust anything anymore.

Sanjay must have felt it too. "Something's different in here," he said, glancing around the sparse home.

"It's the time of day," Hiro said. "With the large windows, the light makes it feel different at different times of day."

"You broke into Akira's workshop and disabled the security camera," I said, trying to get us back on track. "You were on camera. Even with part of your face covered, Sanjay thought it looked like you."

Hiro nodded. "I broke in. But I did no harm. Sabotage could injure someone. Not only Akira, but—someone else."

Sanjay swore and kicked over the low table in the room. "I trusted you. In spite of my better judgment, I trusted you because you were my friend."

"Please," Hiro said. "I meant you no harm. Sébastien saw my despair at hearing what had happened at Akira's workshop. He knew I could not be guilty of sabotage. That's why he insisted he say I was with him."

"The water escape illusion was sabotaged," Sanjay said. "I saw it with my own eyes."

"I was shocked when Akira called me and accused me not of theft, but of sabotage. I was certain when I left there had been no damage."

"You admit you were the intruder," I said. "But not a saboteur? Why did you break in? If you weren't going to sabotage his equipment, what were you after?"

Confusion flashed across Hiro's face. "I thought you knew."

"Knew what?" I said.

"I have the diary."

"Casper Van Asch's diary?" I whispered.

"You admit to killing Akira now?" Sanjay said, taking a protective step in front of me. "Only the killer could have taken the diary that Akira kept with him."

"I found the diary at the studio, *the day before someone else killed him*."

"Stop lying," Sanjay said. "We know the diary wasn't taken until the day Akira was killed."

"Wait," I said. "Do we?"

They both looked at me.

There was something throwing Akira that day. At the time I took it for fear of sabotage, but now I saw it for what it was. "Akira never showed us the diary that day. Remember, Sanjay? That was the most flustered I'd seen him—when we wanted to see the diary."

Sanjay groaned. "The psychic connection to the diary was such an essential part of his act, he never would have admitted it was stolen."

"I only wanted to prove it was a fraud," Hiro said. "You must believe me. You know me, Houdini-san."

"A few minutes ago I would have sworn I knew you were a murderer," Sanjay snapped. "Now I don't know what to believe. The police will be here any minute, so whatever you want to say, say it now."

"I've always sought to expose the truth. I knew it couldn't have been true that Akira knew how to perform an impossible illusion, so I knew there would be no such explanation inside. I needed to find the diary to expose Akira's deception about his supernatural powers. As the time for his show grew near, I'm ashamed to admit I put on a disguise and followed both you and Akira. I was desperate. This televised show was going to make him a bigger star than he already was.

"When I failed to learn anything by following you, and I heard that Akira would be out of his studio, I broke in. He was an egotistical man who thought more highly of himself than was true. I knew his security would not be good enough to stop me. I was able to easily break in. It wasn't perfect, though. The security camera caught my image briefly before I covered the lens.

"Sébastien saw my genuine horror that Akira was accusing me of sabotage. I swear I did nothing to his equipment. I had only one mission. I needed to find the diary to show that everything he was doing was based on a dangerous lie. That he didn't possess mystical powers that led him to this antique document that would allow him to claim the undisputed title of Japan's premier magician. I spoke to the people at the museum, but they wouldn't tell me anything. I thought they were lying. But when I got the diary, I learned that they weren't. It was real."

"How do you know?"

"The day I borrowed the diary, I took one of the pages to someone who could tell me the document's age—"

"You ripped out a page of a historical document?" I asked, horrified.

"Priorities, Jaya," Sanjay softly admonished.

"Sorry," I said.

"I didn't tell him what it was, of course," Hiro said. "I didn't want him to know. I removed a different page in case he recognized the page that was shown in the media. I said I'd found the torn page tucked into a book at a charity shop and wondered if it was as old as it looked. I didn't think his answer would confirm that it indeed *was* from centuries long past, not a replica.

"After studying the pages some more, he didn't think it would be worth much. I waited patiently, not able to tell him I didn't care about the value. But you can imagine my shock when I learned the diary was real.

"At home, I read the Japanese writing in the rest of the diary. It was written by a Dutchman, just as Akira had claimed. But he didn't reveal the secret of the Indian Rope Trick. At least not in the parts that had been translated into Japanese. The next morning, I hoped to translate the rest of the dairy, but I awoke to the news Akira was dead.

"I knew I would be a suspect. I couldn't let anyone know I had the diary. I made an error when I mentioned bamboo. Was that what gave me away?"

"It was," I said. "Why are you admitting this now? You could have continued to deny it, saying you were just thinking of the classic way in which the trick was done."

"A great burden has been lifted from my shoulders," Hiro said. "I now had nothing to gain. Akira was dead, so there was nothing to expose. And I possessed a diary that might falsely implicate me in a murder, so I did nothing. But guilt has been destroying me."

"That's not quite true," I said. "You dressed up as a ninja, kept wearing the disguise, and ransacked Yoko's apartment to confuse things."

Hiro's eyes grew wide behind his glasses. "That wasn't me. The same person who killed Akira must be the one who broke into Yoko's apartment. I would never do that to her."

"And we're supposed to just believe you," Sanjay said. "After you lied to me all week?"

"I don't expect anything from you," Hiro said, bowing. "But it is the truth."

The sound of police sirens sounded.

"Where's the diary?" I asked.

Hiro went to a wooden bureau along the wall and pulled open a drawer. His face contorted and turned ashen. He flipped frantically through a stack of papers, including what looked like a set of train tickets with pre-printed Japanese characters plus handwritten notations, then ripped the drawer from the bureau as the police banged on the door.

"It's gone," he said, his eyes wide with horror. "The diary is gone."

CHAPTER 48

"You don't understand," Hiro said as the police took hold of him. His eyes were wide, his voice frantic. "I wasn't telling the entire truth."

"We know," Sanjay said.

"No," Hiro said. "Right now. The diary is truly gone. I need to tell you—"

A police officer spoke harsh words to Hiro that silenced him. Another officer spoke to me and Sanjay in English and asked politely if we could stay and tell them what we knew. The officer said he'd return momentarily.

As Hiro was led away, his eyes stayed locked on mine, pleading.

"That was strange," I said to Sanjay.

"He got scared once he realized he was really going to be taken into police custody. That would freak me out too. Did I tell you about the time I thought about doing an escape at Alcatraz?"

Sanjay kept talking, but I was barely listening. Was that all it was?

The English-speaking police officer took brief statements from us outside Hiro's house before departing. I asked if I'd be able to speak to Hiro again. The answer? No. A polite no, but still the same result.

"I don't see why you need to say anything more to that traitor," Sanjay said once they'd gone. "He tried to kill me, Jaya. And he succeeded with Akira."

"Weren't you listening to him?"

"Your naiveté truly surprises me sometimes, Jaya."

"He was your friend. Are you giving up on him that easily?"

Sanjay gripped the sides of his bowler hat so hard a paper butterfly popped out. It dropped straight to the floor without fluttering.

"How am I supposed to know what to believe? It's killing me that Hiro did this, but the evidence—"

"That's where I think you're wrong," I said. "He's not a treasure hunter. He's a debunker. Listening to him, what he said makes sense. I need to talk to Yoko to see if I'm right."

A movement in the distance caught my eye. I looked to the hillside and screamed. Sanjay ducked. I'm not proud of the screaming, but the sight startled me.

Standing in the woods was a fox. A human one. Yoko was watching us.

Tamarind had said she slipped away. She must have known we were coming here. She walked down the hill towards us, giving me a few moments to collect my composure. Once she reached us she bowed before speaking.

"I apologize," Yoko said. "I didn't wish to interrupt." She paused and lowered her eyes. "Matsumoto-san is guilty?"

"Hiro is guilty of theft," I said. "But I don't think of murder."

"I wish this would end," she said, looking away into the hills. "I wish...No. We have no time to waste. I've come to collect Sanjay. We have much work to do before the show tomorrow."

"I need to ask you something first," I said. "Hiro admitted breaking into the workshop, but he seemed genuinely horrified to hear he'd been accused of sabotage."

Yoko pressed her lips together for a few moments before speaking. "I believe Matsumoto-san is telling the truth," she said.

"You—" Sanjay sputtered. "Am I going crazy?"

"Houdini-san," Yoko said. "You know what Akira was like. He had many faults. And many fears. He was self-conscious about his crippled hand and never allowed the cameras to film it up close. He had to learn many new ways to perform magic after his accident. He didn't always succeed. He hadn't succeeded with that water-escape illusion."

"You think Akira used the break-in as an excuse to sabotage his own trick," I said.

Yoko nodded. "I knew him well. When he said only that one illusion had been sabotaged..."

"You wondered if he was lying and had done it himself," I said.

"Akira was the first person to arrive at the workshop after the intruder broke in," Yoko said. "Akira had time to do it. He wished to save himself embarrassment."

"His fear of embarrassment explains something else," I said. "Akira never showed us the diary on the day of the break-in, even though he claimed he had it on him. Since it was such an essential prop for the show, symbolically, would he have admitted the truth if it had been stolen?"

"I wondered the same thing myself," Yoko said. "For Akira, appearance mattered above all else."

"Why are you both trying to forgive Hiro?" Sanjay asked. "He admitted to stealing the diary. He knew he'd been found out, so he spun a story to explain it away, admitting guilt only where necessary."

"I wish to see Akira's death avenged," Yoko said, "but Matsumoto-san's story makes sense."

"It doesn't matter what you two think," Sanjay said. "The police have him now. They'll get to the bottom of this."

"The bottom of what?" Yoko asked.

"The expression means to figure it out," Sanjay explained.

I wished I knew what Hiro had wanted to tell us right before the police took him away. Was I fooling myself to believe Hiro had told us the truth?

CHAPTER 49

Sanjay and Yoko were going to be performing on live television the following day, so we returned to the site of the performance.

"I need to speak with the crew and security," Yoko said as we arrived at the fence that surrounded the once-tranquil field. "Otherwise they won't let Jaya-san any farther. I'll only be a moment."

Sanjay waited with me outside the perimeter fence. The area of the hillside where Akira had died was quite a ways from the main performance area, but bright colors caught my eye.

"Where are you going?" Sanjay asked as I began walking toward it. "She'll be right back."

"I'll only be a second."

Yellow crime scene tape with black Japanese characters had been woven through the chain links of the newly constructed fence, but the tape was partially obscured by something far brighter. Hundreds of flower bouquets lined the fence. White, orange, purple, blue...As many types of flowers as the different types of people who had adored him. I remembered Yoko telling us everyone from schoolgirls to surgeons had loved him. A few of them were there now, crying as they knelt over the flowers, but most had simply left a tribute and gone back to their lives. I agreed with Hiro that their devotion might have been dangerous if it went too far, yet this was still a beautiful memorial from the people whose lives he'd touched. I ran my fingertips over the soft flower petals before walking back to Sanjay.

"You look different today," he said, studying my face.

"Stress will do that." I smoothed out my hair. I must have looked like Medusa.

"No, I meant in a good way. You look...contented. Even in the midst of this crazy situation, it's like you've figured things out."

"How can you say that? I haven't figured anything out."

"In your life, I mean." Sanjay's voice was calm. "You talked to him?"

"You mean Lane?"

Sanjay nodded.

"I did."

He flipped his bowler hat in his hands and let out a long sigh. "I can hardly believe I'm saying this, but...He's good for you."

"But I'd hate to lose my best friend in the world."

"You won't," Sanjay said.

Yoko appeared next to us. I hadn't seen her approach, but I didn't jump or scream this time. I must have been getting used to it.

"You're free to come inside," she said, handing me a lanyard with a security pass. "Your friends are inside already with passes. None of you are required to sign an agreement, but please, don't reveal what you see."

Yoko turned and went through the open gate flanked by two security officers, but Sanjay hung back, gripping the rim of his hat like a security blanket.

"I don't want to talk to him. Sébastien betrayed me. I thought he and Hiro were my friends."

"You need to. You saw what a mess it was when you tried to avoid me."

Sanjay scratched his neck. "That was different..."

"Come on." I took my hand in his, and we stepped through the gate into the performance site.

"I can't even look at him," Sanjay said. "I never imagined Sébastien would lie to me. He's like a grandfather to me, you know?"

"I know." I pulled him forward. "I feel the same way."

Tamarind eyed us as we approached holding hands, but I didn't care. Sanjay and I knew what it meant to us now, and that's what mattered. He would always be my best friend, one of the most important people in my life. And I was going to do whatever it took to get him through the next thirty-six hours.

I felt Sanjay's hand shaking, so I gave it a squeeze.

"I can't do this," he whispered to me.

"The security guard who let us in is a fascinating guy," Tamarind said. She wasn't normally so tone-deaf to a situation. And had she forgotten where we'd gone? Why wasn't she asking about it? Maybe she was nervous. The tension between us all was obvious.

"Did you know," she continued, "that there's a special type of security for protecting pop stars? Mr. Oda told me all about it. You have to know how to deal with the fans respectfully. You see what this means, don't you? It means Sanjay is officially a rock star now."

Tamarind wasn't being oblivious at all. I should never have doubted her. It was exactly what Sanjay needed.

Sanjay let go of my hand. He puffed up his chest with pride and straightened his jacket collar. "Sébastien," he said.

Sébastien's face held a sadness I'd never seen before. "I can't begin to express—"

"A truce," Sanjay said, extending his hand. "Can we please have a truce until I get through the show tomorrow? Otherwise I don't know how I'm going to make it."

After a beat, Sébastien removed his glove and shook Sanjay's hand.

Sanjay's face softened. "You're freezing. Are you sure you don't want to go inside? I can get through final practice on my own."

"The cold is good for me," Sébastien said. "As for water? If it begins to rain, you're on your own, my boy." He chuckled. "What I would appreciate, however, is if you would tell me what happened while you were gone. Then I'll be able to focus and help you."

We filled in Sébastien and Tamarind about what had happened with Hiro, while Yoko led us down the hill to the performance area. As we approached the newly constructed set, I understood why the rain wouldn't matter. A stage had been erected with a roof hanging over it. Camera and lighting rigging were placed in strategic positions. The stage was deep, and the back of it surprised me. A green screen.

That's why Akira had insisted on nondisclosure agreements. Akira Kimura was truly a modern magician. His act was achieved not with sleight of hand, but with modern video technology.

"A green screen?" I said to Sanjay. I was more disappointed than I realized I'd be to learn the secret. "But doesn't the audience see it?"

"You saw how there are two rings of security," Sanjay said, "plus the perimeter fence and a slope of this hillside. Anyone standing where we just were can't see the show itself, they can only view it on the large concert screen. I didn't know myself until yesterday."

"But fans will still gather outside the fence," I said, "because there are so many who wanted to see the act in person rather than on television."

"The one hundred audience members who are lucky enough to 'win' tickets past the fence," Sanjay said, "aren't real audience members."

"Shut. Up." Tamarind said. "They're plants?"

"Actors. Paid actors."

"That's how he was going to perform the Indian Rope Trick," I said. "By not doing it at all. It's completely fake." I now understood why magicians always tell people they don't really want to know how a trick is done.

"What makes something fake?" Tamarind asked. "I mean, aren't we just fetishizing the past if we reject modern advances?"

"Magic," Sanjay said. "That's what's missing."

"Human ingenuity," said the man who invented ingenious mechanical devices in a barn in Nantes, France. "Things people can see with their own eyes, truly seeing what's unfolding before them, but at the same time failing to see the trick. That's the skill that plants the seed of magic."

"Technology takes human ingenuity," Tamarind said.

"But part of what Sébastien was trying to express," Sanjay said, "is that if you're setting things up as one thing, but delivering another, that's trickery rather than magic."

"'Any sufficiently advanced technology is indistinguishable from magic,'" Tamarind said.

"Very good," Sébastien said. "I should have known someone as intelligent as yourself would be so well-read. An Arthur C. Clarke quote, wasn't it?"

Tamarind nodded.

"That principle," Sanjay said, "applies equally well to science fiction and to the fact that it's impossible to perform a proper magic show for children under the age of five. Before four or five, *everything* about the way the world works is magic to them."

"I never thought of that."

"The Indian Rope Trick captured the imaginations of grown men and women across the world," Sanjay said, "precisely because it was something supposedly witnessed up close, in person, with no possible trickery. Its impossibility is what makes it so magical."

He ran his hands around the rim of his bowler hat. "That's why Sébastien and Hiro were helping me work out what I could do on my own that was worthy of co-headlining with Yoko. This"—he flipped the hat through the air, releasing a handful of paper butterflies that fluttered through the wind—"doesn't cut it."

I watched the seemingly enchanted paper catch in the autumn wind, swooping almost like real butterflies before falling gently to the ground.

It was a beautiful effect, but I could see what he meant. It would be perfect on a small stage, with the proper story setup, but for a camera and an audience of tens of thousands? Not so much.

"How did you do that?" Tamarind asked.

"Do you really want to know?"

"Yes. Of course. No. Wait." She bit her lip. "Is that a trick question?"

"Three centuries ago," Sébastien said, "a man called Von Kempelen created a mechanical illusion that riveted the public across Europe and America for more than a century. He created a mechanical chess player. An automaton sitting at a chess board, who became known as The Turk. This automaton played the world's most famous chess players—and he could beat them."

"Shut. Up," Tamarind said. "What was the secret?"

"It was the most ingenious automaton ever created," Sébastien said. "Von Kempelen, and the others who toured The Turk after his death, showed audiences the inside of the desk underneath the chess board, with all of its gears. Still, nobody could understand how the automaton was clever enough to beat the land's greatest minds. It was a great mystery for centuries...In spite of the fact that newspapers reported the truth behind the illusion—dozens of times."

"What was the truth?" Tamarind asked.

Sanjay's lips ticked up into a smile. "Do you really want to know?"

Tamarind grabbed the sides of her short hair. "Why are you two messing with my mind?"

"The point," Sébastien said, "is that nobody wanted to believe the truth. The public simply tuned it out. They were repeatedly told the truth behind the illusion, yet they failed to acknowledge it. People continued to show up for the tours and continued to be baffled by the illusion they saw before their own eyes."

"The magic," Sanjay said, "was better than the truth."

CHAPTER 50

While Sébastien worked with Sanjay and Yoko, Tamarind and I were put to work helping move equipment. Yoko explained that she and Akira had always kept their crew small, to protect their secrets. I didn't know what the numerous coils of rope I was asked to move were for, but I was glad to physically exert myself. The events of the last few days hadn't left me time to go running as much as I would have liked. I missed that time that allowed my mind to relax. When running, thoughts that were stuck in the recesses of my mind allowed themselves to break free. I hoped lugging stage equipment would have the same effect. I was wiping sweat from my forehead when a young police officer approached Sanjay.

"Rai-san," the officer said.

I wondered if Sanjay's sour face was caused by the fact that a policeman was looking for him, or whether it was because the man had used the polite honorific with his real last name. I had a feeling he was getting used to being called Mr. Houdini.

"Ah!" the officer continued, spotting me. "Jones-san. I wished to find you as well."

"You did?"

The man led us a few paces away from the others.

"Matsumoto-san wouldn't speak to our detectives," he said, "unless we came to see you both."

"I don't have time to question your suspect for you," Sanjay said. "I have a performance to prepare for. Hiro can wait in jail."

I'm sure the officer was annoyed, but his face didn't show it. Instead, the tall man bowed and said, "You misunderstand, Rai-san.

Forgive me. I was unclear. Detectives will question Matsumoto-san. But he wished to tell you this message: 'You're in danger,' he says. 'The gravest of danger.'"

"Is that a threat?" Sanjay gaped at the officer. "You're delivering a threat from a murderer?"

"I expect Matsumoto-san is building his defense," the man said. "He claims there's a madman who's the true culprit."

"A madman?" Sanjay repeated.

"*Hai,*" the officer said. "Matsumoto-san said a madman, but says he doesn't know who this madman is. Only that you should trust no one. Not even those you believe you can trust."

Sanjay and I stared at him. *A madman. Trust no one.*

"I can say no more. I have fulfilled my duty. I wish you a most successful performance, Rai-san." He bowed again and left.

Tamarind and Sébastien hurried over to us.

"Spill," Tamarind said. "Did they want you to testify against Hiro? Does Sanjay have to go on the stand against his former best friend?"

"He wasn't my best friend," Sanjay said.

"It's more dramatic that way," Tamarind said. "You should say that when the press interviews you."

"He *was* a good friend," Sanjay said, nodding his head sadly.

"Hiro Matsumoto is a good man," Sébastien said. "I'd swear to it. I don't know how this happened—"

"Hiro is innocent," I said.

I spoke without thinking. But as soon as the words had left my mouth, I knew they were true. How could we all have been so mistaken about his character? There was a simple answer: We weren't wrong.

The three of them stared at me.

"You want to see the best in people," Tamarind said, squeezing my shoulder through my heavy coat. "It's an honorable quality, but from what you told us—"

"I've figured it out," I said. "If we assume Hiro told the complete truth, but just left one thing *out*, I can make sense of everything."

"Please don't pause for dramatic effect," Tamarind said. "I've had about as much adventure as I can take in two days."

"Hiro wanted to show the world that Akira was a fraud. He spied on us and broke into Akira's studio—not to hurt Akira, but to get proof he wasn't a miracle worker. Hiro said he had shown the pages to someone who could authenticate their age, but that he didn't have time to get the Dutch parts translated before Akira was killed and he was scared off. He said he didn't know the details of Casper Van Asch's treasure until we told him about it at his house last night. When we ended our conversation with Hiro as the police arrived, he seemed genuinely horrified that the diary was gone."

"He's a showman," Sanjay cut in.

"Do you remember how he was flipping through a stack of papers inside the desk as well? I realized what they were. I'd seen them in a shop when I was exploring the city. They're receipts from pawnshops. Hiro Matsumoto wasn't only shamed by Akira's lawsuit against him. He was financially ruined. Didn't you notice how his house was amazing but not well maintained? I thought at first it was the Japanese sparse style of home decorating, but it was the house itself as well. Hiro needed money. Casper Van Asch was rich. He allegedly stole a hoard of gold pagoda coins. How else would he have lived so comfortably in Japan?"

"Colonialism?" Tamarind suggested.

I shook my head. "Japan kicked out those who wanted to colonize and convert them. In the 1600s they even kicked out children with European fathers. The government forcibly took kids away from their distraught mothers."

"Children?" she said. "That's terrible."

"Hiro was able to read a portion of the diary," I said. "He's a smart guy. He would have understood enough to know there were riches to be had, even without knowing the exact details of the treasure."

"So you're saying Hiro *is* guilty?" Sanjay said. "I thought you were defending him."

"Yes," I said. "And no."

"If I had time for this nonsense instead of planning a show that's about to be a disaster," Sanjay said, "I'd compliment you on being a great performer, Jaya. But it's time for you to just tell us what you mean."

"There are two people who've been after the treasure."

CHAPTER 51

"Multiple people have been after the treasure," I said. "That's what confused things this whole time." Sébastien had been right. There were two people working independently and therefore obscuring the truth. But he'd been wrong about one of them being Lane trying to protect me.

"Who the hell is the other guy?" Tamarind asked.

"I don't know yet. But everything makes sense if we assume there are two actors."

"I don't have time for this," Sanjay seethed. "You're telling me Hiro is guilty but *not* guilty."

"It's not complicated," I insisted. "It's so simple I can't believe we didn't see it before. Hiro was looking for proof to debunk Akira but accidentally discovered a treasure instead. And a second person who'd read—"

"What are you fighting about?" a voice from the sky asked.

The ghostly image of a *kitsune* in a flowing robe with nine tails hovered in the air. She was nowhere near us, so I realized I must have been shouting in my excitement.

"Impressive, my dear," Sébastien called to Yoko. "If you'd like to come down, the two of us can help Sanjay practice for tomorrow's performance."

I stared at Sébastien. "You're not going to help me figure out the last pieces?"

"I *am* helping," Sébastien said. "Making sure Sanjay performs a safe and successful show is how I help. We're magicians and you're a historian. None of us are detectives."

Sébastien walked across the field to Yoko to help her step down from the lift that had been hidden under her flowing costume. Sébastien turned and shot me a glance, assuring me he understood we couldn't take her into our confidence.

"Just stick together," I said to Sanjay, careful to speak softly enough that Yoko couldn't hear us.

"Don't worry," he said. "This show is a group undertaking."

"I mean you and Sébastien. Not Yoko. You heard Hiro's warning to trust no one. And like I was saying before she interrupted us, the other person after the treasure has to have seen the diary, meaning it might be her."

"Except for all the reasons Yoko doesn't make sense as the killer," Tamarind cut in.

"Thank you," Sanjay said. "A shining voice of reason."

"I'd blush if I did that sort of thing," Tamarind said.

"I have to trust her," Sanjay said, his voice tinged with desperation. "I won't survive the show tomorrow if I don't."

I mentally kicked myself. Of course he had to trust her to perform the show successfully. Which meant I didn't have much time to piece together what was going on.

"I don't think it's her," I said. "I just want you to be careful."

"Aren't I always?" He tossed his bowler hat high into the air. Even with the light breeze, it landed squarely on his head. He had his magic mojo back.

"Looks like it's just you and me, kid," Tamarind said as Sanjay walked off.

"Why aren't they taking this more seriously? Sanjay's denial makes sense, since it's a survival mechanism. Sébastien should be the wiser one."

"His protégé is performing in front of millions of people tomorrow, Jaya. That's what they're taking seriously. I can't say I blame them."

She hooked her arm through my elbow and we walked arm in arm out of the field. The wild grass was damp, and although I was wearing walking boots, my feet were cold.

"What's the plan?" Tamarind asked as we approached the fence that led out of the restricted area.

"Sébastien is right. I'm not a detective."

"I know you. You have something in mind."

I grinned at my friend as two bright yellow leaves floated from a tree onto my shoulder. "Let's find the treasure," I said, lifting the fallen leaves from my coat. "That'll lead us to the killer—hopefully before Sanjay performs."

"Did something just click in your mind?" Tamarind squealed. "This is just like in the movies. A seemingly inconsequential occurrence, like two leaves the color of gold, leads to the solution—hey, why are you rolling your eyes at me?"

I let the leaves fall to the ground. "Nope. No revelations. I was only admiring their natural beauty. They reminded me of paper butterflies."

Tamarind leaned close to my ear. "Those women are spying on us," she whispered.

I glanced past the chain link fence. A group of more than a dozen women, between their teens and thirties, stood on the other side. Tamarind and I had walked in the wrong direction. We were near the spot where Akira had been killed. Most of the fans were wearing black, and some held flowers. Two of them were weaving long-stemmed white flowers around the metal wires of the fence, and one of them waved at me. I waved back.

Two security guards stood nearby. The older and larger man stood aloof as he smoked a cigarette. The younger scrawny one smiled as he spoke a few words to us.

"*Arigato*," Tamarind said, bowing at the man.

"You understood him?"

"I'm pretty sure he was pointing the way to the exit."

We walked along the fence until we saw a larger group of fans hovering on the other side. The main gate would be opened up the following day only for a select group, but a large screen had been erected for more fans to watch the show on site. The guards stationed here were far more serious. Neither one smiled as they unlocked the gate for us to depart.

Trust no one. Hiro's words, delivered by the police officer, echoed through my mind as we pushed past the curious group of men and women. Without knowing who to turn to for help, the logical next step presented itself.

"To the library," I said.

"A Japanese library? You've made me the happiest misfit librarian in the world, Jaya."

As nonresidents, we weren't granted library cards at the prefectural public library. But that wasn't our biggest research hurdle. Though the library looked superficially like the San Francisco Public Library, with a classic stone façade and modern interior, here most of the materials were in Japanese. I suggested we go to a café to do internet research, but Tamarind insisted a library provided magical research vibes.

In a nook of the library, I opened my laptop and showed Tamarind the painting of the ship that had started this nightmare. I hadn't noticed before how the vibrant oranges and reds of the sunset sky in the Dutch painting looked like the fall colors here in Japan.

"Normally I'd start with tracking down the missing ship," I said, "except that's a project that would take months or years, not the single day we have before Sanjay performs a dangerous act. And more importantly, it won't tell us what happened to Casper Van Asch's treasure here in Japan. We need to start with his gold pagodas."

"Which we narrow down how?"

"All through the 1700s the Dutch were losing ground in India," I said, "and the English were gaining it. The British Crown sent money and troops to protect its national interests from the French and Dutch, and pagoda coins were minted by both Indian and European powers in various Indian cities."

"It's like you're *trying* to make this more difficult for us."

"Battles raged for the century leading up to the Anglo-Dutch treaty of 1824. There were many openings for thefts, and Casper Van Asch disappeared with his forgotten ship in the 1790s. Our window is still way too big."

"I hate to do this," Tamarind said, biting her lip, "because it probably means we're about to leave my library sanctuary, but there's one more problem. A big one."

"I know. Even once we have a description of the coins, it'll still take too long to track down coin collectors and museum curators."

"Something far more basic. You're looking at this academically, Jaya. Not practically. It doesn't matter what the treasure is. It matters what Casper did with it."

I closed my eyes. She was right. We were right back where we started. "We need to find the diary."

Hiro was our best lead on the diary. He'd wanted to tell us more before being taken away by the police, and all we had was his cryptic message. I needed to talk to him, but we weren't even certain where he was being held. I hoped I could convince Yoko to call police stations to find him.

Back at the site of the show, the full crew had arrived for a run-through, making it difficult to locate the magicians. We found Sanjay in a trailer outfitted both as a green room rest area and mini workshop.

"Where's Sébastien?" I asked.

Sanjay was wearing his performance tuxedo, but the collar was unbuttoned and the black bowtie hung loose around his neck. He was playing with what looked like a projector and didn't look up at me.

"He's around somewhere."

"You two were supposed to stick together."

"Haven't you noticed the security around here? We're fine." Sanjay slipped a glass plate into the metal contraption and continued to fiddle with the switches.

I lifted his hand from the projector. "This is still serious. Where's Yoko? I need to ask her to make a few phone calls. We need to talk to Hiro."

"Then it's a good thing I'm here." The door of the trailer swung open and Hiro stood before us.

CHAPTER 52

Sanjay jumped up. "How did you get in here?"

"It's unfortunate the security guards are mindful only of fans," Hiro said. "It's not difficult to look like a member of the crew."

Sanjay balled his hands into fists, then took a deep breath. "I can't have these distractions right now. Hiro, what are you doing here? And how did you get out of police custody in the first place? Don't tell me you broke out with lock picks hidden inside your cheek."

"I was only being interviewed," Hiro said, "not arrested. Yoko doesn't wish to dishonor me by charging me with theft of the diary, so I've committed no crime. The police had no choice but to let me go."

"Then I'm sure you won't mind if we call them to confirm that," Sanjay said.

Hiro bowed and held out his cell phone for Sanjay to take.

Sanjay's shoulders deflated. "Put that away."

"I know it's unforgivable that I lied to you all." Hiro gave the lowest bow I'd ever seen. "I never wanted to lie to my friends. I truly only wished to learn how to expose Akira's dangerous deception. But when I realized the diary led to valuable *netsuke*—"

"Wait. Aren't you talking about Casper Van Asch's treasure?"

"*Netsuke* are miniature sculptures. They were popular decorative objects on the ends of cords used by people wearing kimonos to secure pouches or small boxes—whatever people needed to hold things without pockets. They were popular during the Edo period."

"Like the new exhibit at the art museum and the figurines at the cooking museum," I said, remembering the humorous carvings made of ivory and wood. "But what do they have to do with the Dutchman of

Dejima's diary and his gold pagoda treasure?"

"Gold? *Netsuke* can be worth a great deal of money. Many of them are in museums, like the ones you saw. Van Asch had a collection of them."

"That's what he spent his gold on," I said. Of course he wouldn't have hoarded his pagoda coins. He spent the gold he possessed.

Hiro nodded. "I hope you can forgive a poor man...After the lawsuit Akira filed against me, I lost everything. I was barely able to keep my home. Like Sébastien, I teach young magicians, but my students are much younger than his." He gave a sad smile as he raised his hand to the height of a child.

"I don't have much left," Hiro continued. "I had hoped to have a family, but it's not possible for me to do so with my current finances and prospects. I'm not telling you this for pity, but so you'll understand why I acted as I did. When I had the whole diary in my possession, I read about the things Casper Van Asch acquired here in Japan. His collection of *netsuke* could be worth a lot of money. Especially if it contains one particular piece."

"The famous missing piece of the museum's *netsuke* collection," I said.

"I'm not certain. But I had hoped..."

"Wasn't most of the diary in Dutch?" I asked. "And you didn't dare show the diary to anyone after Akira was killed."

"The internet," he said simply. "I translated the Dutch online."

Tamarind patted me on the back. "Jaya's brain is wired for historical and cultural accuracy. Our own online translation of the single page we had wasn't helpful. But Jaya, I think in your quest for perfection you're missing the important point."

"You're correct that much of what I translated didn't make sense," Hiro said. "But I could read enough to understand he collected *netsuke* with his wealth. Even a modest amount of money would help me more than you can imagine."

"Why do you think you can find his collection?" I asked. "What makes you think it's not already in someone's possession and that you can find it?"

"I've got an even more important question," Sanjay said, his arms crossed over his chest. "Why are you all wasting my time when the diary thief is already long gone, in search of this treasure that might or might not exist?"

"Um," Tamarind said, "he kinda killed someone. Not cool."

"The police are handling it," Sanjay said.

"I wish it were that simple, Houdini-san," Hiro said. "But I fear I have something he needs to find the *netsuke*."

Sanjay sank back into his chair and put his head in his hands.

"This," Hiro said, holding up a slip of aged paper in the shape of an oversize bookmark, "is what the killer is after."

The faded red stamp on the worn sheet of paper looked vaguely familiar. It had been created hundreds of years before I was born, but I recognized the style of marking. "Is that a receipt?" I asked.

Hiro nodded. "One that reveals where the Dutchman of Dejima's treasure is."

CHAPTER 53

"You know where Casper Van Asch's treasure is?" I asked.

"I do," Hiro said. "In a pawnshop."

"A pawnshop?" Sanjay repeated. "You're kidding. He lived over two hundred years ago."

"In Japan," Hiro said, "pawnshops have a different history than those in the United States. For many centuries, pawnbrokers have been reputable moneylenders who lived by a strict sense of honor. They wouldn't do business with just anyone. Pawnbroker families were selective in their clientele, lending only to samurai, the wealthy, or others who were referred to them. These were honorable families who would promise to safeguard items for generations. They were paid well for their storage, but even more for their honor and silence. I found the receipt in a pocket of the diary."

"Why would he pawn his riches?" Tamarind asked. "I thought he was rich and didn't need money."

"Pawnshops were places where people could store their belongings if they needed safekeeping. It was about safety as much as money." Hiro looked from Tamarind to me. "And Casper Van Asch believed he was in danger."

"The English caught up with him?" Tamarind asked. "Those English can definitely hold a grudge. What? Don't look at me like that. I dated an English guy once. It ended badly."

"I don't know who he was frightened of," Hiro said. "I only know Van Asch was paranoid about something. Or someone."

"So he hid his valuable possessions," I said. "The pawnshop tickets I saw in your home. They were all because you were looking for Casper Van Asch's *netsuke*?"

"Not exactly. My financial troubles...I've been taking my possessions to a pawnshop for some time. That's why I so easily recognized what the Dutchman spoke of, even though my translation of Dutch wasn't very good. The person who stole the diary from me would know to look for this receipt if they had it translated. The diary and the receipt are both needed to find the location. I visited pawnshops around Kyoto. But I found nothing."

"Did you make a copy of the diary?" I asked. "We could have it properly translated."

"I didn't want to be seen with it at a copy shop."

"Oh..." I said.

"But I took photos with my phone."

"Oh!"

Hiro smiled. "I can email you the images."

"Why do you think it's in Kyoto?" I asked as I wrote down my email address for him. I would have entered it directly in his phone except I was betting his phone was set to Japanese characters.

"The museum where the diary was found is here in Kyoto," Hiro said. "I'd hoped the pawnshop was here as well."

"There's no way a Dutchman would have been granted permission to go beyond Dejima. You know in theory where he stashed his *netsuke* collection, but not the exact pawnshop."

Hiro nodded. "I began to research pawnshops in earnest—only at first. I realized what I was becoming. Instead of helping my friend, I was temporarily blinded by the prospect of wealth. I know this can never excuse my actions, but I'd lost everything, from my sister to my career. Instead of chasing a phantom treasure, I should have been helping my friend with his performance. It shouldn't have mattered that I disapproved of Akira. Houdini-san needed my help." Hiro bowed deeply. "I hope you will forgive me one day, Houdini-san."

I looked to Sanjay. I expected to see him with his arms crossed, scowling at his old friend. Instead I saw a smile spread across his face.

"I understand more than you know," Sanjay said. "And I'll forgive you completely if you'll forget about this damn treasure and help me

figure out what I can do to impress this audience"—he gulped—
"tomorrow."

Hiro smiled. "This, I can do."

CHAPTER 54

"I'm glad you're settled about help with the magic performance," I said, "but we can't forget about Casper Van Asch's diary and Akira's killer."

"Why not?" Sanjay said.

"Hiro didn't give the police the pawnshop receipt," I said. "We have something the killer needs."

Hiro handed me the receipt.

"Hey," Sanjay said. "Don't put Jaya in danger." Before I noticed his movement, he'd plucked the receipt from my hand.

"I don't think that's how she sees it," Hiro said, deftly lifting the receipt from Sanjay and handing it back to me. "She wants to find it. Her face makes that clear. As do the many articles I've read about her."

I cringed. Both at Hiro's description of me, and also at the fact that their casual handling of the centuries-old receipt was contaminating it with the oils from their fingertips. I looked around the trailer for something that could protect the receipt. Sanjay handed me a plastic sheet-protector. He knew me well. I took out the magnifying glass I always carried in my bag and looked over the faded paper. A zing of excitement passed through me as I looked at the soft fibers of the paper, the deft strokes of ink, and the imprint of the stamp that was still visible with a vibrant red that had barely faded. It was a feeling I always got when holding a piece of history.

Hiro was right that I wanted to see this through. With my friends around me, I felt as if I could do anything. But there was a problem. One of us was missing.

"You didn't see Sébastien when you made your way past security, did you?" I asked Hiro.

His lips parted in surprise. "You don't know where he is?"

"He's got to be around here somewhere," Sanjay said.

"You didn't notice when he left?" I asked.

"I've been concentrating. But you're overreacting. Even if the killer knows about this pawnshop ticket, he stole the diary from Hiro so he'll go back to Hiro's house to look for it. That's what we need to tell the police."

I swore. "The police. That's what's still bothering me. Hiro, the message you had the police relay to us said the killer was a madman. Why did you insist the police tell us that before you'd talk to them?"

Hiro hesitated. "I was feeling helpless, which made me more worried than I should have been. I heard the police speaking about Akira's body disappearing...I apologize for worrying you."

"There's got to be a reason you said that," I pressed. I couldn't tell if he was being polite or holding something back.

Sanjay groaned. "You're a psychiatrist now? Can we finally get back to practicing? You're reading too much into things, Jaya."

"No," Hiro said. "Jaya-san is right."

Sanjay groaned even more loudly.

"I know I must be wrong..." Hiro let his words trail off and adjusted his glasses.

"About what?" I asked.

"I was shaken," he said slowly, "that someone had gotten into my home to take the diary. My home is secure. I no longer have a separate workshop. My house holds many secrets of my magic."

"No broken lock?" I thought about Yoko's sloppily broken door. Since traditional Japanese houses were constructed with thinner sliding doors inside, I hadn't thought it would be difficult to break into Hiro's home. But that had been an arrogant Western assumption. Though the inside doors were less sturdy than I was used to, that didn't apply to the outside.

"That's what worried me most," Hiro said. "That the person who stole the diary was someone who was in my home. Someone who has looked me in the eye, yet I could not see his malice. This is why I knew he must be a madman."

I shivered. "Do you have a lot of visitors?"

"No," Hiro said. "That's my worry. That the thief could have been one of you who was at my home last night."

"No," I said. "It wasn't one of us who stole the diary." Me. Sanjay. Sébastien. Tamarind. We were the four people who'd been at Hiro's home. But I was done doubting my friends.

Tamarind bit her lip and raised her hand. "My bad."

"This isn't a joke," I snapped. "You didn't steal the diary."

"I'm not joking," Tamarind said. "I'm pretty sure I accidentally left open a window when Hiro was showing me around the house. I didn't mean to. I didn't know how to close the latch, and Hiro had already left the room. Then I forgot to ask...I'm so sorry."

"There," Sanjay said. "Simple explanation. And no harm done."

"How can you say no harm done?" Tamarind asked. "I let this happen—"

"Sanjay is right," I said. "If you hadn't left the window open, the killer would have found another way in, like he did with Sanjay and Yoko."

"Good," Sanjay said, tapping his foot impatiently. "We're in agreement. We can let this go now. We're all friends, and a bad guy is off in search of a treasure. We'll all look after each other. We'll be safe."

"Except for Sébastien," I said. "I can't believe you let him go off on his own."

"What was I supposed to do?" Sanjay said.

"Not that." I grabbed my phone and tried calling Sébastien.

I should have done that in the first place. He picked up after one ring. But the deep voice that answered wasn't Sébastien's.

"Jones."

It was the voice that never failed to make me melt inside.

I looked at the screen of my phone. Had I accidentally hit Lane's contact information? No, it was Sébastien's number I'd called.

"Lane?" I croaked. "Is that really you?"

"I'm with Sébastien."

"He's okay? And how is it possible that you're with him?"

"Sébastien is fine, except he had the crazy idea I was lurking around Japan to look after you," Lane said.

"I'm not crazy," I heard a soft French-accented voice say in the background.

I looked at the wide-eyed group surrounding me, then covered the receiver of the phone and said, "Sébastien is fine. I'm going to step outside to take this."

"Sébastien said something about a foreigner being sighted?" Lane was saying as I jumped down onto the field. "Why didn't you tell me everything that was going on?"

"It was kind of difficult from across the world."

"I could have come sooner," Lane said. "When Sébastien reached me in my San Francisco hotel room on a video call yesterday, he made me call him back and step outside to convince him I wasn't simply in a hotel room in Japan. But the fact that I really was in San Francisco like I'd said, seemed to make him *more* worried, not less."

Because he knew you weren't the foreigner, I thought to myself.

"I wondered why he was so concerned," Lane said, "so I asked a friend from Nagoya to translate more of the news about Akira. There's a lot more being reported in Japan than here. Akira's body was stolen?"

"His fans are hardcore."

"They also say the Hindi Houdini is going on with the show, and that he's in danger of suffering Akira's fate."

I shuddered. If we didn't figure out who was after Casper Van Asch's treasure before the show, that was a real possibility.

"Sébastien's crazy idea made me realize I could be here in less than a day," Lane said. "I couldn't stand feeling helpless on the other side of the world, once I knew what was going on. I got on the first flight I could catch."

"I didn't know what he'd do," Sébastien's voice said faintly in the background.

"Where are you now?" I asked.

"My flight landed this afternoon," Lane said. "Sébastien is taking me to you."

An hour later, I found myself sitting in front of a traditional tea service at a *Ryokan* inn, waiting for Lane to walk through the door.

Sanjay had insisted he couldn't take any more time away from practicing. Hiro had emailed me his photos of the diary and was now working with him and Yoko, and Sébastien would go straight to the site after he dropped Lane off with me. Tamarind had pleaded that she desperately wanted to go back to the manga museum. I knew she was, in truth, trying to avoid being a third wheel. I can't say I was disappointed that I'd get Lane all to myself.

Sébastien had called his *Ryokan* and gotten Lane a room, and I'd caught a cab back from the magic show Arashiyama site to wait for him there.

I arrived before Lane at the inn. I wasn't surprised to find that Sébastien had requested a room for two, or that he'd insisted a full tea service would be waiting for us on our arrival.

The sweet scents of chestnut and mochi pastries mingled with another one. Sandalwood. Lane was here.

I got up from the tatami mat and met Lane at the thick sliding door of the room. At six feet tall, he had to duck his head to enter. I never knew which Lane Peters to expect. In light brown khakis, a white dress shirt, and heather gray pea coat, he was every inch himself. He dropped a leather duffle bag at his feet and swept me up in his arms. By the time he let me go, his glasses were foggy and the tea had gone cold.

CHAPTER 55

While I ate the vast majority of the pastries that had been set out for us, I told Lane everything that had happened since I'd arrived in Japan. He didn't interrupt, but let me talk at my own pace, in between bites of gooey mochi sweets. I sat back on a floor cushion and waited for his reaction.

"You realize we never properly made up," he said.

"What do you call that performance in the doorway?"

"Saying hello."

"Our relationship can't be our highest priority right now," I forced myself to say.

"I know. Someone is about to get away with a valuable piece of history."

I leaned over the tatami mat and kissed him.

"What was that for?" he asked.

"For being the only person I know who would say that."

On the soft matted floor of the room, he pulled me into another kiss. I ran my hands through his wavy hair, but he stopped me when I tried to take off his glasses.

"About that missing *netsuke* collection," he said, "we're wasting time."

"I know. A killer is out there trying to steal this piece of history, and we don't know what he'll do. We need to get the pages of the diary Hiro sent me translated—"

"What I meant," Lane said, "is that you already know who it is."

I shook my head. "I already explained to you that it's not Hiro—"

"Jones, you already told me who it has to be."

"I didn't."

"I've been running on adrenaline for the last day and a half, so I could be wrong. To be sure I've got the facts straight, I'm going to repeat back to you what you told me about individual people's alibis and motives, not grand ideas about the impossible Indian Rope Trick and the Dutchman of Dejima that were obscuring things. I'm not going to say anything you haven't already said, but I'll organize it differently, around people rather than in chronological order. I think that's why you can't see it. Because you've been living it in real time. Tell me if I get anything wrong."

Though I trusted Lane, I was skeptical. "If you think it'll help more than translating the diary..."

"I do. First we have Hiro Matsumoto, Sanjay's friend who hates magicians who claim to perform real miracles, because of his sister's death at the hands of a cult. He especially despised Akira, whose fans called themselves followers, which Hiro felt was leading people down a dangerous path. He wanted to find proof Akira was a fraud. Hiro was the ninja who chased you through a temple in Arashiyama but didn't try to hurt you. He broke into Akira's workshop in search of the diary, *which he found*, but which Akira didn't want to admit was stolen. Akira claimed he still had the diary, since it was an important prop to make his show believable, and Akira also took the opportunity to destroy the workings of an illusion he was afraid of performing—a water escape, because he'd previously been maimed in a different water escape. Sébastien gave Hiro a misguided alibi, because he correctly believed Hiro wouldn't stoop to sabotage that could hurt someone. Another jealous magician might have, but Hiro admitted he was the thief at Akira's workshop. That means we can stop looking for another magician who either wanted Akira's secrets or to cause him harm.

"Then there's Yoko," Lane continued, "who pretended to be both a *kitsune* and an assistant, neither of which she was. You believe she's smart enough to create any misdirection to steal the diary and kill Akira, but there's no reason for her to have taken the actions the killer took. Which I agree with. She could have easily killed him in their act if she wanted to, and she had the diary long before Akira. She's dedicated to magic, and has the intelligence, skills, and looks to pull it off. But she's not interested in a treasure. She's also not a man or a foreigner, descriptions from the witness to Yoko's break-in. And I don't know why you're grinning at me."

"I don't know how you took the mess that poured out of me and turned it into these coherent ideas."

"I told you," Lane said, "you experienced all this packed into just a few days, with everything jumbled together. You're too close to it."

"No, I think it's because we fit well together."

"If you count distracting me as fitting well together." He couldn't suppress a smile. He tilted his head and his lips hovered next to mine. His lips parted, and mine responded accordingly. But instead of following through on the kiss, he pulled away from me and cleared his throat.

"Next," he said, "there's Akira himself. An arrogant man who claimed to perform miracles, who died shortly before revealing the secret of the Indian Rope Trick to Sanjay. Akira changed plans and called Sanjay asking you both to meet him earlier than Sanjay expected. Why? One theory is that he isn't dead at all, planning to rise from the grave as more proof of his miracles."

"Which he hasn't done," I said, "although his body has disappeared. Which could have been a crazed follower who wanted to be close to him. I'd think it was far-fetched except for the fact that I saw the body. I don't know how he could have faked it."

"We know Sébastien well enough that I think we both agree to rule him out as a suspect. Which brings us to the end of our list of magicians. Now on to Dr. Nakamura. The history professor got in touch with you before you left for Japan. Like everyone else here, he saw the posters and media push for Akira's Indian Rope Trick show. The professor thought he'd use the show to get his students interested in history. He was smart enough to know when he needed an expert. You came through, helping him make sense of conflicting Japanese documents by realizing a historical Dutch trading ship was actually *two* ships—which is simply brilliant, Jones."

"You're the one who showed me how much art history can tell us about subjects unrelated to art."

"From that dank little basement office...But we're getting off track again. You and Dr. Nakamura wanted to continue your joint research once you arrived in Japan. You initiated trying to meet up, and he called you back when you were chasing the ninja. Over dinner, you put your research together and realized you were on to something, though you didn't yet know it was the Dutchman of Dejima's ship, and that the boat had enabled Casper Van Asch to smuggle gold pagodas to Japan. He helped you translate the photographed page of Casper Van Asch's diary, which a Dutch librarian translated similarly. But with a cursory search he couldn't find further information on Casper Van Asch in Japan.

"That leaves us," Lane continued, "with 'X,' the unknown actor who broke into Sanjay's hotel room, Yoko's apartment, and Hiro's home, in search of the diary that Hiro had the whole time. What have I just told you?"

"That nobody we know could have killed Akira and be after the treasures," I grumbled. "Hiro already had the diary so he didn't need to take risks to steal it. Yoko didn't have to go to these lengths if she wanted Akira dead or to read the diary. And Professor Nakamura has me as an alibi."

"Does he?"

"He left me a voicemail message while I was chasing our ninja—" I broke off and sank back onto the tatami mats. I put my hands over my face as the awful truth hit me. Lane was right that I was too close to the situation. I hadn't taken a step back to see the truth.

"Exactly," Lane said.

"Hiro was the ninja," I said, opening my eyes, "but he's not the killer. I originally crossed Professor Nakamura off my list because we thought the ninja and the killer were the same person, because of the throwing star at the crime scene. But Hiro was the only person dressed as a ninja. The witness to Yoko's break-in said she saw a man dressed in black and had a vague impression he was a *gaijin*. I'm the one who asked if he was dressed as a ninja—and I'm the one who drew the conclusion of him being a foreigner ninja."

Lane nodded.

"But even if he had a motive," I said, "which I can't see, especially since he came to me in the first place—he's not a foreigner. You are, which is why Sébastien suspected you of being in Japan to look out for me."

"That's where I can help. Japan was one of the places my father worked for a short period of time. I was young. But old enough to understand Japanese culture about who's considered a foreigner. You said you thought the professor might have a mixed heritage. He speaks English and Dutch in addition to Japanese, and he had English-language books in his office."

"Because he studies foreign populations in Japan's history," I said. "Those things make him a good professor."

"They also make him sound a lot like a foreigner. Being able to teach in English and possessing a collection of English-language books is a double-sided coin: prestigious, but at the same time always separating you as 'the other' and not Japanese."

"He's Japanese, though. He told me he was born in Nagasaki."

"Even Korean families who've lived in Japan for generations are still considered foreigners. In Japan, where context is everything, subtle distinctions are easily missed by those of us who are truly foreigners."

"I don't know," I said. "But if you're up for it, I know one way to find out."

CHAPTER 56

We arrived at the university to find the professor's door closed. Lane's knock was met with no reply. Professor Nakamura wasn't in his office. Disappointment welled up in me. I hoped he'd be there preparing for his lecture, oblivious to a murder and a treasure.

Lane put his hands in his pockets and looked casually from one end of the empty hallway to the other.

"No," I said.

"I didn't say anything."

"I know that look." I lowered my voice. "Do you even know how to pick a Japanese lock?"

"They're the same. Though I believe it's illegal to be found in possession of lock picks."

"Wonderful."

While I kept lookout, Lane picked the lock.

"What's taking you so long?" I hissed.

"I thought you'd be happy I'm out of practice. There. Got it."

Inside the office, guilt washed over me as I looked through Professor Nakamura's papers. I took the bookshelf and folder of mail, and Lane took the desk.

"He's a nice guy," I said. "Just because he doesn't have an alibi and isn't here right now doesn't mean he's guilty...Damn. But this might."

"What is it?"

"Aarse," I read.

"What did I do?"

"Not the insult. Professor Lamont said the caller had said *arse,* which he thought was a joke. But Aarse is a Dutch surname." I held up the envelope in my hand. "The professor is from Japan, but look at this letter with the return address in the Netherlands. His father's surname is Aarse. He's half Dutch. He's the person who called Professor Lamont before I did."

I looked at the photo of Professor Nakamura with the older Japanese woman who looked like him. There were no photographs of his father. *Context is everything*, I thought to myself. Because he used the name Nakamura and was from a Japanese university, I'd thought of him as Japanese, but as Lane had rightly pointed out, the Japanese might not.

"But why use his father's name when he called the professor, and not use it elsewhere?" I said. "He goes by his mother's name here in Japan."

"Married couples here are required to have the same surname. It doesn't matter whose name they take, as long as they share the same name."

"That doesn't explain why he'd use his father's name for his research on the Dutchman of Dejima. If he wanted to use a fake name, why use one that led back to him?"

"Unfortunately," Lane said, "I don't think we'll be able to ask him."

"Why not?"

Lane held up a notepad with numbers.

"A code?" I asked.

"Flight times. They're flights from Kansai to Nagasaki. He's gone to Dejima in search of the treasure."

"I should be relieved he didn't need the receipt to locate the pawnshop and isn't coming after us," I said. "But he's on his way to Casper Van Asch's treasure. And more than that..." I looked around his cozy office, both smaller and much neater than mine, but the same love for history was evident in the books and keepsakes that lined the bookshelf.

"He let you down."

"I shouldn't feel so disappointed in someone I barely knew, but when we were working together I thought of him as another kindred spirit."

Lane took my hand as I moved toward the door. "Where are you going?"

"After him. Where else?"

Lane took a moment before answering, keeping my hand firmly in his. "I'm not sure when we switched roles, but that's a terrible idea. He's killed over this. But if we give the police this information, they can catch up with him in Dejima so he won't get away with the historical collection. Then we can stay out of danger and go see the magic show that you came here for. I know how much it means to Sanjay for you to be there."

"You're right. I think it's time to go to the police." I reached for the doorknob. Lane pulled me back.

"Wait," he whispered. He put his ear to the door and listened for what felt like an eternity, while I felt my heart beat in my throat, then cracked the door an inch. Then he nodded. If he hadn't stopped me from yanking open the door, we could have been caught.

We went from breaking-and-entering to a police station. I thought to myself not for the first time that I wasn't cut out for this.

"What's the matter?" Lane asked.

The sun had set, a storm was holding off, and after meeting with the police we were making our way hand in hand across the field to where the magicians were practicing. A lone security guard who recognized me let us through the main gate.

"It's eerie," I said. The night was dark, but moving spotlights cast light across the field, presumably as a security measure.

"I think it's rather beautiful, with the colorful leaves of the trees surrounding the field. But you're not worried because of the harsh lighting."

"No," I admitted. "Though this place is creepy after dark, especially with Akira's fans who believed in his miracles on the other side of that fence."

"Then what is it?"

"I'm still worried for Sanjay."

"I know I'm not always the biggest advocate for going to the police, but this is one situation where it was the right decision."

"I don't mean I'm worried about the police catching Akira's killer before he can get away with Casper Van Asch's treasure. I'm talking about this. The magic show. The audience expects the Indian Rope Trick. That knowledge died with Akira, so I don't know if the show Yoko and Sanjay are putting on will be good enough."

"Jones, from what I know of your best friend, he's going to do just fine."

I stopped abruptly as we reached the crest of the hill. From here, we could see into the valley where the show would take place. Lane's hand fell out of mine as he took a step beyond me.

"Where is everyone?" I said. "I thought Sanjay said they'd meet us here."

"They're probably in one of those trailers down there."

"Why would they have us meet them here if the camera crew and stagehands had already gone home for the day?"

"Let's go find out." Lane held out his hand to me.

I hesitated. I turned but didn't see any of the security guards. None of the fans had gotten past the fence either. By all appearances, we were alone.

Then why couldn't I shake the feeling someone was watching us?

I shook my head. I was in one of the world's most beautiful and historic cities, had solved a crime and hopefully saved a historical treasure, was with the man I loved, and the next day I would be witnessing one of the most spectacular magic shows ever presented. Why couldn't I stop being paranoid and simply enjoy the moment?

I pushed aside my unwarranted fears and took Lane's hand. He pulled me closer to him and we walked into the valley of the field, his arm around my shoulder.

When we reached the heart of the next night's stage, the roving spotlights snapped off. The night was plunged into darkness.

I felt my throat grow tight as Lane let go of my shoulder.

A moment later, barely giving me time to panic, a more diffused light came on. This one was soft and tinted blue. It filled the air like mist, illuminating Lane's surprised face.

The soft sound of fluttering wings filled the air, immediately followed by a movement out of the corner of my eye. Before I could turn, the sky was filled with butterflies.

I knew they couldn't be real, but as I reached out my hand, my fingertips brushed against two of them.

"Paper," Lane whispered, an uncensored look of wonder on his face. "Thousands of paper butterflies."

I twirled around in the field. Dozens of soft wisps of paper touched my face and hands. A soft breeze blew upward, carrying the majestic creatures through the air.

"Not all paper," I said, watching the light cast images of butterflies onto Lane's clothes and face. Video images were being projected, catching in the foggy air as well as on our bodies and the nearby vegetation. It was a perfect mix of classic butterfly magic and modern technology.

"How—" Lane began, but I stopped his words with a kiss.

I don't know how long we stood there in the magical field with wondrous butterflies encircling us, but it was the sound of clapping that brought me to my senses.

Sébastien stood leaning against the nearby trailer, wearing a contented grin on his face as he clapped. The sounds of additional clapping hands joined in. I looked up and saw Yoko and Hiro sitting cross-legged on top of the trailer, smiling down at us. Yoko tucked a runaway lock of her red hair behind her ear and waved.

The trailer door opened and a bowler hat appeared, followed a second later by Sanjay. He jumped down to the ground and his gaze caught mine. He nodded knowingly. This had been his doing. I wouldn't have called the expression on his face one of happiness, but I saw approval there. He was letting go of me, and doing what he did best. Magic.

CHAPTER 57

It was the day of the show.

I'd barely slept. Not only because of Lane, although he was part of the reason. For the rest of the night, I had butterflies in my stomach. And not the beautiful paper or projected butterflies from the night before. The nerve-wracking kind.

When I got up, a text message from Sanjay was waiting for me, asking me and Lane to join him and the others for coffee before they headed to the site.

Coffee? How did they have time for a coffee break?

We met at Doutor coffee house. Lane and I bought expensive coffees and sat at a large table next to the window, overlooking a uniform row of single-person tables, all of which were filled with single people focused on their laptops. It was the space people paid for here.

"Your knee bouncing up and down is making me nervous," Lane said, twirling a wooden coffee stirrer between his fingers.

"Don't you want to keep me company?"

"I'm sure everything is fine. If it wasn't, he'd have asked us to meet them at the show site or the police station."

Ten minutes later, the four magicians and Tamarind walked into the café. Yoko carried a gift-wrapped box in her arms. Hiro followed closely behind her, with Sanjay and Sébastien leisurely strolling in behind them.

Yoko handed me the box with a bow. "We can't thank you enough. You made it possible for the Indian Rope Trick to be performed."

"I did?"

Yoko gave a wicked smile that reminded me of her *kitsune* alter ego.

"Shall I be the one to explain?" Hiro asked.

"Tamarind and I will get everyone coffee while you do," Sanjay said.

"For many years," Hiro said, "I've been working on an idea to perform the most fabled illusion of all time. In my version of the Indian Rope Trick, I wanted to make it a Japanese illusion, using Japanese history and mythology to tell the story of a servant of the emperor and a *kitsune*. I called it Shinobi's Trick—in English, 'The Ninja's Illusion.'"

"That's why you had a ninja costume," I said. I thought back on the first time I laid eyes on Hiro, without knowing it was him. The stealthy ninja with the moves of a magician who'd stopped to make sure Sanjay wasn't injured. I'd misread everything at the time. My whole stay in Japan had been an illusion of the ninja's creation. The Ninja's Illusion.

Hiro lowered his eyes and adjusted his glasses. "I'd never performed my Ninja's Illusion in public, because I wasn't fully able to realize the illusion. Something was missing."

"Matsumoto-san is too humble," Yoko said. "His secret to performing the illusion is magnificent. His only error was not realizing he needed two other magicians to help him." She and Hiro shared a smile. The day was becoming more and more interesting.

"Akira had a way to perform the illusion," Yoko continued, "but his way was fake. Trickery with video cameras and a paid 'audience' who pretended they saw a baffling illusion. I tried to convince him to perform with truth, incorporating the traditional Japanese magic style of *Edo Tezuma*, knowing he had the skill to do it. I couldn't convince him, because I had figured out only part of the Indian Rope Trick illusion."

"But this week," Hiro said, "after all of you forgave me, Yoko and I shared our ideas with each other."

"It turned out," Yoko said, "we each had the missing piece that the other did not."

"The three of us will be performing it tonight," Sanjay said as he and Tamarind set coffees on the table, plus a cinnamon roll in front of me. "It's brilliant, Jaya. I hope you'll enjoy the illusion. They figured out it can be done by—"

"No!" I shrieked.

The nearby row of solitary men and women on their laptops looked up at me.

"Don't tell me," I said, getting control of my voice. "Please don't tell me how the trick is done."

Sanjay grinned. "I knew it. I knew I'd convince you of the wonder of magic one day."

"I'd say she passed with flying colors," Sébastien said.

I stared at them. "He wasn't really going to tell me?"

"Of course not," Sanjay said. "Why don't you open your gift."

"I have one question first. Something that's been driving me crazy. Yoko, when we were at your apartment, I saw the mystical spirit ball Akira always kept with him. The object that's supposed to return to its *kitsune*."

She laughed. "A police officer returned it to me. He was a fan and thought I might want it back. You believed I was truly a *kitsune*?"

"Me? No." I tugged on the gold bow. The silky material untied easily, and I lifted the lid. Inside was a cuddly fox stuffed animal. It looked like the ones I'd seen near the Fushimi Inari shrine, except instead of a white mask, this fox wore a black magician's top hat on its head, and a magnifying glass around its neck.

Throngs of fans were gathering outside the field's fence. They were there early to get a good spot to watch the show on the projection screen set up for the fans who wanted to be close to the show but hadn't been lucky enough to get tickets. They didn't know the tickets were a fraud, just like Akira, and that the hundred audience members with tickets were in fact paid staffers.

But now that the three magicians were performing their magic in the classic tradition, they no longer needed the subterfuge. That morning, Sanjay and Yoko had made the decision to open up the field past the gates for all the fans who wanted to see live magic. With the slope of the hill looking down at the bowl of the stage, more than a thousand would fit.

The challenge now was getting everyone in safely, while also allowing the stage to remain clear for the performers, plus have access for the camera crews. The crews conferred and decided it could work. The fans who had thought they would be watching the Indian Rope Trick live on a screen would now get to witness it with their own eyes.

The fresh scent of the nearby bamboo forest and excitement were both in the air. Camera crews were in place. The show would be starting soon. Sébastien was helping the stagehands, but Lane, Tamarind, and I were given all-access passes to simply relax and enjoy the performance.

I'd silenced my phone for the show, but I felt it vibrating in my coat pocket. My bag was locked inside one of the trailers so it wouldn't get crumpled by the crowd.

"Fish!" I said.

"JJ. Can you hear me? Is that a circus behind you?"

"Something like that. Hang on a minute." I looked to Lane and Tamarind. "My brother. I'll be right back."

As I slipped through the crowd, I felt a hand on my arm and turned to see Tamarind. "Bodyguard, remember?" She grinned. "Actually, I need some air. I could crowd surf with the best of 'em in my youth, but now it's stifling."

We moved to the back of the stage area and cut through the trees. Though it was dark, the spotlights from the nearby show cast enough ambient light that we could see.

"I can hear you better now," I said.

"Happy Thanksgiving, JJ."

"It's the day after Thanksgiving here," I said. "But it's still good to hear your voice. I need to get back in a minute—"

"You'll never guess who's here."

Wasn't that supposed to be my line? My brother didn't know Lane was in Japan.

"Who?"

"Guess," he said.

"The last time we talked Nadia was already back."

"No. You'll never guess. Ava."

I choked.

"Isn't it wonderful?" he said.

Of all the things it might be, *wonderful* wasn't one of them. Lane's ex had lied to us about many things. The only reason I hadn't told my brother the truth about her was the one thing I knew was genuine about her: she loved my brother.

I sat down on the grass. "Wonderful," I repeated, my voice shaking. What was I supposed to do?

"What's wrong?" Tamarind mouthed.

I shook my head. Looking to the dark hillside, I recognized where we'd gone. We were near the temple of statues that Sanjay had shown me.

"How long will Ava be in San Francisco?" I asked, finding my voice.

"Don't worry. You'll get to see her. She'll still be here for the belated Thanksgiving dinner."

"Where are you two staying?" I asked. "My studio isn't big enough—"

"She doesn't need much space."

"She's staying in *my house*?" *Breathe, Jaya.*

"She's practically family, JJ. Why are you being so weird?"

Anything I could possibly say would sound petty. I couldn't tell him the truth about the love of his life on the phone like this.

"Gotta run, but wanted to let you know. Love you."

"Love you too, Fish."

I hung up the phone and put my head in my hands.

I expected Tamarind to say something, but instead all I heard was a strangled gasp.

I looked up and saw Professor Nakamura. He held Tamarind by the hair, the pointed tip of a traditional Japanese sword pointed at her neck.

CHAPTER 58

"Don't move," he said.

My eyes grew wide, but aside from that I don't think I could have moved if I wanted to.

"The receipt. The diary said there would be a receipt in the back pocket. But it was missing."

I nodded, my eyes transfixed on the sword tip inches from Tamarind's quivering neck. Where had he gotten a samurai sword?

"I won't hurt her," he continued, "if you bring it to me." His voice was calm and his hands steady. But his stylish hair was a mess and his collar askew. He wasn't as relaxed as he was pretending to be.

"I don't have it," I said, slowly holding up my hands.

"One of you does. The pawnbroker won't give me access without the receipt. I hope for her sake you can get it."

I nodded. "I can."

"Good."

He relaxed, and Tamarind took the opening. She elbowed the professor and lunged forward. She was big and brave, but he was stronger. He grabbed her hair more tightly in his fist, and moved the blade of the sword to a more stable position: her stomach. She squawked.

"Try that again," he said, "and you'll know what a ritual suicide feels like."

Tamarind scowled, but she remained motionless.

"Why?" I said.

"Don't stall. Get me the receipt, then you can have your friend back. Toss your phones away. Both of you. If you call the police or tell your friends, she'll die a painful death." He pressed the sword against Tamarind's ample midsection.

"It's real," Tamarind whispered, her lip trembling. "The sword is real."

"One of the benefits of being a historian," Professor Nakamura said, "is receiving historical gifts."

He smiled a sickening smile and looked from me to the weapon. Tamarind must have sensed his grip relax as he looked at his beloved sword. She stomped on his foot with her combat boot. The professor stumbled and she kicked him in the groin. He grunted and fell over.

"And one of the benefits of being a librarian at a public university," Tamarind said as I rushed over to them, "is that you learn how to fake someone out. That first move"—she wrestled him for the sword—"was to test your weaknesses."

It was no use. He wasn't giving up the sword. I tried to help Tamarind, but the blade slicing through the air stopped me from coming closer. I was trained in jiu-jitsu, but I would be a fool to think I could disarm a man with a sword who was much stronger than I was.

I cried out for help, but the opening music of the magic show drowned out my scream.

Professor Nakamura was still on the ground in a weakened state, but he wasn't giving up his grip on the hilt of the steel blade. With his other arm, he elbowed Tamarind in the chin.

She stumbled backward, and I caught her.

One of the first rules of self-defense, regardless of the discipline, is that the best defense has nothing to do with skill or strength. It's getting yourself out of harm's way.

"Run," I said.

"You don't have to tell me twice." Tamarind took my hand and ran. "But we're not going to make it back to the show. Too far. No cover."

And Tamarind was breathing hard already. She was right. We wouldn't make it back to the stage and crowd. We had to hide.

"This way." I pointed toward the hillside as we ran. When Hiro had been spying on us dressed as a ninja, he'd been able to hide in the midst of the thousands of moss-covered statues. If we could get there enough ahead of him, it was our best shot at hiding.

The farther we got from the show, the darker the hillside became, so we kept a hold of each other. Tamarind's breath was heavy beside me, but she kept up. All the way to a locked gate.

Tamarind swore. "Isn't this the place you were taking us?"

I looked up at the thick wooden beams of the temple gate. "There's got to be another way in."

We felt our way along a rough stone wall to an even steeper hillside.

"Climb," I said.

She swore again but obliged. I heard her mumbling that dying in a fall was better than having her guts sliced open.

We'd gotten a good head start, but our scrambling was making too much noise.

I looked back and saw a moving figure. I hoped for a moment it might have been a wild fox, until the faint moonlight caught on something shiny. Foxes didn't carry swords.

"We're in," I whispered as I came face to face with the smiling face of a moss-covered statue.

"But it's too late," Tamarind said as we stumbled through the rows of statues.

"No," I said, "it's not." My knees knocked into the rough stones, but I didn't stop. I knew where I was heading. I hoped.

"Why are we headed this way?" Tamarind whispered. "There's more cover the other way—"

"I'm looking for something." I tripped but kept going.

Here. This was the smiling disciple of Buddha I'd noticed on the day of my arrival. Not for his expression—but because his head was loose.

I twisted the stone head in my hands.

"Whatever you're doing," Tamarind said, "hurry."

"We have time," I said. "I didn't see him climbing up behind us."

It took all my strength to lift the stone head. If I hadn't had so much adrenaline pumping through me, I doubt I would have been able to lift it at all. But when he came for us, I'd be ready.

I nearly dropped the head when I saw I was too late.

I hadn't seen Professor Nakamura climbing the hillside behind us because he'd found another way in. He stood above us, brandishing the sword. Tamarind yelled as the blade of the sword sliced across her body.

A scream that sounded more like a banshee than my own voice cried out as I smashed the stone head onto Professor Nakamura's head. He crumpled next to the smiling disciple of Buddha. He was out cold.

But so was Tamarind. Blood covered the front of her coat. The dark liquid was spreading.

CHAPTER 59

Tears escaped from my eyes as I examined Tamarind. She awoke with a start, her fists flailing.

"It's only me," I said, stumbling away from her fists.

"Oh, God," she said. "Who died?"

"I don't think he's dead." I glanced at the prone body of the professor.

"Then why are you crying?"

"I thought *you* were dead." I looked at the blood spreading across her coat.

She gasped. "Help me up. The bastard sliced my arm...Oh...I don't feel so good."

I was relieved the blood was coming from her arm rather than her chest, but there was a lot of it. Too much.

"I didn't get to see you knock him out," she said, her eyelids fluttering closed. "Bummer. But don't worry. All is right with the world. We got him. The princesses saved themselves."

She slipped out of consciousness.

Tamarind was bleeding far too much. Professor Nakamura was unconscious, but I had no idea how long that would last. I glared down at him and saw he was wearing a belt. I could use it either to secure him or tie Tamarind's injured arm. Not both. I opted to save my friend. I used the belt as a tourniquet on her arm so the blood loss wouldn't spread.

I looked between the two unconscious figures. Professor Nakamura had made us leave our phones behind, so there was no way to get help. And no way to know how soon the professor would wake up.

I picked up his sword. I couldn't kill an unconscious man, but I could hide his sword. I stashed it behind an especially chubby statue, then leaned over his unconscious body and searched his pockets until I found his phone. I felt a small glimmer of relief—until I realized it was password protected.

"No," I whispered to the statues, falling to my knees. The people who'd carved these thousands of statues hadn't given up after the temple was destroyed by natural disasters. Out of destruction came a far more breathtaking result.

I wasn't giving up either.

My jiu-jitsu training kicked in. I squatted next to Tamarind and used my leg muscles to lift her onto my back. I couldn't get more than a few steps, though. Carrying someone twice my size down an uneven stone path in the dark was far more difficult than flipping and lifting a person. I placed her back on the ground as gently as I could, and sank down beside her.

I didn't want to leave Tamarind, but what else could I do? But first I needed to find a way to tie up Professor Nakamura. I was wearing a blouse and sweater under my coat. I scrambled out of my clothes, taking off my blouse before hastily putting my sweater back on. I'd seen movie characters rip their shirts to create strips of fabric. I yanked on the silk black blouse. A six-inch square of fabric tore off in my hand. Perhaps the whole shirt would work. Except silk fabric probably wasn't the most secure material to bind wrists.

A clank sounded behind me. The world stopped as I turned and saw Professor Nakamura standing over me with the samurai sword.

So this was what it was like to see your life flash before your eyes. I thought of my big brother holding my hand as we ran along the beaches of Goa, colorful boats along the water and our parents smiling in the distance. The teachers who'd inspired me, both in the classroom and on my travels. The first time I met Sanjay, when he'd pulled a flower out of his hat for me the day I was unpacking my roadster in front of Nadia's house. The feeling of Lane's fingers intertwined with mine on a coastal trail in the Scottish Highlands the first moment I realized I might love him.

Time slowed down. I became aware of my own breathing on a

more primitive level than I'd ever been before. Sanjay and Lane both joked I was a bad Indian, for reasons including the fact that I hated both yoga and meditation. Who could sit still for so long? But now I understood the feeling of being fully attuned to your own breath.

No, this wasn't right. Time couldn't have slowed down this much. Especially not for someone who'd never been able to meditate for more than two minutes. Time hadn't slowed down. It was Professor Nakamura who was standing still.

"Why?" he whispered. "Why are you making me do this?"

"You don't have to do anything."

"It's different when it's not an accident. I didn't mean to kill him."

"I know," I lied as calmly as I could. Could he hear how loudly my heart was beating?

"You don't believe me. But it's true. It wasn't supposed to come to this."

"I do," I said, surprising myself for believing the words. He looked so distraught, and he wasn't plunging the sword into me, even though with me defenseless on the ground he could have easily done so.

"The evening you and I had dinner, I told you I had something else to look up. I went through our online library archives that night. I found more information about our ship, and a name. The one you later came to me with. Casper Van Asch. The Dutchman from the magic show was real. The diary Akira claimed was genuine wasn't only a prop. It was authentic history. I knew my students would love it." His face lit up as he spoke of his students, but the emotion was short-lived.

"I called Akira's publicist to schedule a meeting," he continued, "but she told me since I wasn't a reporter, I wouldn't be able to talk with him. Since you knew him, I planned to ask you about it when we met the following day. But I hardly slept that night. I continued my research through the night, including calling a Scottish scholar."

That's why he'd called Professor Lamont.

"He gave me more details about Van Asch before he reached Japan," he continued. "Sleep was impossible. I knew from my students that Akira had a habit of being alone first thing in the day, to prepare for his miracles on the site where they would take place. I knew where the show was to take place, so I went there at dawn and waited, hoping to speak with him. I only wished to see the diary...but he laughed at me." Professor Nakamura's face filled with rage, and he gripped the sword.

"I only wanted a few minutes with the historical diary, but he said it belonged to him, he'd never show it to me. I grabbed his arm as he walked away. When he pulled away, he fell. But he wasn't dead. He'd knocked his head on the rock, but he stood up and began yelling at me. He screamed that both the magician diary thief and I would pay. I ran away, hoping he wouldn't remember my name. When I reached my home, I saw the news." He took a step back, but kept the sword solidly in his hand.

"He'd died from his head wound," he said softly. "It was my fault. I was a coward and didn't get him medical care. Once I learned he was dead, there was nothing I could do. I knew the police would catch up to me. I was again a coward. I couldn't bring myself to come forward. I began packing to leave. I didn't have enough money to be a fugitive. But I knew someone who did."

"Casper Van Asch," I whispered.

Professor Nakamura nodded. His hands were shaking now. "I needed to find the gold pagodas so I would have enough money to escape. I thought back to when Akira was shouting at me. He said I would regret what I'd done, and so would the *magician diary thief*. That's why he wouldn't show me the diary. Because he didn't have it. A magician had already stolen it from him. I believed it was Houdini-san, the opening performer in the show. I followed him and crept into his room through an open window when he left, but he didn't have it. Neither did Akira's assistant. I followed you to the home of the failed magician. He was the one who had the diary. A diary that tells, in Dutch, where Van Asch hid his riches. He left part of it in Dejima. But the family of pawnbrokers in Dejima wouldn't give it to me. They—"

He broke off and looked around. I'd heard the sound too. But we were alone. It must have been Tamarind, starting to come around.

"It's Tamarind," I said softly. "My friend. She needs medical attention. You didn't mean to kill Akira. I can see that. You regretted not getting him medical attention. Please...Please don't make the same mistake again."

I wasn't sure he'd told me the complete truth. Akira's injuries had looked too serious for him to be walking around before passing out.

But even if the professor had shoved or hit Akira purposefully, I believed he hadn't meant to kill him.

"Why did he have to laugh at me? I couldn't take his mocking laugh. I've never been respected."

"That's not true. Your students must love you. I can tell what a great teacher you are." I was speaking the truth. His desire to bring history to life is what had gotten him into this mess.

"I told you the truth when I first got in touch with you. That I wanted to engage my students using the magic show. But that wasn't the entire truth. I also wanted to make a significant discovery to get respect. My whole life, many people have only seen me as a foreigner. But this is my home. I was born and raised here. Japanese history means so much to me. But it doesn't matter. You wouldn't understand."

"I do," I said. I understood better than he knew. "I also understand you enough to know you're not going to hurt me with that sword."

I held my breath, hoping my instincts were right.

"You're right." His shoulders sagged, but instead of releasing the sword, he gripped it with both hands. It was only once he lifted the sword that I realized what he was doing.

"I'm a dishonorable coward, but I can do one honorable thing."

"No!" I cried as he turned the tip of the sword on himself.

He sliced the blade across his belly. The historian was committing *seppuku*, the honorable ritual suicide from medieval Japan.

CHAPTER 60

My shout echoed through the temple grounds. But mine wasn't the only voice crying out.

A priest in long robes ran toward us as Professor Nakamura fell over with a gasp of pain. He kicked the bloody sword aside and knelt at the professor's side.

"Your jacket," the bald priest said. "Press it to his stomach. I'll call an ambulance."

I obliged, but I didn't know if it would do any good. The professor slipped out of consciousness.

"There," another voice called. "There they are."

It was Sébastien's voice. Two flashlight beams fell on my face.

Blinded by the bright lights, I couldn't see who held the second one until Lane Peters lifted me off the ground and into his arms.

"We need to stop the bleeding until the ambulance arrives," I said.

"I'll call," Lane said.

"The priest already did that."

"What priest?"

"A bald guy in long robes. You can't miss him. He has a scar or a birthmark on his head."

"There's nobody else here, Jaya."

I looked around the dark forest of statues. "He was here a second ago..."

Where had the priest gone? And why did I have a vague feeling I knew him? Had I seen him the first time I visited the temple?

Professor Nakamura was still unconscious, but the sword was too large and unwieldy to turn it on himself with precision. He was still alive, but he needed more help than we could give him.

The sirens that filled the air were a welcome sound. We roused Tamarind enough that she could half-walk out of the temple, leaning on Lane's shoulder for support. A female officer emerged from a police car, and an ambulance pulled up behind it. .

"We'll need two ambulances," I told her.

"No way," Tamarind said. "I've been through too much to miss this magic show. What? I wasn't unconscious so long that we missed the whole show, was I?"

Lane's lips twitched. "You didn't miss it. The show started late, and Yoko was performing a tribute to Akira when we left to find you."

"No ambulance," Tamarind said, "until I see the Indian Rope Trick."

I knew better than to argue with Tamarind.

The ambulance took Professor Nakamura away. We explained to the police what had happened, and Sébastien stayed behind with them while Lane and I helped Tamarind back to the show. An ambulance technician had bandaged her arm while we spoke to the police and declared the wound wasn't as bad as I'd feared. While we retrieved our abandoned cell phones, Lane gave her his coat in place of her own blood-soaked one. I was coatless as well, but had enough adrenaline running through me that I barely felt the cool night air.

"I can't take your coat," she said. "How will you stay warm?"

"Don't worry about me," Lane said, kissing the top of my head. "I have my ways."

With Tamarind's injury, we didn't want to squeeze through the crowds. Instead we watched from the back. On the sloping hillside, even though we were far away, we had a perfect view of the stage below us. Lights from a magic lantern cast shadows of butterflies fluttering through swaying stalks of bamboo. Only the video camera rigging near the open stage and the clothing worn by our fellow spectators signaled we were in the twenty-first century instead of the eighteenth.

As we got into place, the shadows flickered out and fog rolled in. Yoko stood alone in a solitary spotlight, fog swirling behind her. She wore flowing red robes that matched her red hair, which was tied into nine ponytails. Her face was painted white, and even at a distance I could see the bright red of her lips.

A second spotlight appeared and drew my eye to a sparkling object in her right hand. The *kitsune* spirit ball. She tossed it into the air and it disappeared. The spotlight flickered, and her face was transformed into that of a fox. The crowd exploded in applause and squeals.

Yoko bowed and stepped back. The spotlights didn't follow her. The lights flickered in place, and when they came back, a fox sat in the spotlight. If it hadn't been translucent, I would have sworn the fox was real.

Beside me, Tamarind gasped. Lane and I both checked to make sure she was gasping from awe rather than pain.

The fox watched the audience for a few moments before darting off the stage and disappearing from view. As it did so, Yoko fell to her knees, as if her own life force was attached to the fox. Her voice echoed through the field. Yoko spoke Japanese, but the performance transcended language. Through the actions that unfolded on the stage, I understood the story she was narrating. The story of a traveler who'd come to Japan and witnessed its magic.

Flickering spotlights cast the shadow of a sailing ship in the fog. The wavering light made it appear the ship was sailing in a fierce sea. A man appeared from the darkness and jumped out of the shadow ship. It was Hiro, dressed as an eighteenth-century merchant.

Hiro lifted Yoko to her feet. The flickers of light on her white face showed her as a woman one moment, and a fox the next. Trapped between forms, she fell back to the ground.

Hiro spun around, and when he again faced the audience, he was dressed not as a merchant, but as a ninja. He knelt over Yoko and shook his head. In the blink of an eye, Sanjay appeared next to him. They were in a field without the trap doors of an elaborate indoor theater. Where on earth had Sanjay come from?

"I'd clap if I could use my damn arm," Tamarind whispered in my ear.

Sanjay wore the white robes of an Indian *fakir* and held his bowler hat in his hands. He set the hat on the ground and waved his arms above it. A length of rope emerged from the hat and stretched slowly skyward.

The *fakir* commanding the rope motioned for the ninja to climb it. To my surprise, Hiro was able to do just that. Wrapping his hands around the rope, Hiro deftly climbed to the sky, high above the audience—then disappeared.

The crowd went wild. The film crew swung their cameras from the stage to the sea of faces filled with wonder. The impossible Indian Rope Trick was possible.

Sanjay shouted up at the disappeared Hiro. Getting no reply, he climbed up himself. Once he too had disappeared, Yoko jumped up and grabbed the bowler hat that rested under the rope. With a wicked smile on her face, she clasped the hat and pulled a series of objects from it, beginning with a flower and ending with a bottle of sake. Her spirit ball wasn't inside. She shrieked with rage.

A meteor-like object fell from the sky, causing me and half of the audience to jump back. Was it my imagination, or had the ground shaken? Emerging from a puff of smoke next to Yoko was the object that had fallen from the heavens: Hiro. He held an object in the palm of his hand. A shiny glass ball, flecks of gold reflected in the light.

Yoko lunged for her spirit ball. Hiro ducked out of the way and ran to the rope, which still hung in the air. He gave it a tug and the rope fell to his feet. As it fell, it wound itself into a neat pile, almost two feet high. Out stepped Sanjay from the center of the coil of rope. He was now dressed in his black tuxedo. Hiro tossed the spirit ball into the pile of rope, and the desperate *kitsune* followed. She jumped into the coil of rope disappearing from view. Sanjay raised his arms, again commanding the rope to stretch into the sky. In place of Yoko, what remained on the ground was a heap of silky red fabric and a smiling fox. It ran off into the night.

The *fakir* and the ninja had performed an impossible feat, and the *kitsune* had recaptured her spirit ball. She was going home. They all were.

Tamarind, Lane, and I slipped away while the crowd was still applauding wildly.

"We need to get you to the hospital now," I said.

"Okay, Mom." Tamarind accepted Lane's arm for support as she rolled her eyes at me. "Hey, why aren't either of you calling an ambulance?"

"Do you need an ambulance?" I asked as we walked across the trampled grass. "You refused one."

"That was only because I wanted to see that amazing show. Now it's time to ride in a cool ambulance. Did you know they don't just have sirens but also a person who speaks politely through a megaphone letting people know exactly what they're doing? Like 'We're turning left at the intersection' and 'Please be advised we're going through a stop sign.'"

I heard more cheering behind us. The magicians must have been doing an encore. I hoped Tamarind wouldn't insist on going back. Even though I didn't think she needed an ambulance, she did need to get to a hospital.

We weren't the only people leaving early. A bald man in black and yellow robes was walking away as well.

The field began to sway before my eyes.

"Jones?" Lane said. "What's the matter?"

"I forgot something," I said, trying to steady my breathing. "Take Tamarind to the hospital. Let me know where you end up, and I'll meet you there."

I heard Tamarind speaking to Lane as I ran after the priest.

"Do you believe her?" Tamarind was saying. "She's terrible at lying. I bet she wants to see the encore."

The priest was walking away in the direction of the site of Akira's death. Or rather, what I now knew was the site of the magician's faked death.

CHAPTER 61

I found the man dressed as priest standing next to the flower memorial. His right hand was tucked into his robes. Thinking back to the temple, I remembered he'd kicked the sword away rather than picking it up. And getting a better look at his head, the mark I'd mistaken for a scar or birthmark was a recent injury.

"Akira," I said.

He turned and smiled at me. Not the snarky smile I'd known a few days before. But one that was both genuine and forlorn. He looked so different with his hair shaved off, and in the clothing of a religious man rather than his old flamboyant attire.

"I'm sorry I didn't reach him in time," he said. "I didn't think he'd hurt either of you. After all, he hadn't meant to hurt me."

"The professor told me the truth," I murmured. "You were walking around after you fell down the hill."

Akira nodded. "After he ran away, the idea came to me. I've been miserable for a long time now. My persona...it had gotten out of hand. I didn't know how to stop it."

"Your fans who called themselves followers."

"They'd do anything for me. It wasn't right. All I wanted was to recapture that feeling from when I was in Flash. Not this. But there was no stopping it. My promoters spent millions of Yen on this show. I wasn't allowed to break character anywhere in public. Yoko thought it was me who insisted on my persona, because it was at first. But not any longer. It was my financial backers who forbade me to stop. I was trapped."

"This was your way out."

"I wished I'd had time to plan, but when I saw what was possible in that moment...I did wonder if a *kitsune* was guiding me. Though it now appears she was a malevolent one."

"How did you do it?"

"One of my biggest fans works in a hospital. Not one of my fans who considers herself a follower, but a woman who loves magic. The body of a car crash victim had recently been brought to the morgue. She...borrowed it. We dressed him in my clothing and glove."

"That's why the body had to disappear immediately."

Akira kicked the fence. A shower of flower petals rained down on his feet. "And why nobody would have been found guilty of a murder that never happened. Nobody was supposed to be implicated or get hurt. We left enough behind to obscure things."

"Like the ninja's *shuriken* throwing star."

"This all became so much more complicated than it was supposed to be." He hesitated. It was a humble gesture I would never have imagined him capable of on the day I met him. "Are you going to turn me in?"

Was I? Akira had been resurrected as a humble man, no longer the danger Hiro had feared. And it was my fault he was "dead" in the first place. I was the one who found Casper Van Asch's missing ship, without knowing what I'd found at the time. It was the anchor that had pulled the Dutchman to Dejima to Japan, and dragged Professor Nakamura underwater.

"I'll leave Kyoto tomorrow," he continued.

"I'd have thought you'd be gone already. Even without your hair, you're bound to be recognized."

"I doubt it. There are few women like you and Yoko. But can't you guess why I stayed?"

"The magic show."

The smile that spread across his face was filled with genuine happiness. "She did it. She was always the star of the show. Now she can have the recognition she deserves. And without a dangerous following like mine." His smile faltered. "I'm only sorry two deaths may cast a shadow over her stardom."

"Two deaths?"

"Mine, and that of Nakamura-san. I received word he was no

longer alive when the ambulance reached the hospital. He succeeded in killing himself. The damage he did to himself in an attempt to atone for his mistakes was too much for the doctors to fix. That's something I'll always have to live with—" His voice broke.

I wasn't sure my own voice would be steady if I tried to speak.

"What do you say?" Akira said. "Are you going to turn me in?"

"For what?" I said. Now that Professor Nakamura was dead, I didn't think justice would be served by revealing Akira's secret. "You're simply a man who wishes to be left alone to live your life."

CHAPTER 62

Tamarind stayed one night in the hospital. She was recuperating well, and enjoying much better food than she remembered from a trip to a hospital in Texas when she was a child.

The next morning, we scattered in different directions. Sébastien looked after Tamarind at the hotel. Sanjay, Yoko, and Hiro were appearing on two talk shows, responding to the media requests that were pouring in after their successful performance. And Lane and I flew to Nagasaki.

The metropolitan port city of Nagasaki was located next to the tiny artificial island of Dejima as it had for centuries. With our authentic pawnshop receipt, plus a phone call from the police apprising them of the situation, the family of pawnbrokers who had been there for centuries handed us a copy of the inventory that had been recorded. We graciously accepted the list, even though we couldn't read a word of it. We were then handed the box that had been left with their ancestors by Casper Van Asch.

The *netsuke* carvings he'd collected were bewitching. Lifting a smooth wooden amulet into my hand, I thought of the skill and imagination that had gone into creating lifelike and humorous details in miniature sculptures. One in particular caught my eye. A lacquered wood fox that looked a lot like the fox *netsuke* the museum was missing from their otherwise complete collection.

"He'd fallen in love with Japan," Lane whispered. "Working hard to learn the language and collecting this distinctive Japanese art form."

"I believe you're right. I wonder if he stole the gold so he could come back to Japan and live out his days here."

What would life have been like for the Dutchman of Dejima? Grand adventures in India and Japan, but also danger and loneliness so far from home. He'd been a thief, but I didn't know his story, so who was I to judge? Both he and the *netsuke* carvings held more secrets than I knew. Maybe I'd discover them one day. In the meantime, I thought of my own home, my friends, my students—and Lane, the man who Sanjay always joked was a better Indian than either of us. The man with secrets of his own that he'd shared with me.

It was time to fly home to San Francisco for a belated Thanksgiving meal with my friends and family. Plus my brother's girlfriend, Ava. I wasn't sure where she fit, but I was about to find out.

There was one last thing I needed to do before leaving Japan. I was handing over the *netsuke* collection to the Japanese government. They could figure out whether Casper Van Asch had legitimately purchased the *netsuke* and if his descendants would get them. I was glad I wasn't going to be there for that fight.

A government representative would be meeting me to take possession of the box of *netsuke* and the inventory list. The police were in possession of the diary Professor Nakamura had stolen.

As I waited with my backpack at my feet and the antique box in my hands, I couldn't resist taking a last look at the figurines. I lifted the wood carving of the fox into my palm.

The figurine rattled.

That was odd. As with most *netsuke*, it had a hole that could be used to attach it to a kimono tie, but otherwise it should have been solid. I hoped it wasn't coming apart. I glanced around the lobby. Nobody was paying attention to me. I gently shook the figure again. That's when I noticed it. The fox's head was a different color than the body.

I took my magnifying glass from my bag. It wasn't my imagination that the fox had been made from separate pieces of wood. Yet the segments weren't loose. What was the noise I'd heard?

I twisted the wooden head. It protested for a moment, before easing loose and revealing a hollow body—with a rolled sheet of paper inside.

Holding my breath, I tilted the miniature carving upside down so the paper fell into my hand, then put the head back in place. I set the *netsuke* inside the wooden box and turned my attention to the scroll of paper.

The writing was faded, but one thing was clear. It was a map. I stared at it, barely believing my eyes. I'd been wrong. Casper Van Asch hadn't been able to take all his gold with him to Japan. This was his map to retrieve his treasure on a day that never came.

"Jones-san?" a voice said, nearly giving me a heart attack.

I tucked the paper into the pages of a magazine I'd picked out for my flight home. I acted without thinking. It felt instinctively like the right thing to do. I told myself it was for everyone's safety. More murders might follow if word got out there was a treasure map.

But in truth, I knew there were two more reasons I'd kept the map for myself. Casper Van Asch's collection would be tied up for a long time while it was decided what would be done with it; there was no use tying up a treasure map in bureaucracy.

I also knew it was inadvertently my fault that Professor Nakamura had been set on the path that led to murder. I'd helped him with the research that showed him there was a real treasure to be found. I'd started this mess. Maybe I could redeem myself by finishing it. One day.

I handed over the box of *netsuke* with a bow and a smile.

Author's Note

The Ninja's Illusion is a work of fiction, but the historical backdrop is real. The incredible history of the Indian Rope Trick is true as I describe it, as is the mythology of the *kitsune*, the types of historical treasures Jaya uncovers, and the heartbreaking history of Japan's isolationist period.

Kyoto is depicted as I experienced it when I visited Japan in 2016. I took some liberties with specific locations, and therefore they remain nameless in the pages of this book. But if you'd like to visit a Buddhist temple very similar to the one described here, Otagi Nenbutsu-ji in the Arashiyama neighborhood is worth visiting. It's off the beaten path and one of the less visited temples of Kyoto, but it was a favorite of mine.

The characters both past and present are fictional, with the exception of real-life historian Peter Lamont, who sportingly agreed to be featured in a cameo after I read his highly entertaining nonfiction book, *The Rise of the Indian Rope Trick*.

More details, plus recommended reading, can be found on my website: www.gigipandian.com.

GIGI PANDIAN

USA Today bestselling author Gigi Pandian is the child of cultural anthropologists from New Mexico and the southern tip of India. She spent her childhood being dragged around the world, and now lives in the San Francisco Bay Area. Gigi writes the Jaya Jones Treasure Hunt mysteries, the Accidental Alchemist mysteries, and locked-room mystery short stories. Gigi's fiction has been awarded the Malice Domestic Grant and Lefty Awards, and been nominated for Macavity and Agatha Awards. Find her online at www.gigipandian.com.

The Jaya Jones Treasure Hunt Mystery Series
by Gigi Pandian

<u>Novels</u>

ARTIFACT (#1)
PIRATE VISHNU (#2)
QUICKSAND (#3)
MICHELANGELO'S GHOST (#4)
THE NINJA'S ILLUSION (#5)

<u>Novellas</u>

FOOL'S GOLD (prequel to ARTIFACT)
(in OTHER PEOPLE'S BAGGAGE)

Henery Press Mystery Books

And finally, before you go...
Here are a few other mysteries
you might enjoy:

COUNTERFEIT CONSPIRACIES
Ritter Ames

A Bodies of Art Mystery (#1)

Laurel Beacham may have been born with a silver spoon in her mouth, but she has long since lost it digging herself out of trouble. Her father gambled and womanized his way through the family fortune before skiing off an Alp, leaving her with more tarnish than trust fund. Quick wits and connections have gained her a reputation as one of the world's premier art recovery experts. The police may catch the thief, but she reclaims the missing masterpieces.

The latest assignment, however, may be her undoing. Using every ounce of luck and larceny she possesses, Laurel must locate a priceless art icon and rescue a co-worker (and ex-lover) from a master criminal, all the while matching wits with a charming new nemesis. Unfortunately, he seems to know where the bodies are buried—and she prefers hers isn't next.

Available at booksellers nationwide and online

Visit www.henerypress.com for details

A MUDDIED MURDER

Wendy Tyson

A Greenhouse Mystery (#1)

When Megan Sawyer gives up her big-city law career to care for her grandmother and run the family's organic farm and café, she expects to find peace and tranquility in her scenic hometown of Winsome, Pennsylvania. Instead, her goat goes missing, rain muddies her fields, the town denies her business permits, and her family's Colonial-era farm sucks up the remains of her savings.

Just when she thinks she's reached the bottom of the rain barrel, Megan and the town's hunky veterinarian discover the local zoning commissioner's battered body in her barn. Now Megan's thrust into the middle of a murder investigation—and she's the chief suspect. Can Megan dig through small-town secrets, local politics, and old grievances in time to find a killer before that killer strikes again?

Available at booksellers nationwide and online

Visit www.henerypress.com for details

THE AMBITIOUS CARD

John Gaspard

An Eli Marks Mystery (#1)

The life of a magician isn't all kiddie shows and card tricks. Sometimes it's murder. When magician Eli Marks very publicly debunks a famed psychic, said psychic ends up dead. The evidence, including a bloody King of Diamonds playing card (one from Eli's own Ambitious Card routine), directs the police right to Eli.

As more psychics are slain, and more King cards rise to the top, Eli can't escape suspicion. Things get really complicated when romance blooms with a beautiful psychic, and Eli discovers she's the next target for murder, and he's scheduled to die with her. Now Eli must use every trick he knows to keep them both alive and reveal the true killer.

Available at booksellers nationwide and online

Visit www.henerypress.com for details

THE DEEP END

Julie Mulhern

The Country Club Murders (#1)

Swimming into the lifeless body of her husband's mistress tends to ruin a woman's day, but becoming a murder suspect can ruin her whole life.

It's 1974 and Ellison Russell's life revolves around her daughter and her art. She's long since stopped caring about her cheating husband, until she becomes a suspect in Madeline Harper's death. The murder forces Ellison to confront her husband's proclivities and his crimes—kinky sex, petty cruelties and blackmail.

As the body count approaches par on the seventh hole, Ellison knows she has to catch a killer. But with an interfering mother, an adoring father, a teenage daughter, and a cadre of well-meaning friends, can Ellison find the killer before he finds her?

Available at booksellers nationwide and online

Visit www.henerypress.com for details

CPSIA information can be obtained
at www.ICGtesting.com
Printed in the USA
LVOW13*0028121117
555919LV00007B/108/P